THE LAST GUNFIGHTER
Winter Kill

THE LAST GUNFIGHTER
Winter Kill

William W. Johnstone
with J. A. Johnstone

PINNACLE BOOKS
Kensington Publishing Corp.
www.kensingtonbooks.com

PINNACLE BOOKS are published by

Kensington Publishing Corp.
119 West 40th Street
New York, NY 10018

Copyright © 2010 William W. Johnstone

PUBLISHER'S NOTE
Following the death of William W. Johnstone, the Johnstone family is working with a carefully selected writer to organize and complete Mr. Johnstone's outlines and many unfinished manuscripts to create additional novels in all of his series like The Last Gunfighter, Mountain Man, and Eagles, among others. This novel was inspired by Mr. Johnstone's superb storytelling.

All Kensington titles, imprints, and distributed lines are available at special quantity discounts for bulk purchases for sales promotions, premiums, fund-raising, educational, or institutional use. Special book excerpts or customized printings can also be created to fit specific needs. For details, write or phone the office of the Kensington special sales manager: Kensington Publishing Corp., 119 West 40th Street, New York, NY 10018, attn: Special Sales Department; phone 1-800-221-2647.

ISBN 13: 978-0-7860-2122-2
ISBN: 10: 0-7860-2122-5

First printing: March 2010
10 9 8 7 6 5 4 3 2 1

Printed in the United States of America

Chapter 1

Frank Morgan dropped to one knee and fired twice. Muzzle flame spurted from the thick shadows in the alley across the street, and Frank felt the wind-rip of a bullet going past his head. He triggered again, aiming just above the muzzle flash he had seen, and this time he was rewarded by a yell of pain.

The bushwhacker in the alley wasn't the only one yelling. The street had been rather crowded when the shooting started, and men shouted curses and questions as they tried to scurry out of the line of fire.

Frank lunged to his feet and darted behind a parked wagon. He crouched low and took off his high-crowned hat so that he could risk a look past the end of the wagon's sideboards. A man stumbled out of the alley, gun in hand. His other hand was pressed to his belly, where Frank's slug must have caught him.

"Damn you!" he screamed. "You've killed me!"

The man jerked his gun up and fired again. Frank drew a bead and put a bullet through the bush-whacker's head, knocking him off his feet. Gut-shot like that, the varmint might have lived long enough to empty his revolver, and innocent folks might get hit by the stray bullets flying around. Frank didn't want that. The citizens of Seattle, and visitors to the town, had already been endangered enough by this fracas.

Frank stepped out from behind the wagon and clapped his hat back on his head. He still had one round left in the Colt. He kept the gun trained on the fallen man as he approached. Light spilling through the open doors and windows of buildings along the street showed him that the bushwhacker wasn't moving, but Frank hadn't survived all those long, dangerous years on the frontier by taking unnecessary chances.

Frank Morgan was a gunfighter. He was known as The Drifter, because ever since leaving his home in Texas not long after the Civil War, he had never stayed in one place for very long. A little more than three decades had passed since then, and he was still as fiddle-footed as ever.

He had to be. Every time he attempted to settle down, somebody tried to kill him. That was part and parcel of the reputation he had as maybe the fastest gun alive. Of all the famous gunfighters who had lived in the West during its wild and woolly days— Smoke and Matt Jensen, John Wesley Hardin, Matt Bodine, Ben Thompson, Falcon McAllister—Frank Morgan was the last one who hadn't either crossed the divide or hung up his guns. The only shootist remaining in his league was the mysterious Kid Morgan, who had taken to roaming the Southwest in recent months. People might have remarked on the two of them having the same last name and wondered if they were related, but nobody knew for sure.

No one but a handful of people were aware that Kid Morgan was really Conrad Browning, Frank's son.

Frank was a long way from The Kid's stomping ground at the moment. Seattle, Washington, to be precise. He had no real reason for being here, but everybody had to be somewhere. He had drifted up the coast from San Francisco, living up to the nickname that had been given to him many years earlier.

Now he stood over yet another hombre he had shot, the latest in a long line of men who had fallen to The Drifter's gun. Frank saw the neat black hole in the man's forehead, just above the right eye, and knew that he wasn't a threat anymore. Taking cartridges from the loops on his shell belt, Frank began thumbing them into the Colt's cylinder to replace the rounds he had fired.

"You killed that fella, mister," one of the bystanders said as they began to crowd curiously around Frank and the corpse.

"Seemed like the thing to do at the time," Frank said. Even after all these years, his voice still held a trace of a Texas drawl.

Another man spoke up. "Yeah, he fired at you first. I saw the whole thing. Self-defense, sure as hell."

"You know him, mister?" the first man asked. "He have a grudge against you?"

"Must have," Frank said, "but I don't know him."

He snapped the revolver's cylinder closed. "I never saw this hombre in my life until just now."

A burly, blue-uniformed policeman shouldered his way through the crowd. "All right, all right, step aside," he ordered. "What the devil's goin' on—"

He stopped short as he caught sight of the Colt in Frank's hand and the dead man at his feet. Reaching for his own pistol, he went on excitedly. "Drop that gun, mister!"

"You don't drop guns," Frank said. "That can damage them, or make them go off." He pouched the iron. "But I'll put it away while we talk, friend."

The policeman glared at him. "I ain't your friend. What the hell happened here?"

The man who claimed to have witnessed the shooting said, "I saw the whole thing. That fella"— he pointed toward the dead man—"ambushed this other fella. He shot at him from the alley. And all he got for his trouble was a bullet in the gut and one in the head."

The policeman looked around at the crowd. "Anybody else see anything? Is that what happened?"

Several other men spoke up, agreeing with the first witness. The policeman turned back to Frank and said, "I guess maybe you didn't do anything wrong after all, mister. But you'll still have to sign a statement and give testimony at the inquest."

Frank shrugged. "Fine by me."

"And we'll need to know why this man tried to kill you," the policeman added.

"Now, there, you're out of luck," Frank said. "I don't have any earthly idea."

The policeman frowned again. "A man tries to shoot you, and you don't have any idea why?"

"Afraid not."

"I suppose this happens to you all the time," the policeman said with a snort.

"More than you'd think," Frank said with a note of dry humor in his voice. "And more than I'd like."

The policeman stared at Frank, obviously confused, until one of the bystanders said abruptly, "Hey, I recognize that fella. He's Frank Morgan!"

That caused a stir in the crowd. "The gunfighter?" one man asked, while another added, "The one they wrote all those dime novels about?"

Those dime novels were one of the banes of Frank's existence. The gaudy, yellow-backed, luridly overwritten stories wildly exaggerated a reputation that didn't need any exaggeration. Judging by them, Frank had killed more men than all the other infamous shootists put together. That just made even more would-be fast guns eager to test their speed against him. Sometimes he was able to just wound them, but mostly he had to kill the young, stupid firebrands.

"Are you him?" the policeman demanded. "Are you the notorious gunfighter Frank Morgan? The one they call The Drifter?"

Frank didn't see any point in denying it. He nodded wearily and said, "That's right."

The policeman gestured toward the corpse. "Then this fella probably just wanted to be known as the man who killed Frank Morgan. He didn't care that he had to do it from a dark alley."

That theory was probably correct. Similar things happened all too often.

"I'll have the undertaker fetch the body and then I'll file a report. Where are you stayin', Mr. Morgan?"

"I don't have a hotel room yet," Frank replied with a shake of his head. "I just rode in and found a stable for my horses." He had left Stormy and Goldy down the street at Jessup's Livery, along with Dog, the big, wolflike cur who was also one of Frank's trail partners.

"Well, when you get settled in, let headquarters know where to find you. Somebody'll be in touch with you about the inquest."

The policeman's tone had turned to one of mingled respect and wariness. Lawmen across the West knew about Frank Morgan's reputation. Most of them didn't like him because in their opinion he brought violence and danger to their communities. Many considered him a cold-blooded hired killer like the infamous Jim Miller, although that was the farthest thing from the truth. They never stopped to think about the fact that Frank had worn a lawman's badge himself on several occasions, and he had never killed anyone except in self-defense or the defense of someone else.

Politely, he agreed to do as the policeman said. With that, the blue-uniformed officer turned to the crowd and bellowed, "All right, break it up, break it up! There's nothing to see here!"

"Nothing but a dead body and a famous gun-fighter," one of the men in the crowd pointed out.

That just made the policeman's already florid face flush even darker with anger.

Chuckling grimly, Frank turned and started making his way along the street. The bystanders got out of his way. He spotted a decent-looking hotel down the street and headed for it. MAJESTIC HOTEL, the sign over the door read. The place didn't appear to be all that majestic, but it looked clean and well kept up.

Frank hadn't gone very far when he became aware of a man falling in step beside him. A glance over in that direction revealed a tall, lean man with a lantern-jawed face and steel-gray hair that hung down over his collar. He wore a flat-crowned hat and a long coat. His features had a hard cast, as if he was a man accustomed to trouble. He grinned, though, as The Drifter looked at him, making his face a lot friendlier.

"Howdy, Frank," he said.

Frank stopped short. "Jacob?" he asked. "Jacob Trench?"

"That's right. How long's it been? Ten years?"

"At least that." Frank stuck out his hand. "It's good to see you again." The men shook hands for a moment, then Frank went on. "The hell with that." He pulled Trench into a rough hug, pounding the man on the back as he did so. Trench returned the boisterous greeting.

"What are you doing in Seattle?" Trench asked.

"Same as always. Drifting."

"I thought maybe you were headed up to Alaska to get in on the gold rush. That's why the town is so crowded. Lots of prospectors outfit here before they sail north."

Frank shook his head. "I'm not interested in hunting for gold."

He didn't need to. Thanks to the vast, varied, and highly lucrative business interests he had inherited from Vivian Browning, his first love and his son Conrad's mother, Frank Morgan was one of the richest men west of the Mississippi, though an observer would never know that from his broken-in boots, well-worn jeans, faded blue work shirt, and time- and weather-stained hat. His gun and holster—the tools of his trade, so to speak—were well cared for, but there was nothing fancy about them, either.

"Same as always, all right," Trench said with a laugh. "You're one of the most unambitious men I've ever met, Frank. I think that's one reason I like you. You don't ever try to horn in on a man's plans."

"You have plans, Jacob?" Frank asked. The last time he had seen Trench, ten years or more in the past, the man had been running a freight line down in New Mexico Territory. Frank had helped him deal with some outlaws who had been plaguing the line.

"I always have plans. I'm headed up to Alaska myself."

"To prospect?"

Trench shook his head. "I've got another sort of bonanza in mind, if you're interested."

Frank held up a hand to stop him. "Nope. Whatever it is, I want no part of it. Shoot, Jacob, I'm from Texas. I can't take the cold up there in that country. It's all snow and ice, from what I hear."

"Not just yet," Trench said. "Winter hasn't set in yet. There are a few weeks left before the weather turns bad. That's what I'm counting on, anyway. I'll be in Skagway before the snow starts to fall."

"I hope so." They had reached the hotel. Frank stopped in front of it. "Well, good luck to you, whatever this venture of yours is. It's mighty good to see you again—"

"Wait a minute, Frank," Trench said, interrupting. His smile vanished and was replaced by a serious expression. "Come across the street and have a drink with me." He jerked a thumb toward the Cascade Saloon.

"I don't know . . . I've been in the saddle most of the day, and I was looking forward to a hot meal and then a good night's sleep."

"Before somebody threw down on you from that alley, you mean."

A frown creased Frank's forehead. "You saw that, did you?"

"Yeah, I saw it. I did more than that." Trench took a deep breath. "I caused it."

"What in blazes are you talking about?"

"That bastard wasn't shooting at you, Frank," Trench said. "He was shooting at me."

Chapter 2

Trench's angular face appeared to be completely serious. Frank was intrigued enough by his old friend's claim that after a moment he nodded and said, "All right. I reckon we can have that drink."

"Good. I feel mighty guilty about you almost getting ventilated because of me. Seems like buying you a drink is the least I can do to settle the score."

"That and tell me why somebody wants to kill you," Frank said as they started across the street toward the Cascade. Some of the men they passed must have recognized Frank as being involved in the shooting from a few minutes earlier. He saw the looks they cast in his direction and heard the whispers, but he was able to ignore them.

He'd had plenty of practice.

The Cascade Saloon was a good-sized establishment doing a brisk business. It was noisy enough inside, what with the tinny notes of a piano, the clicking of a roulette wheel, and the bawdy laughter and raucous talk of the customers and the girls who worked there, that Frank was confident nobody would be able to eavesdrop on him and Trench as they sat down at a table in the corner with a couple of beers.

Frank wasn't much of a drinker, but he liked a cold beer now and then. The beer in the Cascade was icy and went down smoothly. After a healthy swallow, Frank set his mug on the table and said, "All right, Jacob. Let's hear it."

Trench took another drink from his mug, then thumbed his hat back on his thinning hair. Like Frank, he was well advanced into middle age, but still a vital, powerful man.

"I was walking along the other side of the street from you," he began, "although I didn't know it at the time. Just as I passed that alley, I heard a little noise, and I reckon I was jumpy enough that it made me duck. That's when the fella who was lurking there pulled the trigger. The bullet came mighty close to parting my hair anyway, but it missed and went on across the street."

"Where it went right past *my* ear and busted out a window in the building I was passing," Frank said. The moment was still vivid in his mind.

"Yep. That's about the size of it," Trench agreed.

"Question is, if he was trying to kill *you,* why did he keep shooting at *me*?"

"Because you were shooting at him," Trench said as if it were the most obvious thing in the world.

And it was, Frank supposed. When he had felt the hot breath of that bullet, his instincts had taken over, making him whirl toward the source of the shot, drop to a knee, and return fire. Once things had gone that far, the man in the alley had kept shooting to try to save his own life. Frank could see now that that was the way it must have been.

He took another sip of his beer. "All right, that explains part of it," he said. "Where were you while the rest of it was going on?"

"I got the hell out of the line of fire, of course. Once Haggarty opened the ball and you accepted his invitation to dance, there was nothing I could do to stop it."

Frank grunted. "You knew the fella, then?"

"Damn right. His name was Leon Haggarty. Mean as hell."

"Had a grudge against you, did he?" Frank guessed.

Trench shrugged. "Yeah. He and his brothers think I killed a cousin of theirs over in Idaho a while back."

Frank's eyebrows rose. "Brothers?" he repeated.

Trench rubbed a hand over his jaw and grimaced. "Yeah."

"How many brothers are there?"

"Three more."

"They as mean as Leon?"

"Meaner," Trench admitted with a sheepish grin.

Frank shook his head. Despite his reputation, he had the most peaceful intentions in the world, especially now that he was getting on in years, and yet he still managed to walk right into trouble, usually through no fault of his own, again and again.

Both men drank from their mugs, then Trench went on. "It wasn't until after you'd plugged Leon that I got a good look at you and realized who you were. I didn't know my old compadre Frank Morgan was anywhere close to Seattle."

"I wasn't until today," Frank said. "This cousin of the Haggarty brothers they think you killed in Idaho . . . did you?"

"Well . . . yeah. But I didn't have any choice. He was trying to open me up from one end to the other with a bowie knife. He found an extra jack somewhere in a game of cards we were playing and took exception to it when I pointed out that fact."

Frank nodded slowly. He supposed he couldn't blame Trench for getting in that jam. He couldn't abide anybody who cheated at cards, either.

So it wasn't really Trench's fault that Leon Haggarty had tried to ambush him from that alley, or that the bullet had come within a whisker of Frank's head. It was just bad luck all around.

Not too bad, though, considering the fact that Haggarty was dead and Frank and his old friend were still drawing breath.

"Anyway, when I recognized you, I knew I had to talk to you and let you know what was going on," Trench continued. "It's on my account that the other Haggarty brothers will likely come after you, too, now, just like they're after me. I figured I had to warn you."

"I appreciate that," Frank said. "To tell you the truth, though, this won't be the first time I've had people gunning for me."

Trench laughed. "I should hope to smile it's not.

Hell, you're Frank Morgan, The Drifter. You must be used to it by now."

"I didn't say that," Frank drawled.

Trench drained the last of the cold beer from the mug and then said, "Well, you don't have to worry too much about it, because I've got a plan."

"You do, do you?"

"Yeah. You're coming with me to Alaska."

Frank started to shake his head. "I already told you—"

Trench lifted a hand to stop him. "Just hear me out, Frank. I've got a good deal working. The money's not great, but it's not bad, either. The work's easy and downright pleasant."

"The money's good enough to split two ways?" Frank still wasn't interested in whatever Trench was proposing, but he was curious to hear what the man would say.

Trench hesitated. "Well . . . sure. I guess."

Frank knew then what was going through Trench's mind. Trench was afraid that the Haggarty brothers would follow him all the way to Alaska to settle their grudge, and he wanted Frank along to help him handle that trouble. Frank didn't really blame him for that, but he didn't want to be roped into Trench's ruckus, either.

"You said that in a few weeks, it'll be winter up there. Do boats get in and out once that happens?"

Trench grimaced a couple of times, then admitted, "Not to speak of."

"So if I go with you, we'll be stuck up there until next spring."

"You could look at it like that. But we'll be in Skagway, Frank. It's a new town, a boomtown. All the prospectors go through there on their way to the Klondike, just over the border in Canada. That's where the big strike is going on. The closest, easiest way in and out is through Skagway."

"Have you been there?"

"Not yet, but I've heard plenty about it. There'll be saloons and whorehouses, and all we'd have to do all winter is sit by the stove and roast our old bones. Maybe sip a little whiskey and cavort with the soiled doves when the mood struck us." That infectious grin appeared on Trench's face again. "Doesn't sound like a bad way to spend the winter, now does it?"

"I sort of had in mind staying here."

"In Seattle?" Trench sounded like he couldn't believe it. "Hell, it'll rain for three or four solid months, Frank. You don't want that."

"I don't want to sit in the middle of a blizzard for three or four months, either."

"It won't be that bad. I give you my word."

"Thought you said you'd never been there."

Trench leaned back in his chair and shook his head. "All right. I'm not going to argue with you. I was just trying to show my gratitude to you by letting you in on a good deal, but if you're not interested . . ."

Frank heaved a sigh. "When are you leaving? I'm not saying that I'll go with you, but I reckon it won't hurt anything to think about it."

Trench leaned forward again, the eager grin reappearing. "That's all I'm asking," he said. "The boat's called the *Montclair.* It sails day after tomorrow. I'm expecting the cargo to arrive tomorrow."

"You didn't say anything about any cargo, Jacob," Frank pointed out. "Are you in the freight hauling business again?"

"Not exactly . . . Anyway, I can tell you all about that if you decide to come along, which I sure as hell hope you will."

Frank downed the last of his beer. "I want to get on to the hotel now and get something to eat. Why don't you drop by there tomorrow? I'll have made up my mind by then."

Trench nodded. "Sure thing, Frank. Thanks for considering it."

Somewhat to Frank's surprise, he actually was considering Trench's proposition. He still wasn't sure about spending the winter in all that snow and ice up in Alaska, but he didn't like the idea of being waterlogged by spring in Seattle, either. Maybe he ought to turn around and ride south instead, he thought. He had spent a number of winters in Mexico.

Mexico was a hell of a long way off, though, and there was something to be said for passing the long winter months with a friend. Trench didn't make Skagway sound half bad, either. The idea was worth thinking about.

But not until he got some hot food in his belly. He put his hands on the table and pushed to his feet. Trench stood up as well. "I'll walk across to the hotel with you," he said.

Frank nodded. "All right."

They threaded their way through the crowd in the

saloon and stepped out onto the Cascade's porch. A fine mist had started to fall, a precursor to those rains Trench had mentioned, Frank supposed. He could see the mist haloing the lights in the hotel across the street, and he felt its cool caress on his cheek as he and Trench stepped down off the porch, clearing the overhanging awning.

"You murderin' sons o' bitches!" a man yelled to Frank's right.

His eyes flicked in that direction as instinct once again caused the Colt to leap from its holster into his hand as if by magic, in a blur of speed too fast for the eye to follow. He saw a man rushing toward them, pistol in hand.

From the corner of his left eye, though, he caught another flicker of movement in front of them. Men in the street yelled and jumped for cover as a second attacker leveled a shotgun at Frank and Trench. That was the most immediate threat. At this range, a double-barreled shotgun blast would blow them to bloody pieces.

Frank's gun came up smoothly, flame stabbing from its muzzle. His bullet went into the chest of the shotgun wielder, rocking the man back on his heels. He didn't go down, though, and the Greener was still in his hands, so Frank shot him again.

As he pulled the trigger, he heard guns roar from both left and right, which came as no surprise to him. Trench had said there were three more Haggarty brothers. They had bided their time, waiting for Frank and Trench to come out of the saloon, then

attacked from three directions at once. It was a good
strategy.

At least it would have been if they were throwing
down against anybody but The Drifter. As the shotgunner fell, discharging both barrels almost straight
up into the air as his dying fingers spasmed on the
triggers, Frank pivoted back toward the first man he
had seen. The man fired again, but he rushed his shot
and the bullet plowed into the dirt next to Frank's
right boot. Frank took his time and drilled a slug
through the hombre's throat. Blood fountained from
the wound as the bullet's impact sent the man reeling
backward.

Frank kept turning, dropping into a crouch as he
leveled his gun at the spot where he thought the third
Haggarty brother would be. The man was down,
though, kicking out his life in the street as Jacob
Trench stood over him, gun in hand. Trench had
never been anywhere near as fast on the draw as
Frank, but he didn't lose his head in a fight, and that
counted for a lot when it came to gun-handling. Obviously, Trench had been able to deal with the threat
of the third man.

Frank moved quickly to check on the other two.
He nudged the shotgun and the pistol well out of
reach. The man he had shot in the throat lay with his
head in a rapidly spreading pool of blood that was
black in the light from the saloon. He was either dead
or soon would be. The shotgunner lay on his back,
arms spread, his chest heaving as he struggled to get
some air in his bullet-riddled lungs. Frank heard the
whistling as the air went right back out again. It was

an ugly sound, as was the dying rattle that came from the man's throat a moment later.

As Frank turned back toward Trench and the third man, he started to reload. "You all right, Jacob?" he asked.

"Not . . . really."

The painful rasp in Trench's voice made Frank's head jerk up. He took a hurried step toward his friend as Trench turned toward him. Frank saw the black trails of blood leading down from both sides of Trench's mouth and the dark stains on the front of his shirt. The gun slipped from his fingers and thudded to the ground.

Then Trench doubled over and pitched forward.

Chapter 3

Moving with the same speed that had made him a frontier legend for his gun-handling, Frank holstered his Colt and leaped to catch Trench before the man could hit the ground. He eased Trench down, resting his old friend's head on his leg.

"Hold on," Frank said. "Somebody can fetch a doctor—"

"Too . . . late for that," Trench cut in. "I'm shot . . . through and through . . . Frank."

Trench was smart and experienced enough to know that he had only moments to live. Frank didn't see any point in lying to him. So he said truthfully, "I'm sorry, Jacob. At least you can cross the divide knowing that we sent all three of those bastards to hell."

"Yeah, but . . . I'll just have to deal with 'em again . . . when I get there." Trench chuckled, and more dark blood welled from his mouth. His right hand came up and fastened desperately on Frank's forearm. "Frank . . .

you gotta promise me . . . you'll finish . . . that job for me."

"The deal you were trying to get me to come in on with you?"

"Y-yeah. People are . . . countin' on me. I can rest easier . . . knowin' they won't be . . . let down."

Frank bit back a curse. It was true that he had been considering Trench's offer, but if he'd accepted, it would have been his own choice. This way, he felt like he had an obligation, and that was never a feeling he liked.

Trench's fingers clawed spasmodically at his arm. "Frank . . . you gotta . . . promise . . ."

"All right," Frank said. "What do I do?"

"Go to . . . the *Montclair* . . . tell Captain Hoffman . . . what happened. You'll need to talk to—"

The blood in Trench's throat choked him then, so that he coughed and gagged as he tried to continue speaking. He got a few more words out, but the only one Frank understood was a name: Devereaux.

"All right," he said as he leaned closer over Trench. "I'll talk to Captain Hoffman and this fella Devereaux, and whatever that cargo is you were taking to Skagway, I'll get it there, Jacob. You have my word on that."

Trench's eyelids started to droop, but a smile curved his mouth. "Knew I could . . . count on you, Frank," he murmured. "And you're gonna have . . . a hell of a time . . ."

Frank wasn't sure about that, but he didn't argue with the dying man.

"Just . . . one more thing . . . Something you . . . need to know."

"What's that, Jacob?"

"The fella who played . . . the extra jack . . . in that poker game . . . that was me, Frank . . . not the Haggartys' cousin. But he really was . . . tryin' to gut me—"

Trench's eyes were still half open, but his head suddenly lolled to the side against the arm that Frank had around his shoulders, supporting him. Frank said, "Jacob?" But Trench didn't respond. Frank lifted his other hand, searched for a pulse in Trench's neck, and didn't find one. The man's eyes were already starting to turn glassy in death.

"Is he dead?" a familiar voice asked from behind Frank.

"Yeah." Frank lowered Trench's head to the ground, then looked back over his shoulder and saw the beefy policeman who had shown up after the first gunfight.

The man said, "You again, Morgan? The dead bodies just pile up around you like cordwood, don't they?"

Frank suppressed the urge to stand up and throw a punch at the policeman. It would feel good to plant his fist right in the middle of the son of a gun's smug face.

But it wouldn't actually accomplish anything except to maybe get him thrown in jail. He got to his feet, but he just said curtly, "There were plenty of witnesses to this shooting, too. Those three men—there and there and there—attacked me and my friend as we came out of the saloon. We defended ourselves. If you ask around, that's the story you'll get."

"How'd your friend wind up dead while you're still alive?"

"He wasn't quite as fast as me, or quite as lucky. He did for one of them, but the bastard got him, too."

"You know why these fellas came after you? Or was it just another case of some hotheads trying to kill the famous Frank Morgan?"

Frank's jaw tightened in anger, but again, he controlled it. "As a matter of fact, I do know why this happened." Quickly, he sketched in the story of how the Haggarty brothers had followed Jacob Trench to Seattle to try to avenge their cousin's death. He left out the part about how Trench was really the one who'd been cheating at cards and provoked the fatal fight.

"Sounds like you're in the clear again, Morgan," the policeman said when Frank was finished. "I'd say you were a mighty lucky man."

An old friend was dead, and he had been roped into some deal that might be shady or dangerous or both, Frank thought.

Yeah. Mighty lucky.

After warning Frank that he would have to testify at the inquest into these deaths, too, the policeman let Frank go on about his business. "Just try not to kill anybody else," he added.

"Not unless they try to kill me first," Frank replied.

He went into the Majestic Hotel and rented a room

from an inquisitive clerk. "There was all sorts of uproar out there in the street a little while ago," the man said. "Shooting and yelling and everything. Did you happen to see what was going on, Mister . . ." He glanced at the register, reading upside down the name Frank had written there. "Morgan?"

Frank shook his head. "Sorry. Didn't see a thing. I try to avoid trouble whenever I can."

With that, he took his room key from the clerk, tipped his hat at a rakish angle on his head, and went into the hotel dining room to get that long-delayed hot meal.

Like everywhere else in Seattle, the dining room was busy. The clerk at the desk in the lobby had informed Frank that he was lucky the hotel even had a vacant room. Looking at the crowd in the dining room, Frank could believe it. He didn't even see an empty table.

"Sir?"

It was a woman's voice, and at first Frank didn't figure she was talking to him. Then she said, "Sir?" more insistently, and he looked in her direction. She was alone at one of the nearby tables. She gestured at the chair across from her and went on. "You can join me if you like. I don't think you'll find a table to yourself. Unless you have some objection to my company . . ."

Frank didn't think many men would object to this lady's company. If they did, there was sure as hell something wrong with them. She was about thirty, old enough so that the few lines on her face were interesting, rather than unattractive. Short, dark brown hair framed her features. She wore a dark blue, high-necked traveling gown that was snug enough to reveal a mature, shapely figure. Her voice had a slight rasp to it that made it intriguing and distinctive.

She also had a plain gold band on the third finger of her left hand.

Frank took his hat off and held it in front of him as he stepped over to the table. "I appreciate the invitation, ma'am," he said, "but I don't reckon your husband would appreciate it if he came in and found you sharing a table with a strange man."

She smiled up at him, and he saw that her eyes were a rich brown, like her hair. "First of all," she said, "my husband doesn't appreciate anything anymore, since he's dead—"

"I'm sorry," Frank said.

"And secondly," the woman went on, "I pride myself on being a good judge of character—a woman on her own has to be, you know—and you don't strike me as strange at all, Mister . . . ?"

"Morgan," he supplied. "Frank Morgan."

"My name is Fiona," she said. "Please, sit down."

Frank didn't hesitate. He placed his hat on the table and took the empty chair opposite the woman called Fiona.

"I know it was terribly forward of me to speak to you like that," she went on.

"I'm glad you did. Otherwise I'd still be looking for a place to sit."

She returned the smile he gave her. He saw that she had a cup of coffee in front of her, but no food.

"You haven't eaten yet?"

"No. In fact, I just gave the girl my order a short time ago." Fiona lifted a hand. "I'll get her attention, and you can tell her what you want."

"As long as it's hot and halfway cooked, it'll be fine with me."

A waitress in a long, starched white apron made her way through the tables to them a moment later. When Frank asked for a steak, she shook her head.

"Sorry, we're out of 'em. The way these gold-hunters eat, I'd be surprised if there's a cow left in the whole state of Washington! We've got pork chops and potatoes and greens, though."

Frank chuckled. "Bring 'em on. And coffee."

"Right away, mister."

When the waitress was gone, Frank looked around the room and commented, "I'm not sure I've ever seen so many men bound and determined to make their fortune."

It was true. Most of the men in the dining room already wore the flannel shirts, canvas trousers, and laced-up work boots of prospectors. The clothes were new, though, which told Frank that the men hadn't yet set out on their quest for gold. As Jacob Trench had told him, Seattle was the place where the Argonauts outfitted before leaving for Alaska.

The thought of Trench made Frank grow sober for a moment. Fiona must have seen the reaction, because she asked, "Is something wrong?"

"I lost an old friend earlier tonight," Frank told her.

"Oh. I'm so sorry."

"He brought it on himself in a way. Doesn't make it any easier, though." He shook his head and changed the subject by saying, "You didn't tell me your last name."

She smiled at him. "That's right, I didn't. No offense, Mr. Morgan, but a woman traveling alone can't be too careful. I give you my word, though, that I'm not one of those . . . what do you call them? . . . soiled doves."

Frank's eyes widened in surprise. "I swear, ma'am, that's not what I was thinking. Not at all. I mean, a fella can tell just by looking at you that you're not . . . well . . ."

"That's all right, Mr. Morgan. I know what you mean. And I take it as a compliment, I assure you. I've always tried to conduct myself as a lady."

"Yes, ma'am, I'm sure you have."

Their meals arrived a few minutes later. The orders had gone in close enough together so that the waitress brought them to the table at the same time. Frank dug in. He tried to be polite about it, but he was hungry. Fiona didn't seem bothered by his hearty appetite. She even smiled slightly as if she enjoyed watching him eat.

The food was good, and Frank followed it with a serving of apple pie that hit the spot. Fiona passed on the pie. "I don't keep this girlish figure by indulging too often," she said, the rasp in her voice giving the words a touch of dry humor.

When Frank was finished, he leaned back in his chair and sipped his coffee. "What brings you to Seattle?" he asked. "Or is it improper to ask?"

Fiona shook her head. "Not improper at all. I'm here on business."

Frank arched an eyebrow.

"I know, not many women are involved in business," Fiona said. "But as I told you, I'm a widow, and I have to do something to provide for myself."

"You're still young. You could—"

"Marry again?" she broke in. "I suppose I could. If I could ever find someone I wanted to marry. The problem is that I'm very selective. Are *you* in the market for a wife, Mr. Morgan?"

Frank sat up straighter and frowned. "Me?"

She laughed. "Take it easy. I was just joshing you."

"Oh. Well, that's good, because I'm not looking to get married."

Not after he had buried two wives because of the violence that followed him.

"What brings *you* to Seattle?" Fiona asked.

"My horse." Frank smiled. "I'm what they call a drifter. A saddle tramp, I guess you could say." He paused, thinking again of Jacob Trench. "But as it turns out, I've got some business I need to take care of, too."

Fiona lifted her coffee cup. "Well, then, here's to good luck for us both in our endeavors."

"I'll drink to that," Frank agreed.

"Although it would be more fitting with a nice slug of brandy in this coffee, wouldn't it?"

He grinned. "I reckon so. You think we should ask the waitress?"

"I think we'd give the poor girl palpitations if we did."

The coffee cups clinked together.

Chapter 4

Over the years, Frank had seen too much violence and sudden death to let it affect him too much. Because of that, he was able to sleep soundly that night, although as he dozed off he did feel a moment of regret over what had happened to Jacob Trench.

He thought about the mysterious Fiona as well. They had parted company in the lobby after dinner. She was staying at the hotel, too, and Frank had a feeling she didn't want him to know which room she was in. That was fine with him. He wasn't looking for a romance, although he had definitely enjoyed her company during dinner.

He woke rested the next morning. The bed was comfortable, and after decades of spending a lot of nights on the trail, he enjoyed a few creature comforts every now and then. When he went downstairs to eat breakfast, he looked around the dining room, thinking that Fiona might be there. He didn't see any sign of her, though.

When he had finished washing down a mound of

flapjacks, eggs, and bacon with several cups of strong, steaming coffee, he went out to the lobby and stopped at the desk to see if there were any messages for him. There was one, from the coroner's office: The inquest into the deaths the night before would be held at eleven o'clock that morning, at the King County courthouse.

Frank left the Majestic. He planned to go by the livery stable to check on Dog and the two horses, and then he supposed he needed to locate the *Montclair* and have that talk with Captain Hoffman, as Trench had asked. He figured he would have time to tend to those two errands before the inquest.

The misty rain of the night before had blown on out of the area. It was a beautiful morning. The air was crisp and cool and so clear that Frank could see Mount Rainier, miles away to the southeast along with the rest of the Cascade range. Across Puget Sound to the west lay the Olympic Mountains, also clearly visible.

Frank hadn't been to Seattle in a number of years, and the town had changed some, he saw now that he got his first good look at it in the light of day. He recalled hearing that a disastrous fire had destroyed much of the downtown area seven or eight years earlier. The buildings that had been rebuilt were of brick now, rather than wood. That give the town a modern look, but it still retained its rugged frontier atmosphere. How could it not, when the streets were full of prospectors, loggers, cowhands, and Indians?

A different hostler was working at the livery stable

this morning. He greeted Frank by asking, "Are you the fella who owns that blasted wolf?"

"I don't own him. We just travel together. And he's not a wolf," Frank said. "He just bears a certain resemblance to one."

"Enough of a resemblance to spook all my other customers. They're a mite leery of leaving their horses around a creature like that."

Having heard Frank's voice, Dog came bounding up the big barn's center aisle from the stalls where Stormy and Goldy were being kept. The hostler flinched nervously as the big cur went past him. Dog reared up, put his front paws on Frank's shoulders, and licked his face. Frank laughed and roughed up the thick fur around Dog's neck and ears.

"If he's gonna stay here, I may have to charge you a little more," the hostler went on. From the sound of it, he was the owner of the stable as well.

Frank had been debating what to do with Dog and the two horses, whether to take them with him on the ship or leave them here in Seattle. He had been leaning toward taking them with him anyway, since it might be five or six months before he was able to return, and the hostler's comments just helped him make up his mind. He didn't want to leave his old friends anywhere they wouldn't be taken care of properly.

"Don't worry, we'll all be leaving in a day or two," Frank said. The look of relief on the hostler's face told him that was welcome news.

After checking on Stormy and Goldy and seeing that they were all right, Frank left the livery stable.

The shore curved inland around Elliott Bay a couple of blocks west. Frank headed for the waterfront. He didn't know where the *Montclair* was anchored, but he figured he could find someone who could tell him without much trouble.

Like the rest of Seattle, the docks were a busy place. Tall-masted ships were tied up at most of the wharves, and there were also a number of steam-powered vessels with tall smokestacks. Not only was there a heavy traffic to Alaska these days, but a lot of shipping plied the Pacific Ocean between here and the Orient, as well.

Frank walked over to a man holding a sheaf of papers who was supervising the unloading of cargo from one of the ships. "Can you tell me where to find the *Montclair*?" Frank asked.

"No, but I'll tell you where to find somebody who can," the man replied. He waved the papers in his hand toward a frame building nestled between two looming warehouses made of brick. "The harbor-master's office is in there. He can help you."

"Much obliged," Frank said with a nod.

"Headed to Alaska, cowboy?"

Frank had started to turn away, but he paused and nodded. "Looks like it."

"Better not waste any time, then. Only a few weeks left before the weather turns bad."

"That's what I've heard," Frank said, once again thinking that maybe he had made a mistake by going along with what Jacob Trench wanted. When it was a man's dying wish, though, what else could you do?

The clerk in the harbormaster's office told Frank

that the harbormaster himself was in a meeting and couldn't be disturbed. However, the man was able to give Frank the information he needed, telling him where the *Montclair* was anchored and how to find the ship.

"That's a popular ship this morning," the man commented.

Frank was about to ask him what he meant by that, when the door of the harbormaster's private office opened and a florid-faced man with a gray mustache looked out.

"Boyd, step in here and bring those manifests with you," the man ordered.

"Yes, sir." The clerk stood up and moved toward the office, already forgetting about Frank, who glanced idly through the open door as he turned toward the street.

He frowned. He had caught a glimpse of a woman sitting in a leather chair in front of the harbormaster's desk. He couldn't be sure because her back was to him and she wore a rather extravagant hat, to boot, but she reminded him somehow of Fiona.

Well, she had said she was in Seattle on business, he told himself as he left the building. That business could easily involve shipping. And most importantly, it was none of *his* business.

He found the *Montclair* without any trouble. It was an impressive, double-masted vessel, but amidships, between those two masts, rose a smokestack, and there were paddle wheels on both sides of the ship, indicating that it was powered by both steam and wind. Frank had never seen a ship like that before, but he had never been around the sea very much, either.

A gangplank with ropes strung along the sides for handrails led from the wharf to the deck. A ship's officer in a blue uniform stood at the top of the gangplank. He smiled when Frank paused halfway up and said, "Am I supposed to ask for permission to come aboard, or something like that?"

"That's right, mister," the officer replied. "But if you're here hoping to book passage to Alaska, I'm afraid you're out of luck. We're full up, and we have been for weeks now."

"I need to talk to Captain Hoffman."

The officer's smile went away. "I told you, it won't do any good. Either you've already booked passage, or you won't be sailing with us tomorrow. I don't care if this is one of the last ships this season. You'll just have to hope that there's still some gold left for you next spring."

"I'm not a prospector. I just need to talk to the captain. A friend of mine was supposed to sail on this ship, but he was killed last night."

"And you want to use his ticket. I see."

Frank's jaw tightened. He didn't much cotton to the officer. He said, "I'll bet that water in the bay is cold."

"I'm sure it is. What's that have to do with anything?"

"You're about to find out firsthand when I toss you into it," Frank said. "Unless you get out of my way, that is."

That was probably a mistake, and he knew it. The

ship's officer could yell for help from the rest of the crew, and likely if anybody went into the drink, it would be Frank himself. But sometimes his temper got the best of him, especially when he was confronted by some stubborn, officious fool.

"What's going on there, Brewster?" another blue-uniformed man called from the bridge.

"This cowboy wants to talk to you, Captain," the officer replied. "Something about a dead friend of his booking passage with us—"

"It's about Jacob Trench," Frank said, lifting his voice so that the man on the bridge could hear him.

"What's that?" The captain came closer. "Trench is dead?" He made an impatient gesture. "Let the man on board, Brewster."

The officer stepped aside. As Frank went past, he said in a low voice, "I don't like being threatened, mister. I'll remember that crack about tossing me in the bay."

"You do that," Frank said. He hadn't set out to make an enemy of the man, but he couldn't help it that the Good Lord hadn't put any back-up in him, either.

He walked along the deck to the steep, narrow stairs that led to the bridge. They were more like a ladder than stairs, he thought as he went up them.

The captain was waiting for him at the top. "I'm Rudolph Hoffman," he introduced himself. He was a tall, thick-bodied man with a broad face and graying blond hair under a black uniform cap. "What's this about Jacob Trench being dead?"

"He was killed in a gunfight last night," Frank

explained. "I'm an old friend of his. Name's Frank Morgan."

"I'm sorry to make your acquaintance under these circumstances, Mr. Morgan."

"Was Jacob a friend of yours, too?"

Captain Hoffman shook his head. "No. In fact, I only met him once. He was coming along on our voyage to Alaska that begins tomorrow."

"As a passenger?"

"In a manner of speaking. He was working for one of our passengers, guarding some . . . precious cargo, I suppose you could say."

Frank didn't care for the air of mystery behind this deal, whatever it was. He told the captain, "I was with Jacob when he died. He asked me to take over for him and see that the job he was supposed to do gets done. I reckon you can give me all the details about that."

Hoffman frowned. "I'm not sure I should do that. It seems to me that you should be talking to Trench's employer. Do you know who that is?"

"Some fella named Devereaux," Frank said. "That's all I know. Can you at least tell me where to find him?"

The captain's frown deepened. "Well . . . not exactly. But as it happens, I can tell you where to find *her.*"

"Her?" Frank repeated as his eyebrows rose in surprise. "Devereaux is a woman?"

"Indeed." Hoffman nodded toward the dock. "And here she comes now."

Frank turned to look along the wharf in the direction Hoffman indicated. He spotted her immediately, making her way through the throngs of dockworkers with an assurance that caused them to step aside and give her a clear path.

Fiona.

Chapter 5

Even with the shock of seeing her and learning of her connection to Jacob Trench, Frank recognized the dress Fiona was wearing and knew he'd been right. That *was* her he had seen in the harbormaster's office.

Even as he saw her, she spotted him as well. She stopped short as they locked eyes. Only for a moment, though, and then she strode forward as if with renewed determination. When she reached the gangplank, she started up it without hesitation.

"Allow the lady aboard, Mr. Brewster," Hoffman called to the officer on duty on the deck.

"Aye, Captain," Brewster replied. He stepped aside to allow Fiona to board the ship.

Hoffman started to leave the bridge to go down and greet her, but she held up a hand to stop him. "Stay there, Captain," she called. "I want to come up and talk to you . . . and to Mr. Morgan."

From the sound of the way she said his name, she wasn't happy with him, Frank thought. He wasn't sure why she would feel that way. He hadn't done anything to offend her, at least as far as he knew. He thought they had parted on good terms the night before.

Fiona came up the steep stairs with ease, and when she reached the bridge, she confronted Frank and Hoffman with her handbag clutched tightly in her fingers. "Are you following me, Mr. Morgan?" she demanded.

"How do you figure that?" Frank asked. "I was here talking to Captain Hoffman when you showed up."

"And before that you were at the harbormaster's office when I was."

So she had seen him, too, or maybe just heard and recognized his voice. He supposed that under the circumstances, she had a right to be a mite suspicious of him.

"I'm not following you," he said. "I didn't know you had any connection with Jacob Trench."

"Mr. Trench? What about him?" Fiona's gaze darted to Hoffman. "Have you seen him this morning, Captain?"

"You . . . don't know?" Hoffman asked heavily.

"Know? Know what?"

Frank broke the news to her. "I'm afraid Jacob's dead, Mrs. Devereaux. He's the old friend I told you I lost last night."

Fiona looked more than surprised. She was shocked. "Dead?" she repeated. "But . . . but that's not possible. Mr. Trench is accompanying me to Alaska."

Frank shook his head. "I'm afraid not. I was with

him when he passed, though, and he asked me to take over for him. I promised him that I would."

The suspicion was back in Fiona's eyes suddenly, stronger than ever. "What are you talking about? Exactly how did Mr. Trench die?"

"I didn't have anything to do with it, if that's what you're worried about. I wouldn't horn in on a friend's business, and I sure wouldn't kill him over it." Quickly, Frank explained how the four Haggarty brothers had followed Trench to Seattle from Idaho, determined to settle the score for their cousin's death. He told her about the two ambush attempts and how the second one had taken Trench's life, then concluded by saying, "If you're not satisfied with what I've told you, you can come to the inquest and hear the official verdict. It's at eleven o'clock this morning."

Fiona's anger and suspicion had faded somewhat as Frank told her what happened. Captain Hoffman had listened with great interest, too. When Frank was finished, Fiona said, "I don't think I need to attend the inquest. I suppose I can take your word for what happened, Mr. Morgan. As I told you last night, I pride myself on my judgment, and you strike me as an honest man." She paused. "That doesn't mean I'm going to take you along with me to Alaska, though. Why, I don't even know you. I have no idea whether you're qualified to take over for Mr. Trench."

He smiled slightly. "Maybe if you'd tell me what the job is, we could figure it out. All I know is that Jacob was supposed to guard some cargo for you. What is it? Supplies? Mining equipment?"

"Not exactly, although my customers are all miners."

Frank suppressed the irritation he felt at the way she was making it difficult for him to find out anything. He asked bluntly, "What is it you're taking to them?"

"Women," Fiona said.

Frank grunted. He couldn't hold in the startled question that came to his lips.

"You're a madam?"

It was Fiona's turn to look shocked again. "I should say not! How . . . how dare you imply . . . Do I look like the sort of woman who . . . who would engage in such . . . such an immoral, despicable—"

Frank broke into her outraged sputtering. "You said you're taking women to Alaska for the gold-hunters up there. What was I supposed to think?"

"Brides, Mr. Morgan! Mail-order brides!"

Frank blinked and frowned, then said, "Oh."

"Oh, indeed! I've never been so . . . so insulted!"

"Now hold on a minute," he said. "It was a natural mistake."

"No one *else* has ever mistaken me for a purveyor of fallen women."

"Maybe not, but I meant no offense." She would probably just be more upset if he told her that he had known some madams who were fine women. The salt of the earth, in fact. She wouldn't think that was possible. So he went on. "I've heard about such things, even known some fellas who sent off for brides like that. I don't think there's anything wrong with it."

"Well, I'm so glad my business meets with your approval, Mr. Morgan."

Frank glanced at Captain Hoffman, who seemed to be having a hard time not laughing at him. He supposed the situation was a mite comical. It would have been more so, though, if it hadn't been brought about by the death of a friend.

"Is there someplace Mrs. Devereaux and I can talk in private, Captain?"

Fiona said, "I'm not sure we have anything to discuss."

"I made a promise to an old amigo, and I intend to carry it out."

Hoffman said, "You can talk in my cabin, if Mrs. Devereaux agrees."

Fiona sniffed. "I suppose it woudn't hurt anything to hear you out," she said with obvious reluctance.

"Thanks," Frank said. He nodded to Hoffman. "Captain?"

"Follow me, please."

He led them down to the main deck and opened a door that revealed some more stairs, heading down this time. They descended into a corridor with several doors on each side. Hoffman opened one of them and stepped back, holding out a hand to usher them inside.

Fiona went in first, followed by Frank. The cabin wasn't very large, especially considering the fact that it belonged to the captain, but Frank supposed that space was at a premium on board a ship. There was a narrow bunk, a comfortable-looking chair, and a table strewn with maps, along with a sextant and some other things that Frank didn't recognize but supposed were navigation instruments.

"I'm sorry, it's not very fancy," Hoffman said, "but make yourself at home anyway. I'll be topside, if you need me."

"Thank you, Captain," Fiona said. She waited until Hoffman was gone, then put her handbag on the table, crossed her arms over her chest, and looked steadily at Frank. "I think I'd like to know more about your relationship with Jacob Trench, Mr. Morgan."

"Wasn't really a relationship," Frank said with a shrug. "We ran into each other a few times over the years. For all its size, the West is a smaller place than you might think. Jacob and I backed each other's play a few times, when there was trouble. Out here, that makes a man your friend. Last time I saw him was in New Mexico Territory, ten or twelve years ago."

"And was there trouble then?"

"There was. He was running a freight line, and outlaws were raising he—I mean, stealing shipments from him. I helped him put a stop to that."

"How?"

Frank smiled. "Well, there are some folks who seem to think that I'm pretty good with a gun."

"Are you saying that you're a . . . gunfighter?"

"Yes, ma'am. For want of a better term, I reckon I am."

"Then you're as capable of handling trouble as Mr. Trench was?" Fiona didn't give him a chance to answer the question. Instead she shook her head and went on.

"Of course you are. You must be more capable. You're still alive, and Mr. Trench isn't."

"One thing doesn't always follow the other. There's some luck involved sometimes, too. But yeah, not bragging or anything, I can take care of myself. I can handle the job of guarding you and those mail-order brides of yours, too."

"You sound quite confident."

"If a man's honest with himself," Frank said, "he knows what he can and can't do."

She looked at him for a moment, then slowly nodded. "I suppose that's true. It's true of a woman, as well." A smile curved her lips. "And I know that I'm not capable of taking a dozen young, eligible ladies all the way to Whitehorse by myself."

"Whitehorse? I thought you were going to Skagway."

"That's just the first stop," Fiona explained. "Our ultimate destination is the settlement of Whitehorse. That's across the border in Canada, in the Klondike country, where the most valuable gold diggings are. From what I've heard, the terrain is very rugged. We'll have to cross over something called Chilkoot Pass to get there."

Frank didn't know anything about the geography of Alaska or Canada, but he supposed he could learn. It was also possible that they could pick up a good guide when they got to Skagway. His job would just be to make sure that Fiona and her charges were safe . . . assuming, of course, that she agreed to let him come along.

If she didn't . . . well, he might have to try to

follow them and keep them safe, anyway. A promise was a promise.

She seemed more amenable to the idea now, though. She had said *we* when she was talking about crossing Chilkoot Pass, wherever that was. So he said, "I give you my word I'll do my best to get you there safely, ma'am."

"Oh, for goodness sake. Don't ma'am me. And you don't have to call me Mrs. Devereaux, either." She laughed softly. "We shared a very pleasant dinner last night with you calling me Fiona. I don't suppose there's any real reason to change that. Especially not if we're going to be traveling together."

"You're agreeable to that, then?"

"Well . . . I think I'd like to attend that inquest after all. If you're going to be with us for hundreds of miles, I think I should be sure you've been officially cleared of any wrongdoing."

Frank fished his pocket watch from his jeans and flipped it open. "I reckon we'd better be going, then. It's closing in on eleven o'clock."

He opened the door and let her precede him back to the deck. They paused there to look up at the bridge, where Captain Hoffman stood with his hands on the railing around it.

"Captain, it appears that Mr. Morgan will probably be joining my party after all," Fiona said.

Hoffman tugged on the brim of his cap. "Aye, ma'am. Whatever you say. That's your business."

Fiona smiled. "It certainly is."

As they left the ship, they passed the officer called Brewster, who was still at the head of the gangplank.

He smiled and nodded to Fiona, then glared darkly at Frank, who just gave him a cool, level stare in return. Brewster didn't like him, and Frank didn't give a damn one way or the other.

As they walked away from the waterfront, Frank said, "I'll have to talk to the captain about my horses. I hope the ship can accommodate them."

"You're bringing horses along?"

"We'll have to have some sort of transportation once we get to Alaska."

"Well, certainly, but I assumed we could hire a couple of wagons once we get there."

"Wagons may not be able to get over Chilkoot Pass," Frank pointed out. "We'll have to look into that. You and the ladies may have to ride all the way to Whitehorse. Seems like I've heard that they sometimes use dogsleds to get around up there, too, but only when there's a lot of snow on the ground."

"There'll be a lot to figure out once we get there, won't there?"

"Yes, ma'am . . . I mean, Fiona."

"And I'll call you Frank."

"Fine by me."

"There's one thing you haven't mentioned, Frank . . . your wages."

He chuckled. "To tell you the truth, I hadn't even thought about it. Whatever you were going to pay Jacob will be fine by me."

He didn't try to explain to her that he wasn't doing it for the money, that he already had more money than he could ever possibly spend. That would just complicate matters unnecessarily. All he really cared about was keeping his word to Trench.

"We can discuss that," Fiona said. "Isn't that the courthouse up ahead?"

"Yep." Frank checked his watch again. Not quite eleven o'clock. "Let's get this over with. I never did like court."

The inquest went smoothly, however. Frank was sworn in and testified as to what had happened, and several witnesses who had been on hand for the shoot-outs agreed with his story. The police had also taken statements from a number of witnesses who weren't there to testify, and those were entered into the record, too. The coroner's jury didn't have to deliberate. They rendered a verdict of murder in the case of Trench's death at the hands of one of the Haggarty brothers, and the other four deaths were ruled to be self-defense on the part of Frank and Trench. The coroner dismissed the proceedings, and Frank was free to go.

"Satisfied?" he asked Fiona as they left the courthouse.

"As a matter of fact, I am. There's just one more hurdle you have to clear, Frank, before you officially become a member of our party."

"And what's that?" he asked.

She smiled at him. "You have to meet the brides."

Chapter 6

Frank and Fiona went back to the Majestic Hotel. Along the way, Fiona explained, "These are fine, upstanding young ladies from respectable families in places like New York, Philadelphia, and Boston, you understand. Many of them are quite well educated. I'm sure you're wondering why such women would want to travel thousands of miles to a wilderness such as Alaska to marry men that they've never met."

"The thought crossed my mind," Frank admitted. "I can understand why a man might send off for a wife when he's in a place where there aren't any women, but I can't quite figure why a woman would be interested in a deal like that."

"There are a number of reasons. Some of them simply have a thirst for adventure. Others have suffered tragedies of some sort—the loss of a loved one, a failed romance, things like that—and want to make a fresh start somewhere else."

"I reckon Alaska's about as much 'somewhere else' as you can get," Frank commented with a smile.

"Indeed it is. To these young women, it's as faraway and exotic as, say, China would be." Fiona paused. "But to finish my thought, and to be totally honest with you, Frank, some of the women who enter into arrangements like this are rather unattractive and don't believe they'll ever have a man any other way. Also, some are looking for a degree of financial security. If a man can afford to engage my services and have a bride brought to him, generally he's either already well-to-do or has excellent prospects for being so. The women know that." She laughed. "So, if you want to look at it that way, I suppose what I do *is* sort of like being a madam. I shouldn't have been so offended when you mentioned it earlier."

Frank shook his head. "I wouldn't say that at all. Seems completely different to me."

"I *am* in the business of selling women for money."

"Nope, not the same thing," Frank insisted.

"Well, I'm glad you feel that way." She looked up at the front of the hotel. "Here we are."

They went inside the redbrick building and up the stairs to the second floor. Fiona said, "We'll go to my suite, and I'll have the ladies assemble there. I engaged six rooms for them, two to a room."

The mail-order bride business must pay pretty well, Frank thought. The Majestic wasn't the fanciest hotel in the world, but Fiona had to be doing all right if she could afford to rent a suite and six more rooms for her charges.

The sitting room of Fiona's suite was comfortably furnished. She discreetly closed the door to the bedroom, then told Frank, "Wait here. I'll be back in a moment."

He felt a mite odd, standing there holding his hat in the sitting room of a lady's suite, but luckily Fiona wasn't gone very long. When she came back in, she had a dozen young women trooping along behind her.

They were all shapes and sizes, Frank saw right away, with hair that ranged from palest blond to black as dark as a raven's wing. The only thing they had in common was their age. Frank estimated that all of them were around twenty-five, past the first blush of youth but hardly getting on in years. Although some people uncharitably figured that a woman past the age of twenty who had never been married was an old maid, Frank thought.

As Fiona had pointed out, some of the women were rather plain, but there wasn't a single one of them Frank would have called downright ugly, and a few were pretty darned good-looking, in his opinion. One blonde in particular was really pretty, he thought. She had a nice quirky smile and cornflower blue eyes.

She was the one Fiona introduced to him first, as well. "Frank, this is Margaret Goodwin. Meg, as she's called."

Frank nodded. "Miss Goodwin."

"Meg," she said. She held out a hand to shake, just like a man would have. "I'm pleased to meet you, Mr. Morgan. Mrs. Devereaux tells us that you're a famous gunfighter."

"Well . . . some folks might say infamous," Frank said as he shook hands with her. "Or even notorious."

"Yes, but if you're going to be protecting us on our voyage, I prefer to think of you as famous."

Fiona motioned forward a little brunette with a lush figure. "This is Jessica Harpe."

Frank said, "Pleased to meet you, Miss Harpe."

For the next few minutes, Fiona continued the introductions. The names began to run together in Frank's head: Elizabeth Jenkins, Ruth Donnelly, Marie Boulieu, Gertrude Nevins, Maureen Kincaid, Ginnie Miller, Constance Wilson, Wilma Keller, Elizabeth Tarrant, and Lucy Calvert. Elizabeth Jenkins went by Elizabeth, Elizabeth Tarrant by Lizzie, so Frank tried to make a note of that in his head. He knew it would take him a while to remember all their names, though. They were all unfailingly polite, and Frank instinctively liked them.

When the introductions were finished, Fiona said, "Well, ladies, you've met Mr. Morgan. What do you think of him?"

"He's very handsome, in a rugged way," Meg said with a smile.

"I don't care much for that gun, though," Gertrude added. "Would a gentleman wear a weapon out in the open like that?"

"Not in Philadelphia, where you're from, my dear," Fiona said. "I assure you, Seattle is *not* Philadelphia."

Gertrude sniffed. "I know. I heard all sorts of shooting and yelling in the street last night. It frightened me."

Frank said, "No offense, miss, but where you're headed will be a lot more rugged and dangerous than

Seattle is. You may have to ride horseback for miles up and down mountains, and there'll be men who won't hesitate to try to take what they want . . . which might include you."

A pink flush spread over Gertrude's face. "That's not really a proper thing to say, Mr. Morgan."

"I was raised to believe that it's always proper to speak the truth. And the truth is, you ladies are in for a long, difficult journey. You may be faced with bad weather, bad food, and bad men. I promised a friend of mine that I'd do my best to see to it that you get where you're going safe and sound. That's what I intend to do if Mrs. Devereaux agrees, and the way I understand it, she'd like for you ladies to agree, too."

"That's right," Fiona said with a nod. "I had originally engaged his friend Mr. Trench to accompany us, but unfortunately, Mr. Trench was killed last night." She looked at Gertrude. "It may well have been some of the shots you heard that were responsible for his demise."

Gertrude paled. "How terrible."

"Yes, it is. But Mr. Morgan has offered to step in for Mr. Trench. I appreciate that gesture on his part and intend to allow him to travel with us. What do you say?"

"I'm all for it," Meg said.

"So am I," Lucy added. She was a tall, lanky young woman with long, light brown hair.

Several other women nodded or voiced their agreement, and one by one they all joined in until only Gertrude and Marie hadn't said one way or the other. Marie, a slender young woman with a lot of curly black hair, shrugged and said with a slight French accent, "One gunman is much the same as another, I suppose."

"Well, I'm not going to vote against everyone else," Gertrude said. "I do hope you won't have to use that awful gun, though, Mr. Morgan."

"So do I, miss, so do I," Frank said.

He was going to be damned surprised if that was the way it turned out, though.

With the question of whether or not Frank was going with them settled, Fiona sent the young women back to their rooms. Then she said, "Would you care to join me in the dining room for dinner, Frank? We can discuss the arrangements for the trip."

"I'd like that," Frank replied with a nod. "I've got some questions about supplies and things like that."

They spent the next hour in the hotel dining room, eating and discussing the trip. With Skagway being the jumping-off point to Whitehorse and the rich gold fields of the Klondike country, it made sense to buy as many of the supplies needed for the journey as they could here in Seattle. Goods were cheaper and more plentiful than they would be in Skagway.

"We'll have to buy some fresh meat when we get there, of course," Frank said, "and then I can probably bag some game while we're on our way from Skagway over the pass to Whitehorse." He smiled. "Did you ever have moose steaks?"

A little shudder went through Fiona. "No, not that I'm aware of."

"Well, I bet you'll be trying them before we get where we're going. But we'll stock up on sugar, flour, salt, things like that, before we leave here. Also ammunition."

"How many bullets do you think you'll need?"

"It's not just for me," Frank said. "I intend to pick up some pistols for the ladies, and a couple of extra rifles."

Fiona's eyes widened. "You intend to arm them? They're mail-order brides, Frank! I doubt if any of them have ever even held a weapon."

"I don't know. That Meg strikes me as the sort who might've burned some powder sometime," Frank said with a grin. "She's pretty feisty." He grew more serious as he went on. "I can give them some pointers while we're on board the ship. But I think it's important that the ladies be able to protect themselves, at least a little. There's no telling what might happen along the way. If I wound up dead, the bunch of you wouldn't be totally defenseless."

"Don't even *say* such a thing! We're relying on you, Frank. Nothing can happen to you."

He frowned. "Out here, it's best to be able to rely on yourself as much as possible. I'm not trying to scare you, Fiona. I just want you—and those gals of yours—to go into this with your eyes open. Seattle can be a rough place, but it's still civilization. Alaska's not. It's just as much an untamed frontier as the country west of the Mississippi was fifty or sixty years ago."

"Bad weather, bad food, and bad men, as you said earlier, eh?" she said, cocking an eyebrow at him.

"That's right. And I forgot to mention the bears and wolves and varmints like that."

Fiona shook her head. "Why would men even want to go to a place like that?"

"For what they think is the best reason of all . . . gold."

"But you don't think that?" she asked with a shrewd look on her face.

"I'm old enough to know that there are a lot of things in this world gold *can't* buy you."

"Then you're a wise man, Frank Morgan."

"I don't know that I'd say that. Anyway, maybe you'd better not say anything to the ladies about the guns until we're on board the *Montclair*. I think Miss Gertrude might have a fit if she thought she was going to have to learn how to shoot a pistol."

"I think you're right about that," Fiona said.

After they finished their meal, Fiona went back upstairs to her suite, while Frank headed for the waterfront again. He wanted to talk to Captain Hoffman again and make arrangements for Stormy, Goldy, and Dog to come with him.

A different officer was on deck this afternoon instead of the surly Brewster. He was pleasant enough as he told Frank to come aboard and said in answer to Frank's question, "Captain Hoffman is in his cabin, sir. Do you know where that is?"

"Yeah, I do. Thanks."

Frank went below to the captain's cabin and rapped on the door. When Hoffman asked who was there, he said, "Frank Morgan, Captain."

"Come in, please."

Frank went in and found Hoffman sitting at the desk, looking over some of the charts spread out there. The captain glanced up with a smile.

"Is your business with Mrs. Devereaux all squared away, Mr. Morgan?" he asked.

Frank thumbed his hat back. "Yeah, she's agreed that I'll be coming along to Alaska with her and her young ladies."

"Mail-order brides," Hoffman said with a shake of his head. "I'd heard of such a thing, of course, but this is the first time I've encountered it. Have you met the young ladies?"

"I have," Frank said. "Seems like a fine bunch. I'm not sure how well some of them are going to like living in the Klondike, but that's not my business. All I have to do is get them there."

"Much like me," Hoffman said. "I'll deliver my passengers and cargo to Skagway, and there my responsibility ends." He tapped one of the charts. "I was just looking at the route I intend to follow."

"You've sailed to Alaska before?" Frank asked as he leaned over and looked at the map. This late in the season, he wasn't too fond of the idea of setting out with an inexperienced captain.

"Oh, yes, many times," Hoffman replied. "Don't worry, Mr. Morgan. We'll have no trouble."

"What about the weather?"

"It'll be at least three weeks, probably a month, before the weather represents a danger. We'll be in Skagway in less than a week."

Hoffman seemed to know what he was doing, Frank thought. That eased his worries.

"Is it going to be all right for me to bring my horses along?" he asked.

"Horses?" Hoffman frowned. "The *Montclair* normally doesn't carry livestock." He thought about it for a moment and then shrugged. "But I suppose we could make a place for them in the hold. We could open one of the hatches for light and air. It might not be very comfortable for them, being cooped up that way, though."

"They can stand it for a few days," Frank said. "I want my own mounts with me when we get there."

"I don't blame you for that. A man likes to have what he's accustomed to."

"I have a dog, too, but he won't take up much room or be any trouble."

"That's fine, as long as he doesn't fight with cats. We have a couple who sail with us to keep the rats out of the cargo."

"Dog will leave them alone as long as I tell him to." Frank added, "I'm going to see about having some supplies delivered for us to take along. Better to stock up on things here in Seattle rather than waiting until we get to Skagway."

Hoffman nodded. "I believe that was Mr. Trench's plan as well. There should be adequate room in the hold for whatever you want to bring along. Although having those horses in there will cut down on the available space."

"We'll work it out," Frank said. He held out his hand. "Sounds like it'll all be fine. I'm looking forward to sailing with you, Captain."

Hoffman shook with him. "I hope it's a pleasant journey for you, Mr. Morgan."

Frank said so long and went up on deck again. He was headed for the gangplank when he heard a step behind him. A man said, "Morgan."

Frank turned and saw the ship's officer called Brewster. He gave the man a curt nod.

"You're coming along to Alaska?" Brewster asked harshly.

"That's right."

"I think we should get something straight between us, then, before the voyage starts."

"What's that?" Frank asked, his voice cool.

"This," Brewster said. He sent a punch rocketing at Frank's jaw.

Chapter 7

The attack didn't take Frank totally by surprise. Over the years he had learned how to sense the intentions of other men. That was one thing that had helped him stay alive as long as he had. As soon as he turned around and saw Brewster's hostile stance, he knew the officer was looking for trouble.

With that much warning, Frank was able to pull his head aside so that Brewster's punch missed completely, sailing past his ear by a good two inches. Thrown off balance by the missed blow, Brewster stumbled forward. Frank twisted at the waist, grabbed Brewster's arm, and kept pivoting, hauling hard on the arm as he did so.

With a startled yell, Brewster lost his footing and crashed to the deck. He rolled over a couple of times before he came to a stop.

"You took your shot, mister," Frank said in a hard, flat voice. "Let it go at that, and we'll call it even."

"The hell we will," Brewster snarled as he climbed to his feet. He lowered his head and charged at Frank.

That bull rush was just a feint, though. When Frank started to dart aside from it, Brewster stopped suddenly and lashed out again with his fist. This time the punch landed cleanly on Frank's jaw and knocked him back several steps. Like most sailors, even officers, Brewster obviously had plenty of experience as a bare-knuckles brawler. He charged again while Frank was off balance, and this time it was the real thing. Brewster wrapped his arms around Frank in a tackle that sent both of them slamming down onto the deck. Frank was on the bottom, and the impact drove the air out of his lungs.

As he gasped for breath, Frank was vaguely aware of shouting and knew that other members of the crew were probably gathering around to watch the fight. That meant he would be heavily outnumbered if the other sailors decided to take a hand.

He could only fight one battle at a time, though, so as Brewster tried to lock his hands around his throat, Frank sent a short punch straight up at the officer's chin. It rocked Brewster's head back and kept him from getting the choke hold he sought.

Frank arched his back off the deck, grabbed the lapels of Brewster's uniform coat, and flung him off to the side. Frank rolled the other way, came up on hands and knees, and paused long enough to drag a deep breath back into his lungs.

A rush of footsteps told him that Brewster was charging him again. Frank twisted in that direction and saw Brewster swinging a foot at him in a vicious kick. Frank got his hands up in time to catch hold of Brewster's ankle and stop the blow from landing. He surged up, still holding on to Brewster, and sent the officer toppling over backward. Brewster landed so hard on his back that Frank felt the deck vibrate a little under his feet.

"Damn it, stay down," Frank growled.

"You go to . . . hell, Morgan," Brewster panted as he climbed laboriously back to his feet. Chest heaving, he came toward Frank. He weaved a little from side to side as he bunched his hands into fists and got ready to start swinging again.

Frank didn't wait. He stepped in, hooked a left into Brewster's midsection, and then when Brewster hunched over in pain, Frank brought around a looping right that landed with devastating impact on the officer's jaw. Brewster hit the deck again and didn't move this time. He was out cold.

With that threat taken care of, Frank looked around to see if any of the other members of the *Montclair*'s crew wanted to take a hand in this game. Half a dozen roughly clad sailors and a couple of blue-uniformed officers were standing there with surprised expressions on their faces. Clearly, they hadn't expected Frank to emerge triumphant from this fracas.

"Mr. Morgan!" Captain Hoffman's voice came sharply from the door that led belowdecks. "What's going on here?"

Instead of answering right away, Frank looked around for his hat, which had fallen off when Brewster tackled him. Spotting it on the deck, he bent and picked it up, then punched it back into shape and settled it on his head. Then and only then did he turn to face the captain.

"That fella Brewster didn't care much for the idea of me sailing with you," he said.

Hoffman stalked across the deck, his face set in grim lines. He looked around at the other members of the crew and asked, "Is this true? Did Brewster attack Mr. Morgan?"

No one answered him. Frank figured the men wanted to be loyal to their fellow seaman. But then one of the sailors spoke up, saying, "Aye, that he did, Cap'n. The cowboy didn't do anything except defend hisself."

Another man said, "Aye, that's the way it happened, Cap'n," and the other sailors nodded. Frank began to sense that Brewster wasn't well liked among the crew, at least not by the common sailors. The other officers were reluctant to speak against him, though.

"I see," Hoffman said. He turned to Frank. "My apologies, Mr. Morgan. I'll deal with this matter. I'll tell you right now, though, I don't plan to dismiss Mr. Brewster. He's a very competent seaman, despite his touchy nature at times."

"Wouldn't ask you to throw him off the ship," Frank said. "Just tell him to steer clear of me, and we'll get along fine."

"That much I can and will do," Hoffman vowed.

Frank nodded. As far as he was concerned, the ruckus was over and done with, and he was willing to leave it that way.

As Frank started to turn away, the captain added softly, "Thank you for not killing him."

"That would've been a hell of a way to start the trip, wouldn' it?" Frank said.

Since Fiona agreed with him about the advisability of stocking up on supplies here in Seattle, she had left it to him to make those arrangements. Frank went to the largest general store he could find and talked to the proprietor, laying out a list of what he needed. The man's advice came in handy. He had outfitted plenty of travelers to Alaska and knew what was necessary and what wasn't. Of course, this was a little different, since the young women traveling with Fiona weren't going to prospect for gold themselves. But they needed the same sort of warm, heavy clothing and easy-to-carry provisions as the gold-hunters.

The storekeeper raised his bushy eyebrows in surprise, though, when Frank asked for twelve .32-caliber pistols. He didn't figure the young women could handle anything heavier than that.

"I thought you was takin' mail-order brides to Skagway, Mr. Morgan," the man said, "not puttin' together a small army."

So word had gotten around town about the "cargo" he and Fiona were delivering to Alaska, Frank thought. He wasn't surprised. News traveled fast in frontier settlements, and that's what Seattle still was.

"Just because they're women doesn't mean they can't protect themselves," he said. "They're going to some rough country."

"They sure are," the storekeeper agreed. "And I

reckon it's a good idea for them to be armed. I wouldn't have thought of it myself, that's all."

"I want a couple of Winchesters, too. .44-40s."

The man nodded. "I can do that. If you're goin' over Chilkoot Pass, you'd better be armed for bear . . . or worse."

"What do you mean by that?" Frank asked with a slight frown.

"Just that there's things up there worse'n wild animals. From what I've heard, that Yukon and Klondike country is full of two-legged varmints, too. Outlaws, claim-jumpers, and just pure-dee mean hombres lookin' for trouble. A bunch of young women travelin' together . . ." The man shook his head. "That's gonna be a mighty temptin' target. I don't reckon I'm tellin' you anything you don't already know, though."

"No," Frank said, "you're not."

The storekeeper agreed to put the order together and have it delivered to the *Montclair* the first thing in the morning. Captain Hoffman intended to sail by ten o'clock.

"Do I send the bill to Mrs. Devereaux at the hotel?" the man asked.

"Send her the bill for half of it," Frank said. "I'll take care of the other half right now, if you'll accept a draft on my bank in San Francisco."

"Well, now . . ."

"The draft is good."

"Oh, I never doubted that, Mr. Morgan," the storekeeper said quickly. "I didn't mean no offense."

The story of Fiona's trip to Alaska with the

mail-order brides wasn't the only information that had gotten around Seattle, Frank thought. So had the news of the two gunfights in which he had been involved the night before. The storekeeper knew that he was dealing with the notorious Drifter.

"I'll be glad to take your draft, Mr. Morgan," the man went on. "I was just a mite confused, that's all. I was under the impression you're workin' for Mrs. Devereaux."

"I am," Frank said. "I just thought I'd help her out a little."

The amount was more than a little, of course, but Frank knew he would never miss the money. When his attorney, Claudius Turnbuckle, got wind of the expense, as Claudius always did, he might raise an eyebrow, but he had learned over the years that Frank usually did as he damned well pleased, and arguing about it didn't serve any purpose.

The arrangements concluded, Frank left the store and headed back to the hotel. It was late in the afternoon by now. Along the way he stopped at the livery stable and informed the proprietor there that he would be picking up Stormy, Goldy, and Dog first thing the next morning. The man's sour expression as he nodded indicated that it couldn't be soon enough to suit him.

By the time Frank got back to the hotel, people were going into the dining room for supper. He looked through the arched entrance for Fiona, but didn't see her. Turning instead to the stairs, he started up to the second floor.

Fiona appeared at the landing when Frank was

halfway up, followed by the twelve young women. Frank stopped and watched as they started to descend, talking and laughing among themselves. It was a sight to behold, he thought. True, not all of them could be considered beauties, but they were all sweet and appealing, even the somewhat prissy Gertrude. Frank was old enough to be their father, of course, so he didn't feel drawn to them himself, but he could imagine how some miner stuck in the wilds of Alaska would react to any one of them. It was no wonder that Fiona's business was successful. A man could get mighty lonely, and only the soft touch of a woman could ease the ache he felt inside.

Fiona paused and smiled at him. "Is everything ready, Frank?" she asked.

"It will be. Our supplies will be delivered to the boat tomorrow morning in plenty of time for Captain Hoffman to sail on schedule."

"That's wonderful!" She came on down the steps and linked her arm with his. "You'll join us for supper?"

"Well, I thought I might clean up a little . . ." He didn't mention that he'd been rolling on the deck of the *Montclair* a couple of hours earlier, tussling with Brewster.

Meg came down the steps and took his other arm. "I think you're fine just the way you are, Mr. Morgan," she said. "Don't you, girls?"

Several of them smiled and nodded. Frank had no choice but to say, "All right, then. I'd be honored to join you ladies."

He thought about all the solitary meals he had

eaten on some lonely trail, often with men pursuing him who wanted to kill him, not knowing if he would live to see the sun rise the next morning. Now he was about to sit down to eat at a table with a snowy white cloth on it, set with fine china, surrounded by a dozen young women and a somewhat older one who was even lovelier. He regretted Jacob Trench's death, of course . . .

But right now he was sort of glad he had come to Seattle.

Chapter 8

The next morning dawned cold and blustery, with gray clouds scudding through the sky and occasional bursts of light rain spitting down on Puget Sound. Frank wore a sheepskin coat as he left the hotel and headed toward the livery stable to collect Stormy, Goldy, and Dog.

The horses and the big cur were glad to see him. Frank settled up with the liveryman, then saddled Stormy himself and rode out of the barn, leading Goldy. Dog trotted along beside them. His ears were up and tilted forward a little as he took in all the sights and, more importantly where he was concerned, the smells of the port settlement.

Frank rode along the waterfront until he came to the wharf where the *Montclair* was anchored. A couple of wagons were drawn up on the dock and crates were being unloaded from them and carried aboard. Frank spotted the storekeeper he had dealt with the day before. Obviously, the man had come along to supervise the loading of the supplies himself.

He raised a hand in greeting when he saw Frank. "Mornin', Mr. Morgan. Got everything you wanted." He waved toward the crates. "It'll all be on board in a little while."

One of the boxes seemed to be pretty heavy. Frank watched two men pick it up and lug it up the gangplank.

"Rifles, pistols, and ammunition," the storekeeper told him. "Just like you said."

"Much obliged. I'm sure the ladies will appreciate it, too."

The man looked around. "Are they, uh, here yet?"

Frank suppressed the urge to grin. The storekeeper hoped to catch a glimpse of those mail-order brides he had heard about, Frank figured. That was another reason he had come along with the wagons.

"I think they're still at the hotel," Frank said. "They'll be along directly."

"Oh." The storekeeper tried not to look or sound too disappointed. All the supplies had been unloaded now, so he no longer had an excuse for hanging around the dock. "I wish you good luck, then, Mr. Morgan."

Frank leaned over in the saddle and reached out to shake hands with the man, who was sitting on one of the wagon seats. "Thanks. I'm hoping we won't need luck . . . but I'll bet a hat that we will before we get where we're going."

The wagons rattled off a minute later. Frank swung down from the saddle and tied the horses' reins to one of the pilings that stuck up at the edge of the dock. Then he went up the gangplank with Dog following him.

Captain Hoffman himself was at the head of the gangplank today. He looked past Frank and said, "My God. I thought you said you were bringing a dog with you, Mr. Morgan, not a wolf."

Frank grinned. "Don't worry about him. He's all dog. Well, mostly, anyway. I can't be sure about all his ancestors, though." He gestured toward Stormy and Goldy. "There are my horses."

"I suppose we can rig some sort of sling and boom to lift them onto the deck and lower them into the hold," Hoffman said with a frown.

"No need. I'll just lead them aboard, if that's all right with you."

"Up the gangplank?" Hoffman sounded like he thought that wouldn't be possible.

"They're pretty sure-footed," Frank said. "I've trusted my life to them on ledges that are even narrower than that plank, with a sheer cliff going up on one side and a drop of several hundred feet on the other."

A shiver went through Hoffman. "I don't see how anyone does such a thing," he said. "Give me the sea any day."

Frank looked out at the cold, gray waters of the sound, which were pretty choppy this morning, and felt the same way about it that Hoffman did about those high mountain trails.

"The weather's taken a turn for the worse," he commented.

"This?" Hoffman made a casual gesture toward

the leaden sky. "This is nothing to worry about. I'd be more concerned if it was clear and warm. Now, if you're sure about bringing those horses of yours aboard, we can lower some boards through the hatch into the cargo hold to make a ramp."

Frank nodded. "I'll go get 'em."

One at a time, he led Stormy and Goldy up the gangplank, onto the deck, and then down the make-shift ramp into the hold. As he expected, neither of them had any trouble. They were both almost as nimble as mountain goats. The sailors had put up some partitions to form stalls in one corner of the hold, and buckets of fresh water and grain were al-ready in place. Hoffman had done a good job of preparing for the unexpected four-legged passengers, and Frank intended to thank him and compliment him for his efforts. He left Dog belowdecks as well, telling the big cur to stay with Stormy and Goldy. Dog didn't seem to like it much, but he would do whatever Frank told him.

When Frank started topside again, he heard women's voices before he even emerged from the hold. As he came out on deck, he saw that Fiona and the young women had arrived at the wharf in several carriages, followed by a wagon piled high with baggage.

Captain Hoffman stood at the railing, a frown on his face. He glanced at Frank and said, "I hope we have room for all those bags. Women don't travel lightly, do they, Mr. Morgan?"

"Don't ask me a question like that when there are ladies in earshot, Captain," Frank responded with a grin. Fiona had reached the top of the gangplank.

"Good morning, Frank," she said. "Captain Hoffman, do we have your permission to come aboard?"

"Indeed you and your charges do, Mrs. Devereaux, ma'am," Hoffman said. "Welcome to the *Montclair*, all of you."

Chattering excitedly, the young women came up the gangplank and onto the ship. Hoffman had one of his officers show them to their cabins. It wasn't Brewster who got the job, Frank noted. In fact, Frank hadn't even seen Brewster this morning. He wondered if Captain Hoffman had assigned him to duties belowdecks to keep him out of the way. If so, that was fine for now, but Frank doubted if Hoffman would be able to keep the two of them apart all the way to Skagway.

The rain began to fall harder, which drove everyone inside except the sailors who had to be on deck. Frank lingered for a moment with moisture dripping off the brim of his hat as he said, "We're putting ourselves in your hands, Captain."

"Don't worry," Hoffman said as he buttoned up the slicker he had put on. "In less than a week, you'll be in Skagway. And once you've seen that hellhole, you may wish you were back on my boat, Mr. Morgan!"

The captain's prediction stayed with Frank as the ship weighed anchor a short time later and used its steam engine to push itself away from the dock, out into Elliott Bay and then Puget Sound itself. Just how much of a hellhole *was* Skagway?

Frank had seen many boomtowns in his time, most

recently the silver mining town of Buckskin in Nevada. He had served as the marshal there for a while, and he had to admit that it had been an exciting, violent time. It was entirely possible that Skagway was worse, since it was more isolated. Frank didn't know if there was any law up there beyond what the settlers themselves made.

He wondered if Whitehorse would be better or worse. At least across the border in Canada, the Royal Canadian Mounted Police had jurisdiction. Frank had run into a few Mounties in the past and knew them to be tough, capable hombres.

But he was getting ahead of himself. They still had several days worth of sailing to go before they arrived in Alaska. He went to the tiny porthole of the cabin he had been assigned and looked out at the rain-lashed waters of the sound. He felt the faint vibration of the deck under his feet from the engines and heard their deep-throated rumble. That was reassuring. The engines were powerful enough so that they sent the vessel through the water at a steady pace. The ship pitched some—enough to make Frank a little queasy, in fact—but he thought he would get used to it without much trouble. He hoped so, anyway.

But even if he did, he would still be mighty glad to have dry land under his feet again.

He remembered looking at one of the maps in Captain Hoffman's cabin. From Puget Sound, the ship turned west and headed through the Strait of Juan de Fuca, which led to the Pacific Ocean. Frank had seen the Pacific on numerous occasions, most recently during a dustup in the redwood country of northern California, but it was always an impressive sight, stretching out endlessly to the horizon. Frank looked out at the mountains that wore a gray shroud of clouds and rain and knew that he was bidding farewell to land for a few days.

A knock sounded on his door, taking him a little by surprise. He turned away from the porthole and went to answer the summons. When he swung the door open, he found Fiona standing there. She had shed her coat and hat and wore an elegant traveling gown of some dark gray fabric that clung to her body.

"Well, we're on our way, Frank," she said.

"Yeah, I know. I was just watching the shoreline fall behind us."

She lifted a bottle that had been partially concealed behind the folds of her dress. "I thought we might have a drink to commemorate our departure and the start of our new venture."

"It's your venture, not mine," Frank pointed out. "I'm just a hired hand."

"I was hoping that wouldn't be the case. I could use a partner, Frank. I was considering making that offer to Mr. Trench, once I got to know him better, but since he's gone . . . I'm making it to you."

"Me? In the mail-order bride business?" Frank managed not to laugh at such a loco notion. "I don't think that would be a very good idea. I don't have much of a head for business."

That was why he had firms of high-priced lawyers in San Francisco and Denver looking out for his interests, he thought . . . but he didn't say that to Fiona.

"Don't worry about that," she said. "I'd handle all the business end of the operation. What I need is a man to make the details run smoothly, and I must say, I've been very impressed with the way you've handled everything. I'm sure that if we run into trouble, you'll handle that, too."

"That's what I figure, but you don't need a partner for things like that, Fiona. You just need somebody to work for you, like Jacob was going to. Like I am."

"A man does a better job if he has a personal stake in something," Fiona said as she moved closer to him and shut the cabin door behind her. "That's why I thought we could have a drink and talk about extending your involvement."

He was slow as molasses sometimes, Frank thought as he suddenly realized why she had really come to his cabin. He said, "I'm still not sure that would be a good idea . . ."

She was right in front of him now, only inches away. She laid her free hand on his chest and murmured in that intriguingly hoarse voice of hers, "I think it would be an excellent idea."

Frank was as human as the next hombre, and Fiona Devereaux was a beautiful woman with what appeared to be an excellent bottle of whiskey in her hand. He slid his left arm around her waist and pulled her closer.

"Sailors have a saying," she said as she tipped her head back to look up into his eyes. "Somewhere in the world, the sun is over the yardarm."

"I reckon I'll drink to that," Frank said. "Later."

Chapter 9

Despite the rough seas, the *Montclair* handled the waves easily that first day. Frank went up on deck when the rain stopped that afternoon and saw that Captain Hoffman had ordered the crew to raise the sails. They were full and billowing as the ship tacked back and forth, running before the wind. The engines still chugged along, but they didn't have to work as hard with the sails raised.

Frank quickly discovered that being on deck where he could see the horizon rising and falling with each wave made his stomach feel worse. He was about to turn around and go below when Captain Hoffman hailed him from the bridge.

"Mr. Morgan! How are you doing?"

Frank raised a hand in a gesture that was more casual than he felt. "All right, I reckon," he replied. "I'm just not that fond of the water."

"You'll get used to it," Hoffman called down reassuringly. "We'll make an old salt out of you!"

Frank doubted that. He didn't figure he'd be on

board long enough to get too accustomed to the sea's motion.

He was on his way back down to the belowdecks corridor when he encountered Fiona coming up. She wore a grim look on her face, and Frank thought he knew why. He heard sounds of retching coming from behind many of the closed cabin doors.

"Nearly all of the girls are sick as dogs," Fiona said. "I don't know what to do. I was on my way to ask the captain."

"I don't think there's anything that can be done," Frank said. "You'll just have to let them get over it."

"What if they don't?"

Frank shrugged. "Some will. The ones who don't will just have to be sick all the way to Alaska. It won't kill them . . . although they're liable to wish they could go ahead and die before it's over."

"Did you know it would be like this?"

"I figured as much," Frank admitted. "But I knew there was no way around it. Shoot, I don't feel too good myself."

Fiona pressed a hand to her stomach. "Neither do I. In fact . . . oh, my God, Frank . . ."

"There's a bucket in your cabin," he told her, "or you can hurry on topside and maybe make it to the railing."

"Ohhh . . . let's try that."

Frank took hold of her arm, hustled her up onto the deck, and over to the railing. They reached it in time, and he looked away discreetly while she was sick. When she was finished, she straightened and pushed back several strands of dark hair that had fallen over her washed-out face. Frank patted her lightly on the back, for whatever good that did.

"I'm not sure it's worth it," Fiona muttered.

"You'll feel differently once we get to Skagway and start out for Whitehorse."

"That may be even worse, just in different ways."

Frank couldn't argue with that, so he just shrugged again.

He helped her below to her cabin and told her, "If any of the girls want to come topside, let me know and I'll come with them to make sure they're all right."

"You think some of the sailors might try to bother them?"

"I doubt it. Captain Hoffman runs a pretty tight ship." Frank smiled wryly. "I was more worried about one of 'em falling overboard while they're feeding the fishes."

Fiona looked like she wanted to punch him. "Don't even talk about it," she said.

Frank skipped the midday meal, but by nightfall his stomach had settled down enough so that he was hungry again. When he checked with Fiona and the rest of the women, none of them wanted to eat. He was planning to rustle something for himself from their supplies when he ran into one of the other passengers in the corridor outside the cabins, a man outfitted in the rough but new clothes of a gold-hunter, a sure sign that he was making his first trip to Alaska.

"You're Mr. Morgan, aren't you?" the young man said as he held out his hand. "I'm Peter Conway."

The youngster was trying to grow a beard, no

doubt to make him look more like a sourdough, but he wasn't having much luck with it. The blond whiskers were coming in sort of wispylike. He was tall and broad-shouldered, though, and his grip was strong as Frank shook with him.

"Yeah, I'm Morgan. Call me Frank, though."

Conway grinned. "All right. I'm pleased to meet you, Frank. Everyone's talking about you."

Frank raised an eyebrow. "Everyone?"

"All the other prospectors, I mean. We heard about the things that happened in Seattle, before the boat sailed, how you were in those gunfights and that brawl with one of the ship's officers." Conway's grin grew even wider. "And of course, we've all heard about those women traveling with you. We've been waiting to get a look at them, but they're still shut up in their cabins."

"They're pretty sick," Frank said, "and they may stay that way the whole voyage."

"I hope not."

"You know they're already spoken for, don't you?"

"Yeah, of course. They're mail-order brides, right? But we'd still enjoy talking to them. Where we're going, we may not see any respectable women for a long time."

"That's true enough, I reckon," Frank said. "Some of 'em might not mind socializing a little on the way, but that's up to them. It's my job to keep them from being bothered."

Conway nodded, his expression solemn now. "I understand, and I'll pass the word along. Better yet, why don't you come have supper with us? That is, if you don't mind eating with a bunch of cheechakos."

"What's that?"

"That's what they call us newcomers up there in the Klondike, or so I've heard. It's some sort of Indian word."

Frank nodded in understanding. "Like a tenderfoot or a greenhorn back where I come from in Texas."

"Yeah, I suppose. Anyway, we have plenty of food if you'd like to join us."

"Sure. I'm much obliged." Frank would be glad for the company, and he didn't think it would hurt anything to get to know some of his fellow passengers.

He followed Conway up on deck. The wind was cold, but the rain had stopped and a group of gold-hunters had gathered around a Primus stove where they were cooking a pot of stew. Conway introduced Frank to the men. One of them said, "You're the gun-fighter they call The Drifter, aren't you?"

"That's right."

"I've read books about you, mister. Never thought I'd meet you, though."

"Those books are mostly made up," Frank advised him. "And the hombres who write them have pretty wild imaginations." He took a cup of the stew that Peter Conway handed to him. It smelled delicious.

It tasted as good as it smelled, he discovered as he began to eat. Earlier in the day, he had thought that he wouldn't have an appetite again until the ship docked and he had dry land under his feet. He was surprised now by how hungry he was. He'd always had an iron constitution, though, and he supposed that included his stomach.

The dime-novel reader sidled over to him again. "How many men have you killed, Mr. Morgan?" he asked.

A frown creased Frank's forehead. "I don't carve notches in my gun butt, if that's what you're asking."

"There are so many, you don't even know anymore, do you?"

"I never killed anybody who wasn't trying to kill me or somebody else," Frank said, trying to keep the irritation out of his voice. "I don't see any point in keeping count of how many fools there are in the world. That'd be a never-ending job."

"I just can't imagine what it would be like to shoot all those men, to have that much blood on my hands. How do you sleep at night?"

Frank didn't answer the question. Instead, he asked curtly, "Where are you from, mister?"

"New York City. Why?"

Frank nodded and said, "I figured as much."

The man bristled. "What the hell do you mean by that?"

Conway came up in time to hear that last exchange. He said, "Take it easy, Neville. I asked Mr. Morgan to join us. I don't want you getting in an argument with him."

"I'm not arguing with anybody," Neville insisted. "But he insulted New York."

Frank shook his head. "No, I didn't. I reckon it's a fine place. But it's been settled for a long time. It hasn't been a real frontier for, what, a couple of hundred years? So you folks back there have forgotten what it's like to have to fight to defend yourself and your loved ones. You've never known any real danger."

Neville sneered. "If you'd ever been in certain parts of New York City, you wouldn't say that, Morgan."

"You might be right," Frank said with a shrug. "All I'm saying is that you look at things different than folks who grew up out West do. We're used to relying on ourselves. And if you're going to Alaska to hunt for gold, that'd be a good thing for you to learn, too, amigo."

That seemed to mollify Neville a little. He said, "I suppose you're right. I didn't mean any offense, Morgan." He changed the subject by asking, "How pretty are those girls you're taking to the Klondike?"

The other would-be prospectors crowded around to hear Frank's answer.

"They're nice-looking young ladies," he said. "And they're *ladies,* don't forget that. They're all engaged to be married."

"To men they've never met," Peter Conway pointed out. "It might as well be us."

"But it's not. Like I told you, Pete, they're spoken for, and that's the way it is."

One of the other men suggested in a plaintive voice, "Maybe they wouldn't mind dancin' with us, or just talkin' to us a little?"

"I can ask them," Frank said. "But it's up to them."

Or more likely, it was up to Fiona, he thought. She was in charge of this expedition. He would go along with whatever she said and enforce her wishes . . . within reason, of course.

He polished off the stew and had a cup of coffee with the cheechakos as well. Then he told them good night and started back toward the door that led below-decks.

He went around one of the low, square structures that housed a hatch opening into the cargo hold. As he strode past the corner of it, he suddenly heard the scuff of shoe leather on the deck behind him. Instinct made him pivot sharply toward the sound, but whoever was behind him struck with deadly swiftness. Something hard crashed against Frank's head with stunning impact. The blow drove him to his knees.

He struggled to get up, but his attacker grabbed him from behind, looping an arm around his neck and tightening it like an iron bar. Frank's breath was cut off. His head was already spinning from the hard clout on his skull, and now a red haze began to settle over his vision, brought on by the lack of air. He realized that he was about to pass out.

And as the man behind him began to rush him toward the rail, Frank knew that if he lost consciousness now, he was dead. His attacker intended to shove him over the rail into the icy waters of the Pacific.

Chapter 10

Frank managed to thrust a booted foot behind him, between the legs of the man who had hold of him. Their ankles tangled up, and with a startled curse, the man tripped and fell forward, taking Frank with him. They crashed to the deck about five feet short of the railing.

Frank still couldn't see or think very straight, but again his instincts served him well. He lashed out with a foot. The kick connected with his assailant and drove the man away from him. Frank got his hands on the deck and pushed himself up.

This area of the ship was fairly dark. A light burned on the bridge, but the glow from it barely reached this far. Frank's attacker was only a shadowy shape as he got to his feet and rushed again. Frank recognized that move, though. Brewster had tried it on him the day before. Frank knew it was a feint.

He went the other way, the way he knew Brewster was going to dodge at the last second, and threw a punch. Brewster ran right into Frank's fist. The blow

knocked him back, but Brewster managed to stay on
his feet. He bore in, swinging wild punches. Frank
was able to block most of them, but a few thudded
against his body. Brewster forced him back a step,
then another and another, until Frank reached the
railing. He felt it pressing into his back.

Brewster suddenly changed tactics. His hands shot
out and locked around Frank's throat. With a grunt of
effort, he heaved up, and Frank felt his feet come off
the deck. In another second, Brewster was going to
force him over the railing.

In desperation, Frank lifted his knee into the officer's groin. Brewster groaned in pain but didn't
loosen his grip. That made him hesitate, though, and
in that moment, someone else loomed up out of the
shadows and yelled, "Hey! Let him go!"

Frank recognized Pete Conway's voice. The brawny
young cheechako grabbed Brewster's shoulder and
jerked him away from Frank, turning him so that he
could drive a fist into Brewster's face. The terrific
blow sent Brewster spinning away across the deck.

Frank slumped as Brewster let go of him. He
caught hold of the railing and pushed himself upward.
Brewster recovered and charged at Conway, slugging
ferociously. The young cheechako was big and strong,
but he wasn't an experienced brawler the way Brewster was. Brewster landed several punches that drove
Conway to the deck, half stunned. Then Brewster
lifted a brutal kick into Conway's belly that sent the
young man rolling.

Someone must have seen the struggle and re-
ported it, because Frank heard running footsteps

coming closer, and then Captain Hoffman shouted, "Brewster! Belay that! Stop it, you damned fool!"

Brewster ignored the command. He charged Frank again, and even in the dim light, Frank could see how contorted with hate the officer's face was. He wasn't going to stop. He was trying to barrel into Frank, drive him back against the railing, and either snap his spine or force him overboard.

Frank dived to the deck, going low into Brewster's legs. Brewster let out a startled yell as his momentum carried him on and he pitched forward. Frank rolled and came up on hands and knees, looking around for his opponent.

The man was nowhere to be seen.

A shock went through Frank as he realized what had happened. Brewster had fallen forward, out of control, and went right over the railing. Frank hadn't heard the splash, but he knew that Brewster must have gone into the water.

Captain Hoffman confirmed that by bellowing, "Man overboard! Man overboard!" as he rushed to the rail. He turned toward the bridge, cupped his hands around his mouth, and shouted, "All engines stop! All stop!"

The *Montclair* slowed as whoever was on duty on the bridge relayed the command to the engine room, but the ship didn't come to a stop. The sails were still raised and full of air.

"Strike the sails! Strike the sails!" Hoffman leaned over the rail and searched the black water. "Brewster! Can you hear me? Brewster!"

Frank and Conway climbed to their feet and

stumbled over to join the captain. Frank peered over the railing, but couldn't see anything out there except darkness. He listened, but heard nothing except the slapping of the waves.

Sailors came running with life preservers tied to thick ropes. They threw them out into the area in which Brewster had disappeared. The ship finally shuddered to a dead stop in the water as the sails were lowered. With the engines stopped, there was an eerie quiet on board, broken by the shouts of the crew as they called out to Brewster.

No response came back from the sea.

Some of the officers brought bull's-eye lanterns to the rail and swept the beams from them over the waves. The searching and shouting went on for a good half hour before Captain Hoffman sighed and turned away from the rail, wearily shaking his head. He motioned for the other men to step back as well.

"It's been too long," he said. "Brewster was a good swimmer, but no man could stay afloat for this long in water that cold. He might have been knocked out when he struck the surface. He must have gone down quickly."

Frank said, "I didn't mean for him to go overboard."

Hoffman shook his head again. "I know that. He wouldn't have if he had obeyed my order and stopped fighting. His stubborn pride just wouldn't allow him to admit defeat, either this time or the time he clashed with you before, Morgan." Hoffman looked at Frank and added, "You may not believe this, but that quality was one of the things that made him an exceptional sailor. He never quit."

"I reckon I can understand that. A man needs to stick to what he starts . . . most of the time, anyway."

"Are you all right? Were you injured?"

"He hit me a pretty good wallop with something when he first jumped me," Frank said. He felt of his head and found a sore, swollen lump. "There's a little goose egg up there, but this old skull of mine is too hard to dent very easily. I'll be fine."

Hoffman turned to Conway. "What about you, young man?"

"I'm fine," Conway replied. "The fella got in some good licks, but that's all."

"Did you see what happened?"

"I sure did. That man jumped Mr. Morgan and tried to force him over the rail."

Frank said, "He likely would have, too, if you hadn't pitched in when you did, Pete."

Conway shrugged. "When I saw what was going on, I just tried to help."

"You probably saved my life. I won't forget that." Frank turned back to Hoffman. "I'm sorry for the loss of your officer, Captain, but this wasn't my fault or young Conway's."

Hoffman waved a hand. "No, as I said, it was Brewster's foolish pride that caused his death. An unfortunate tragedy, but no one else is to blame."

"I wouldn't want anybody trying to get back at me by hurting Mrs. Devereaux or the young ladies. Any members of the crew who have a problem with me need to take it up with me."

"There won't be any of that," Hoffman said firmly. "You don't have to worry. I'll make it clear that there are to be no repercussions." The captain paused, then added, "I doubt if there would have been, anyway. Brewster was admired for his qualities of seamanship, but he wasn't well liked."

That was the impression Frank had gotten, so he wasn't surprised by Hoffman's words.

The captain turned to his first mate and said, "Go up to the bridge and tell the engine room to get some steam up again. The wind's dying for the night, so we won't raise the sails."

"Aye, Cap'n. Ahead full, on the same bearing, once we have steam?"

"Aye," Hoffman said. He cast one final look at the stretch of dark water where Brewster had disappeared. "We'll be heading north again."

The rest of the group of cheechakos had come up while the search for Brewster was going on. As the crewmen scattered to go about their tasks, the novice gold-hunters gathered around Frank and Conway. They threw questions about the fight at the two men.

"I guess this is what you meant about a life-and-death struggle, Morgan," Neville, the man from New York, said. "That trouble came at you without any warning, and you had to deal with it. The same thing's liable to happen to any of us in Alaska."

"Not exactly the same thing," Conway said. "Nobody's going to throw us off a ship up there."

"There are plenty of other things that can kill a man," Frank said.

The gold-hunters talked about the fight and

Brewster's death for a while longer. Then Frank finally managed to get away from them. He motioned for Conway to follow him as he started once again toward the door leading belowdecks.

"I'm obliged to you for your help, Pete," he said quietly. "I reckon you really did save my life."

"I'm glad I could lend a hand, Mr. Morgan."

"Make it Frank."

"All right. I'm glad I could help, Frank. I didn't really think about it. I just saw that you were in trouble." Conway hesitated, then went on. "But if you really want to thank me . . . maybe you could talk one of those ladies into having a dance with me before they all have to go off to Whitehorse and get married."

"I'll see what I can do," Frank said.

An air of gloom hung over the ship the next morning. Brewster might not have been well liked, but his loss still affected most of the passengers and crew on board. People couldn't help but think about how easily the sea could claim them, too, if they were unlucky enough to fall overboard.

Fiona was getting her sea legs, and since she felt better, she spend part of the time fussing over Frank. "That man could have killed you!" she told him. "I intend to speak to Captain Hoffman about this."

"No need for that," Frank said. "It wasn't his fault."

"In a way it was. He should have had better control over his crew."

Frank couldn't argue with that, although he wasn't sure anybody could have controlled a stiff-necked son of a bitch like Brewster. He managed to talk Fiona out of filing an official complaint with the shipping line that owned the *Montclair*. He didn't see how that would do any good.

Fiona wasn't too receptive to the idea of the young women spending some time with Pete Conway and the other novice gold-hunters. "How do we know we can trust them?" she asked.

"Well, Pete saved my life," Frank pointed out. "I owe him a favor."

"And since you're working for me, I suppose by extension, I do, too. If I still can't talk you into becoming my partner, that is."

Frank shook his head. "I don't figure that would be a good idea. Once we get these gals where they're going, I'll have kept my promise to Jacob."

"What about making sure I get back safely to Seattle next spring?"

Frank thought about it and nodded. "I reckon I could do that."

"Good." She smiled up at him. "That gives me all winter in Skagway to change your mind about, how do you Westerners say it, throwing in with me. I can be quite persuasive, you know."

Frank didn't doubt that for a second.

Fiona went on. "And as far as having some sort of little . . . get-together . . . with those prospectors, I suppose it wouldn't hurt anything."

Frank smiled. "Good. I'll tell Pete."

"But I'm holding you responsible for their good

behavior," Fiona warned. "If they get out of line, I'm counting on you to put a stop to it."

A short time later, Pete Conway let out an excited whoop when Frank told him about Fiona's decision. "One of the fellows plays the fiddle," he said. "We can have a regular dance, right here on the deck of the ship!"

"Just make sure they all understand that they can't try anything improper."

"Just some dancing and conversation, that's all," Conway said with a grin. "That'll give us some good memories to hang on to when the temperature is forty below, the snow is ten feet deep outside, and there's a bear trying to get into the cabin to eat us!"

"When you put it like that," Frank said dryly, "it almost makes me want to go hunt for gold, too."

Chapter 11

The dance was scheduled for that night. Fiona gathered the young women and spoke to them about it. Most of them were feeling better now as they became more accustomed to the motion of the ship, and all of them agreed that they could go along with the plan, even Gertrude. "Those prospectors had better keep their hands to themselves, though," she said. "I'm a respectable woman, even if I *am* a mail-order bride!"

"Mr. Morgan assures me that they'll be on their best behavior." Fiona looked at Frank. "Isn't that right?"

"Yes, ma'am," he said. "If they give any of you any trouble, just let me know."

Word got around the ship about the gathering. Frank overheard some discussion of it among the crew, and he wondered if some of the sailors planned to show up and ask the women to dance with them, too. That could lead to problems. The gold-hunters might feel that the sailors were horning in and take offense to it. He didn't think it would be anything he couldn't handle, though, so he didn't mention it to Captain Hoffman.

The captain must have heard about it on his own, because he sought out Frank late that afternoon. "I hear there's going to be some sort of soiree on deck tonight involving those young women of yours," Hoffman said.

"Well, they're not exactly my young women," Frank said with a smile. "There's just going to be a little dancing and some conversation with Pete Conway and the rest of those gold-hunters."

"My crew has heard about it, and some of them resent the fact that they weren't included in the arrangements. They'd like to know if they can dance with the young ladies as well."

"It doesn't matter to me," Frank said. "That's up to the young ladies. I promised Mrs. Devereaux there wouldn't be any trouble, though."

Hoffman nodded. "Perhaps it would be best if I spoke to my officers and had them pass the word to the men that they should avoid the activities. That way, there'll be no chance of anything going wrong."

"Do whatever you think you should, Captain," Frank said.

It was possible that the whole thing would have to be canceled, he thought. The sky was still overcast, and there were occasional squalls of cold rain and sleet. The *Montclair* had no ballroom or salon. It was a working ship, transporting people and cargo, and it didn't make pleasure cruises or cater to wealthy passengers.

But just before sunset, the clouds thinned and the chilly wind began to die down. It looked like the weather was going to cooperate, at least as much as it could at this time of year and at this latitude.

Soon after dinner, Frank led Fiona and the young women up on deck. Lanterns had been placed on the hatch covers, and while the setting wasn't exactly what anyone would call festive, it had a certain air of celebration about it.

Conway, Neville, and the rest of the cheechakos were waiting with smiles of anticipation on their faces. They had scrubbed their faces as well, some of them had shaved, and a few had even put on suits. Conway was one of them. As the young women looked over the group of men, Jessica Harpe giggled and said under her breath to Meg Goodwin, "Look at that big blond one. Isn't he handsome?"

Fiona overheard the comment and said, "Don't get too attached to any of these men, ladies. Remember you have husbands-to-be waiting for you in the Klondike."

Conway stepped forward and gave an awkward little bow. "Mrs. Devereaux, ma'am," he said. "Ladies. Thank you for joining us this evening."

"Thank you for the invitation, Mr. Conway," Fiona said in a cool, formal voice. "May I present Miss Goodwin, Miss Harpe, Miss Donnelly, Miss Boulieu . . ."

Fiona went down the line, introducing all the women. Conway, who seemed to have taken on the leadership of the cheechakos despite his youth, responded by introducing all of the men, starting with himself and Neville. Frank stood off to the side, smiling to himself at the stiffness of it. One good thing about getting older. He had long since passed the point where he felt uncomfortable around women. He knew better than to think that they could no longer hold any surprises for him, but at least all those courtship rituals didn't mean much to him anymore.

"Charlie here plays the fiddle," Conway said, gesturing toward one of the older prospectors. "He's going to provide some music, if you ladies would care to dance."

"Are you asking?" Jessica said.

"Well . . . I reckon I am. Would you care to dance with me, ma'am?"

She held out a hand to him. "I'd love to, thank you."

The fiddler grinned and took out his bow. He lifted the instrument to his shoulder, tucked his chin over it, and began to saw on the strings. The notes were a little harsh and discordant, but they were music, the only real melody likely to be found on this rugged ship steaming northward toward Alaska.

Conway took Jessica into his arms, being careful to leave some space between their bodies, and they launched into a rough waltz. The rest of the women paired up with the cheechakos and began to dance as well. There were more men than women, so some of the gold-hunters had to wait their turn.

Fiona sidled over to Frank. "What about you?" she asked.

"What about me?"

"Are you much of a dancer, Frank?"

"Well . . . not really. I can manage not to step on a gal's feet if I try hard enough, but that's about it."

Fiona took his hand. "I don't believe you. I've seen how you move. You have a natural, fluid grace about you."

"Maybe when I'm drawing a gun . . ."

"Nonsense. Come on. We can't let these young people have all the fun."

She wasn't all that much older than the other women, he thought, but he supposed that being a widow, she felt more mature. He went along with what she wanted, taking her in his arms and twirling her around the open area of the deck that served as a dance floor.

The fiddler seemed to be tireless, going from one raucous tune to the next with scarcely a pause and stamping his foot in time to the music. The young women switched back and forth among the cheechakos so that all the men got a chance to swing them around the deck. Sometimes one of the gold-hunters would get impatient and cut in on another while a dance was going on. Frank thought a time or two that this might cause a ruckus, but the men seemed to know that if a fight broke out, the impromptu social would be over. They restrained any irritation they felt.

When the fiddler finally had to take a break and rest a little, the men and women stood around talking. The cheechakos seemed to enjoy that almost as much as the dancing. After a while, the fiddler was ready to go again, and as he lifted the fiddle and bow, the men claimed their partners.

The fiddler had scraped out only a couple of notes,

though, when he abruptly stopped playing. Frank turned toward him to find out what was wrong, and saw more than a dozen members of the ship's crew striding along the deck toward them. The sailors had an air of grim determination about them.

"Oh, no," Fiona breathed beside Frank. "I was afraid this might happen."

"I was worried about it, too," he told her. "Captain Hoffman had a talk with me and promised he'd keep his boys in line, but I reckon they didn't really listen."

He wasn't all that surprised. Having women around usually made it hard for lonesome hombres to concentrate on anything else.

Frank stepped forward, getting between the sailors and the cheechakos. He lifted a hand to stop them and said, "Hold it right there, fellas. This is a private get-together."

"Why should it be?" one of the sailors demanded belligerently. "We got rights, too, you know."

"Yeah, and you can't toss us all overboard, mister!" another man added.

Frank's jaw tightened. No one was really mourning Brewster's death, but they hadn't forgotten about it, either.

"Captain Hoffman gave you orders to steer clear," Frank said. "If you're off duty, I reckon you'd better go back to your quarters. If you're supposed to be on watch, you're neglecting your jobs."

"Just one dance," the first sailor insisted. "That's all we're askin'." He grinned at the young women. "How about it, ladies? Wouldn't you rather dance with some real men, instead of these gold-crazy landlubbers?"

Neville stepped forward, clenching his fists and bristling with anger. "You can't talk about us like that," he snapped. "At least we've got some ambition. We won't spend the rest of our lives swabbing some deck!"

This was turning into just the sort of confrontation Frank had hoped to avoid. He held up both hands this time and said, "There's no need for trouble here. You sailors go on about your business—"

"The hell with that!" one of the crewmen exclaimed. "I want to dance!"

He rushed forward, obviously intending to grab the nearest young woman. That was Jessica Harpe. Frank would have intercepted the sailor, but he didn't get the chance. Pete Conway sprang in front of Jessica and met the sailor with a hard punch that knocked him off his feet and sent him skidding across the deck on his butt.

With howls of outrage, the other sailors surged forward, ready to fight. The cheechakos did likewise, pushing the young women aside. Dancing and socializing were forgotten. The men on both sides were ready to brawl instead.

"Frank!" Fiona cried. "You said you wouldn't let this happen!"

"I'm not," he snapped. He palmed out his Colt, pointed it at the night sky, and squeezed off two rounds.

The pair of shots made everyone on deck freeze in

their tracks. The reports were loud, even out here on the vast, open sea.

"Everybody hold it!" Frank shouted. "The next man who throws a punch will answer to me!"

He didn't actually say he would shoot the next man who tried to hit somebody, but the sailors and the gold-hunters all seemed to take it that way, which was exactly what Frank intended. He knew they were all aware of his reputation as a gunman, so he figured he might as well take advantage of that fact.

One of the sailors pointed at the cheechakos and yelled, "They started it!"

"The hell we did!" Neville responded. "Pete was just protecting Miss Harpe from you lugs!"

"I can take care of myself, thank you!" Jessica put in, clearly annoyed. But when she turned to look at Conway, a smile appeared on her face. "But you really were gallant, Mr. Conway."

That made the big youngster grin from ear to ear.

Captain Hoffman came stalking up from belowdecks, followed by the first mate. The sailors started to scatter before Hoffman reached them.

"Get to your posts!" he shouted. "Right now, by God!" He came to a stop in front of Frank and glared at him. "I assume you fired those shots, Mr. Morgan?"

"I figured that was better than letting these fellas beat each other half to death," Frank said as he opened the revolver's cylinder. He reached under his sheepskin coat and took a couple of shells from the loops on his belt to replace the ones he had fired.

"You said there wouldn't be any trouble."

"I said I'd handle it if there was," Frank corrected. He finished reloading and snapped the cylinder closed. "It's handled. You don't see men fighting all over the deck, do you?"

The group of sailors had dispersed, even the man Pete Conway had knocked down. The young women and the gold-hunters were standing separately, with the fiddler in the middle looking a little forlorn as he held his fiddle and bow at his sides. From the looks of things, his services wouldn't be needed anymore tonight.

"I think all the passengers should return to their accommodations now," Hoffman said tersely.

"So do I," Fiona added. Her eyes glittered with anger as she looked at Frank.

He wasn't sure why everybody was blaming him. He had warned them of the possible consequences. It had been their own decision to go along with the idea.

Fiona started herding the brides below to their cabins. Muttering with disappointment, the cheechakos withdrew to the other end of the deck. Some of them had cabins, but many of them had paid only for deck space, so they were spending the voyage outdoors, under tarps they used as makeshift tents.

"We'll reach Skagway in two more days," Hoffman said to Frank. "I hope you can keep a lid on this trouble until then."

"I intend to," Frank said. "But again, it was your men who disobeyed orders and bulled in where they weren't supposed to be."

The captain sniffed and turned away, refusing to

acknowledge that his crewmen were the ones who had caused the trouble.

Conway came up and said, "I'm sorry, Frank. I suppose I shouldn't have punched that fellow. I couldn't just stand by and let him grab Miss Harpe like that, though."

"He didn't actually grab her," Frank pointed out. "You didn't give him the chance."

"Yes, but he was *going* to. You could tell that."

The young man was right. And if Conway hadn't walloped the sailor, Frank thought, *he* probably would have. That really would have set off a fracas.

"Do you think we'll get a chance to spend any more time with the ladies before we get to Skagway?" Conway went on in a plaintive voice.

Frank clapped a hand on his shoulder. "I don't know, son. Probably not, if Mrs. Devereaux has anything to say about it, and she's in charge of them. But you got those good memories you were talking about, the ones you can hang on to when you're wondering why the hell you came to Alaska in the first place."

"I suppose so," Conway said with a smile. "I just hope that's enough."

Frank did, too, but mostly he hoped that the rest of the voyage to Skagway would pass peacefully.

Chapter 12

He should have known better.

Even before he climbed out of his bunk the next morning, Frank knew something was wrong. The ship was pitching around more than it had been earlier in the voyage, and he could hear the wind howling. He got up, swallowing the queasiness that tried to take hold in his stomach, and pulled on his clothes, including the sheepskin coat. Then he headed for the deck to look for Captain Hoffman and find out what was going on.

His boots slipped as soon as he stepped outside, and he had to grab hold of the side of the door to keep from falling. A thin, almost invisible layer of ice coated the deck. More sleet pelted down, making little thudding sounds against his hat as he started cautiously across the desk toward the stairs leading up to the bridge.

He went up them carefully, and when he reached the top he saw Hoffman at the wheel, huddled there in a slicker and rain hat. "Captain!" Frank called.

Hoffman looked back over his shoulder in surprise. "Mr. Morgan!" he exclaimed. "You'd better get back to your cabin! This isn't fit weather for you to be out!"

"It doesn't look like fit weather to be sailing in!"

"Don't worry about the *Montclair*! She can handle a little blow like this!"

If Hoffman thought this was a little blow, Frank would have hated to see what the captain considered a major storm. The wind lashed viciously at the ship, and the angry waves seemed to be trying to toss it straight up into the sky. The sails were lowered, so the *Montclair* was running on its engines alone. Frank thought the wind would probably rip the sails to shreds if they were raised.

He leaned closer to Hoffman and asked, "We're not that far from the coastline, are we? Maybe you should make a run for shore so we can ride out the storm there!"

"And risk being battered to pieces on some rocks?" Hoffman shook his head. "I know what I'm doing, Morgan! We'll be all right! This squall will blow itself out before the day's over!"

Frank didn't believe that. It looked to him like the first of the winter storms had arrived a few weeks earlier than Hoffman expected it.

But he had to admit that he was no sailor, and certainly no expert where the sea was concerned. Hoffman had made this Seattle-to-Skagway run before. He ought to know what he was doing.

"All right!" Frank said. "But if there's anything I can do to help . . ."

"Just go below, dry off, and don't worry! We'll be fine!"

As the day went on, though, it began to look like they would be anything but fine. The storm continued unabated. If anything, its ferocity seemed to grow stronger. Fiona and all the young women were sick again, as were some of the cheechakos. The ones who had purchased deck space were allowed belowdecks to huddle miserably in the corridors, because they would have frozen to death and wound up ice-covered corpses if they had remained topside.

Frank weathered the storm better than most of the landlubbers. His stomach was a little unsettled, but he never completely lost his appetite. He wound up taking his meals in the officers' mess, at Captain Hoffman's invitation. The officers expressed confidence in the captain and in the *Montclair*'s ability to handle this rough weather, but Frank thought he saw worry lurking in their eyes.

It was the same sort of concern he had seen more than twenty years earlier at Fort Lincoln, in the eyes of some of the junior officers of the Seventh Cavalry as they were about to follow Colonel George Armstrong Custer into Indian country. Frank had been passing through, headed in the opposite direction, and he remembered thinking that he wouldn't have gone with those soldier boys for all the money in the world.

Now he had no choice but to put his trust in Captain Rudolph Hoffman. Hoffman was the only man who could get them where they were going.

The seas were still extremely rough that evening,

but the wind had died down slightly. Sleet showers still lashed the vessel and added to the layer of ice that had formed on the deck. Frank slept only fitfully, and during the night he heard groans coming from some of the other cabins. The women were suffering a lot more than he was, but there was nothing he could do for them.

The next morning, he sought out Hoffman again and found the captain in his cabin, pouring over the charts. "Do you still think we'll reach Skagway today?" Frank asked bluntly. He knew from looking at the maps that they would have to sail through Glacier Bay and then up a long inlet to reach the port city, and he hoped that once they made it to the bay, the water would be calmer.

"I . . . I don't know," Hoffman replied, and Frank didn't like what he heard in the captain's voice. The confidence and decisiveness that had been there earlier were gone now. "I've never seen a gale quite this bad. So early, I mean."

Frank had a feeling Hoffman meant he had never encountered a storm this bad before, period. That wasn't good.

"You *do* know where we are, don't you?"

Hoffman got to his feet and glared angrily at Frank. "Of course I know where we are. Taking readings has been difficult because of the weather, but I've sailed these waters more than a dozen times. We'll be fine, Mr. Morgan, and the best thing you can do is go back to your cabin and wait. If there's anything you need to know, I'll make sure you do."

"All right," Frank said, his face and voice grim. "I

don't mean any offense, Captain, but I promised an old friend that I'd get Mrs. Devereaux and those young ladies safely to their destination. I intend to do that."

"So do I, Mr. Morgan. So do I."

Frank went back to his cabin, and paused in front of the door to shake off some of the ice pellets that clung to his hat and coat before he went in. While he was standing there, the door to Fiona's cabin opened. She peered out at him, her face haggard with strain.

"We're not going to make it, are we, Frank?" she asked.

"I reckon we will," he replied, trying not to sound as worried as he felt. "I just talked to the captain, and he says this is nothing to worry about."

"Of course he says that! He's not going to admit that we never should have left Seattle this late in the season!"

Frank refrained from pointing out to her that she had been just as determined to get to Skagway as Captain Hoffman was, if not more so. That wouldn't do any good.

Fiona pawed hair out of her eyes and moaned. "We're all going to die," she said. "Frank . . . Frank, come in my cabin and hold me. I . . . I don't want to die alone."

"None of us are going to die," he told her. "And I'm covered with melting ice right now."

"I don't care." She clutched at his arms. "I'm so scared, I can't be alone—"

With a grinding racket, the ship gave a sudden

lurch. The deck tilted for a second under Frank's feet, then settled back. That tilt was enough to throw Fiona into his arms. She screamed in fear as she fell against him. He held on tightly to her to keep her from toppling to the floor.

Eyes wide, she stared up at him and exclaimed, "Oh, my God! We hit something! We're going to sink!"

"No, we're not," Frank said, although he didn't know if that was true. "I'll go find the captain and see what happened."

By now, the doors of the other cabins were opening and the brides started to pour out into the corridor. Fear had banished their sickness for the moment. Several of them cried out, demanding to know what was going on.

Meg Goodwin was really the only one who didn't look like she was on the verge of hysteria. Frank called her over and practically thrust Fiona into her arms.

"Take care of Mrs. Devereaux," he said. "I'll go find out what's going on."

"We hit something," Meg said. "It's just a matter of how bad the damage is."

Frank figured she was right about that. He said, "I'll be back as quick as I can."

He left the crowd of panicky women in the corridor and ran up the stairs to the deck. Something felt wrong, and as he emerged from the hatch, he could tell what it was. The ship had started to list a little to the right. Starboard, that was what the sailors called it, Frank told himself, then shoved that thought aside because it didn't matter now. The important thing was that the *Montclair* must have suffered some serious damage, or it wouldn't be tilting like that.

As he hurried toward the bridge, slipping a little on the ice that coated the deck, he saw that a frigid fog had closed in around the ship, but through those billows of white, he saw dark, hulking shapes sliding past. Ice-mantled pine trees thrust up from some of them. The ship was in the middle of a bunch of rocks and tiny islands, Frank realized. That meant they were a lot closer to shore than he had thought they were.

He wondered if Hoffman had known just how close those rocks were. Frank had a hunch that they had taken the captain by surprise.

Unfortunately, the storm was as fierce as ever. The waves tossed the *Montclair* back and forth. Frank felt the deck shuddering under his feet as the engines strained mightily to keep up. As he started to climb the steps to the bridge, he heard a dull boom somewhere from the bowels of the ship, and felt an even stronger shudder go through the vessel.

"Damn it," he said under his breath. He didn't know what the explosion meant, but it couldn't be anything good. A boiler bursting, maybe?

He stumbled onto the bridge, saw Hoffman wrestling with the wheel while he shouted orders to several officers clustered around him. Over the howling of the wind, Frank caught one of the commands.

"Ready the lifeboats!"

Frank Morgan wasn't the sort of man who ever gave in to despair, but even his fighting heart sank a little at the sound of those words. Hoffman wouldn't order his men to prepare the lifeboats unless he planned to abandon the ship, and he wouldn't abandon ship unless it was sinking. Frank glanced out at the storm-tossed waves and the jagged rocks sticking up through them like fangs. The thought of trusting his life and the lives of Fiona and the brides to a little boat in that maelstrom made a chill even icier than the wind go through him.

"Captain!" Frank shouted as he came up behind Hoffman. "Captain, what can I do to help?"

Hoffman spun toward him. "Morgan! Get those women together and into a lifeboat! The ship's going down!"

"Do you have enough lifeboats for everybody?"

"Of course! They'll be crowded, but we can make it! I recognize these islands! We're not far from Glacier Bay. I . . . I miscalculated somehow!" Hoffman's pale face under the rain hat was stricken as he made that admission. "But the current will carry the boats in to shore if they can stay off the rocks! You'll be all right! Take as many supplies as you can, and if you follow the shoreline, it'll take you to Skagway!"

The idea of trekking a hundred miles or more overland in weather like this wasn't very appealing, but it beat the hell out of drowning in the icy Pacific, Frank thought. He nodded and turned to hurry back belowdecks.

Fiona and Meg were waiting for him, and to his surprise, so were Pete Conway, Neville, and a couple of other gold-hunters. Fiona grabbed his arm and asked, "What did the captain say?"

"Get some warm clothes on and grab everything else you can," Frank said. "We're abandoning ship."

"So it *is* sinking!" Conway exclaimed. "We hit a rock or something, didn't we?"

Frank nodded. "That'd be my guess. The same thing goes for you and your friends, Pete. Grab as many supplies as you can and head for the lifeboats."

Conway looked scared, but he didn't waste time asking any more questions. He turned to the others and said, "Let's go, fellows."

The next few minutes were barely controlled chaos. Frank made sure that the women were gathering supplies and understood what they were supposed to do; then he headed for the cargo hold where Stormy, Goldy, and Dog were. The horses would have to swim for shore. They wouldn't fit in a lifeboat. He knew their chances of survival were slim, but he couldn't leave them here. If any animals had the strength, stamina, and gallant hearts to make it through this ordeal, it was Stormy and Goldy.

The horses were frightened but not panicking. Dog barked furiously as Frank swung down into the hold. He came to Frank and reared up to slobber on his face. Frank grinned and roughed up the thick fur around Dog's neck. "Stay with me, boy," he said. "We'll find room for you in the lifeboat."

He looked around for the heavy planks that formed the ramp, intending to put them in place so that Stormy and Goldy could get out of there. He had just found them when a couple of sailors dropped into the hold.

"Captain Hoffman sent us to help you!" one of the men said. "He figured you'd want to get those horses of yours out of there!"

"Thanks!" Frank said. "Let's get that ramp up!"

With grunts of effort, Frank and the two sailors wrestled the planks into place. Then Frank said, "We'll need some of these supplies when we get to shore. Load as many of the crates as you can into the lifeboats!"

The men got busy with that while Frank slipped harnesses on the two horses and led them up the ramp to the deck. It was slippery for them, too, and he worried they might fall and break a leg before they ever got off the ship.

The women staggered up from below, their arms full of bundles. One of the ship's officers had them place the supplies in one lifeboat, then climb into another themselves. "Hang on, ladies!" he told them, lifting his voice over the gale. "We're about to swing you over the side!"

Several of the women screamed as the boat swung out on its davits and then was lowered to the stormy sea. It bobbed and leaped, and they had to hang on for dear life.

Frank bit back a curse as he watched. He wished he was in the same lifeboat, but it was too late to do anything about that. He'd been too busy loading supplies to stop.

Pete Conway came up beside him, grunting with the effort of carrying a crate. "I don't know . . . what's in here . . . Mr. Morgan," the young man said, "but I reckon . . . we can probably use it!"

Frank recognized the crate containing the rifles, pistols, and ammunition and realized that Conway was carrying by himself what it had taken two sailors to load onto the ship. He took hold of it and helped Conway put it in one of the lifeboats.

Captain Hoffman came along the deck, shouting, "All passengers in the lifeboats! All passengers off! Abandon ship! Abandon ship!" He paused and looked at Frank. "God, I'm sorry, Morgan! I . . . I don't know what happened!"

Frank didn't say anything. He didn't know if Hoffman was truly to blame for this catastrophe or if it was purely a case of bad luck, and right now he didn't care. He took hold of Conway's arm and said, "Climb in, Pete! I'll be right back!"

He hurried over to his horses, grabbed their harnesses, and led them toward the edge of the deck where a section of railing had been swung out to let the lifeboats through. "You boys are gonna have to swim for it!" he told them. "I never had a better pair of trail partners! I'll see you on shore!"

Frank didn't know if the horses would jump off into the water or not. He didn't have a chance to find out, because at that moment someone yelled, "Look out! The rocks!" and the *Montclair* gave a violent lurch. A rending crash of wood and metal and rock filled the air. The impact threw Frank off his feet.

He landed on the icy deck and slid toward the edge. Twisting, he slapped at the deck to try to slow himself, but the ship kept tilting. Timbers groaned and snapped and bulkheads crumpled as the waves drove it against a giant rock. Frank had no chance to stop his slide.

Like a rocket, he shot off the deck and plummeted toward the icy water below.

Chapter 13

The fall tried to suck all the breath out of Frank's body. He managed to drag a little air into his lungs just before he hit the water. It slammed against him like a frozen fist, and as he went under, its frigid grip closed around him and threatened to squeeze the very life out of him. Fighting against the panic that welled up inside him, he kicked hard in an effort to propel himself back to the surface.

Something struck a heavy blow against his shoulder. He spun around and grabbed at it. His hand came out of the water. Someone grabbed it and hauled hard, lifting him. Frank's head broke the surface. He gasped for air through teeth that began to chatter involuntarily as the wind hit his soaked body.

His rescuer wrapped brawny arms around him and hauled him up, into one of the lifeboats. The small part of Frank's brain that was still functioning in spite of the cold told him that the boat was what he had rammed with his shoulder.

"Gather around him! Get him out of the wind!"

That was Pete Conway's voice bellowing orders. Obviously, the boat containing Conway and some of the supplies had made it into the water. Frank felt bodies crowding around him, and it was a blessed relief as they cut the wind. He still felt like he was frozen through and through. The water had sapped every bit of warmth out of his body.

Frank couldn't see anything. His eyes seemed to be frozen shut. He lifted a hand and pawed clumsily at them, finally forcing them open.

His sight returned in time for him to see the *Montclair* break up on the jagged rocks. The waves threw spume and broken boards high in the air as the ship splintered apart into sections. Frank didn't know if anyone was left on board, but if they were, he didn't see how they could survive such devastation. It was one of the most terrible things he had ever seen.

He looked around, hoping to see the other lifeboats or maybe even Stormy or Goldy swimming for shore, but there was too much fog, too many crashing waves. As far as he could tell, the narrow boat containing him, Conway, half a dozen other cheechakos, and some crates of supplies was alone on the vast, storm-tossed sea.

"Look out!" one of the men yelled. A rock loomed up in front of them. The lifeboat seemed to be headed straight for it, but somehow the current carried it past.

They weren't as lucky the next time. A man screamed as a wave lifted the boat and brought it crashing down against a rock. The boat broke in half, dumping men and crates into the water. Frank grabbed one of the crates as he fell, and this time he didn't go all the way under. As the crate bobbed up, carrying him with it, he looked around, hoping to spot Conway.

Someone was thrashing around nearby. Frank held on to the crate with one arm and used the other to paddle toward the man. His muscles didn't want to work very well because of the cold, but he managed to make enough headway that he could reach out and grab the man's coat. He pulled the man closer and yelled, "Grab the crate! Grab the crate!"

Pete Conway's head broke the surface. His blond hair was plastered to his skull. He flailed around for a second before he got one arm wrapped around the crate. With both Frank's and Conway's weight on it, the crate rode low in the water. It might not be enough to keep them both afloat. Frank looked around, spotted another crate floating nearby, and kicked them toward it. Once the second crate was within reach, he let go of the first one and grabbed it instead.

It was a struggle to think. His brain seemed to be slowing down more and more in the cold. But Frank could feel the current and remembered what Hoffman said about it carrying them to shore. He yelled, "Pete! Pete!" until he got Conway's attention, then pointed in that direction. "Kick, Pete! Kick!"

Hanging on to the crates, they began trying to swim, helping the current carry them in. Frank's muscles were really stiffening up, though, and he knew that Conway had to be experiencing the same thing.

"Hold on! Kick!"

They would freeze to death in just a few more minutes, Frank knew. The blood would thicken in their veins and cease to flow. Their stiff, brittle fingers would slip off the crates. They would sink below the surface as the cold, briny water filled their lungs, and their lives would be over.

"No!"

Frank didn't know if he yelled the word out loud, or if the defiant shout was only in his head. But he knew he wasn't going to give up and allow death to claim him without a fight. As long as there was breath in his body, he would continue to struggle against fate.

"Kick, Pete! Hang on and kick, damn it!"

Slowly, foot by foot, the two men struggled on, borne ceaselessly toward an unknown destiny.

Later, Frank didn't know if he lost consciousness somewhere along the way, or if he simply blocked out the incredible torment his body suffered on the way to shore. All he knew for sure was that he lying on solid ground again, and his mouth was filled with sand.

He lifted his head, sputtering and choking as he spit out the sand. As he looked around, he saw pine trees nearby, with strands of fog twined around their branches. The trees bordered a narrow beach that disappeared in the fog in both directions.

A few yards away, Pete Conway lay facedown on the sand as well. The crates he and Frank had been clinging to sat there with water swirling in and out around them. Frank forced his frozen muscles to work and crawled over to Conway.

"Pete!" he called as he fumbled to take hold of the young man's shoulder with stiff fingers. "Pete, wake up!"

For a moment, Frank thought Conway was dead. But then the cheechako let out a groan, then coughed and choked on the sand that filled his mouth, too. He managed to roll onto his side and rasped, "Mister . . . Morgan?"

Frank tugged at Conway's sodden coat. "Come on." Through chattering teeth, he added, "L-let's g-get into the trees."

On hands and knees at first, then forcing themselves upright into a stumbling walk, the two men made it to the trees and sank down among them. The thick trunks blocked the wind, and the canopy of interwoven branches was solid enough so that the carpet of fallen needles was somewhat dry.

"A f-fire," Frank said. "We need a fire."

He didn't know if any of the other lifeboats had made it to shore, didn't know about Fiona or the young women, Dog or Stormy or Goldy. But at this moment there was only room in his stunned brain for one thing: survival.

And survival meant a fire.

"How . . . how can we build a fire?" Conway asked. "We're . . . we're soaked . . . we don't have . . . any matches . . ."

Frank's hands felt twice their normal size. If he had to make a fast draw right now, he would have been out of luck.

He couldn't have pulled an iron anyway, he realized, since his holster was empty. His Colt was gone.

But the bowie knife that was sheathed on his left hip was still there, held in place by the rawhide thong attached to the sheath. His heart leaped with hope as he touched the knife's handle. He forced his hand into one of the pockets of his jeans, searching, searching . . .

It was there. The piece of flint that he habitually carried was still in his pocket. He fished it out, fumbling with it, then held it tightly in one hand while he used the other to scrape up a mound of pine needles. They had been falling here for centuries, slowly decaying into a fine, powdery carpet. When he had a nice little mound, he drew the knife.

Flint and steel . . . an ancient solution to the age-old problem of being cold and wet. He struck the flint against the blade and sent a few tiny sparks flying into the air. They fell on the heap of pine needles and duff, but no flames resulted. Frank struck flint and steel together again and again and again . . .

He lost track of how many tries it took before a tiny, almost invisible thread of smoke climbed into the air from the pile. Frank leaned closer, saw the spark still glowing faintly, blew on it gently. The glow became brighter. Frank blew on it again.

A little tongue of flame licked up.

Frank sent up a prayer of thanksgiving to El Señor Dios. A couple more pine needles caught fire and curled as they burned, spreading the flame to the others around them. Frank held his hands over the little fire and winced at the unfamiliar heat it gave off. It seemed like a thousand years since he had been anything except frozen.

"Pete! Pete, warm your hands. We got to get the blood flowing again so we won't get frostbite."

Conway didn't respond. Frank glanced over at the young man and saw that he was leaning against a tree trunk with his eyes closed. Again, Frank thought for a second that Conway was dead, but then he saw the cheechako's massive chest rising and falling shallowly.

He reached over with a hand that was tingling painfully now and shook Conway. "Pete!" he said again. "Wake up, damn it! You go to sleep and you'll die!"

Conway muttered something; then his eyelids flickered open as Frank continued to shake him. "Wha . . . wha . . ." He saw the fire and his eyes widened. He moved closer and extended his shaking hands over the flames.

"Don't leave them there for very long," Frank warned him. "We've got to warm the flesh gradually."

Conway groaned. "It hurts like hell."

"Good," Frank said with a note of savage triumph in his voice.

"G-good?"

"Damn right. Hurting means we're still alive."

During the next hour, Frank kept feeding pine needles into the fire, building it bigger and bigger. His clothes started to dry, and the chill that had gripped him all the way to his core began to ease. Conway was recovering, too.

But they were still a long way from being out of the woods, both literally and figuratively. They had some supplies of some sort, although they didn't know what was in either crate that had washed up on the beach. Not the guns, though, Frank was sure of that. That particular crate had been so heavy it must have gone straight to the bottom.

"It's not sleeting anymore," he told Conway as they huddled under the trees next to the fire, "and the wind's not blowing near as hard. The worst of the storm must have moved on."

"Too late to save the *Montclair*." Conway's voice caught in his throat for a second. "Or those women."

"We don't know that," Frank said. "Their boat could have made it to shore safely."

"Through those rocks?" Conway shook his head. "I don't think so."

"We won't know until we have a look around. That's what I intend to do as soon as I thaw out a little more."

Conway shrugged. "I'll go with you. No reason to stay here."

They stayed by the fire for a while longer; then Frank stood up and waved his arms around to get the circulation going even more. He stomped his feet on the pine-needle-covered ground. So did Conway. Then Frank said, "Let's go."

They stomped out the fire, then stumbled out of the trees onto the edge of the long, curving beach.

"North or south?" Conway asked. "Do you even know which way is which?"

Frank pointed. "That way is south. We'll head that way. The women's lifeboat left the ship first, so they should have reached shore first."

"You can't know that, as crazy as that storm was."

Frank grinned. "No, but that direction's as good as any, I reckon."

"I suppose you're right about that," Conway said with a grim laugh.

They set off, following the treeline. The wind had died down to a breeze, but even that was cold. Frank continued waving his arms to keep as warm as possible.

He couldn't even begin to estimate the distance they had covered when he spotted something on the beach up ahead. Conway saw it at the same time and said, "That's part of our lifeboat!"

The young man was right. A large chunk of the boat had washed ashore intact. Even more important, a couple of crates were still in it. Frank and Conway broke into a stumbling run toward it.

As they approached, Frank dared to hope that one of the crates contained the guns. He fell to his knees in the sand beside the wreckage and wrestled one of the crates around. Conway leaned in to help him.

Relief flooded through Frank as he recognized the crate. Considering the bad luck that had befallen them so far, they were overdue for a stroke of good fortune, and they had just gotten it. This was the crate with the guns and ammunition. Their chances for survival had just gone up.

But then, with a sudden growl, fate smashed those chances down again. The noise made Frank and Conway look toward the woods, where a massive brown bear stood on its hind legs, glaring at them.

Chapter 14

"Don't move," Frank breathed.

"I . . . I thought bears hibernated during the winter," Conway said.

"I reckon this one hasn't quite gotten around to it yet." A grim smile curved Frank's raw, wind-chapped lips. "Maybe he wants to fill his belly with a couple of cheechakos before he goes to sleep for the next few months." He thought back on some things that old-time mountain men had told him. "Bears can't see worth a damn. They rely more on their sense of smell. The wind's from offshore, so he's caught our scent. Or she. Might be a female." He glanced down at the crate of guns and ammunition. "We'll take it slow and easy, Pete, so as not to spook that critter, but we need to get the lid off this crate."

"You think you can get one of those rifles out, load it, and shoot that bear before it charges us?"

"That's not what I had in mind," Frank said. He bent his knees and reached down to the crate. They needed some sort of lever to pry the lid off. "There's a little busted place here. See if you can get your fingers in it."

Conway had to lower himself to one knee in order to slip the fingers of one hand into the opening. He heaved against the lid while Frank took hold of one of the broken boards from the lifeboat's hull and began slowly twisting it back and forth. Meanwhile the bear stood at the edge of the trees, sniffing the air with a confused look on its furry face.

"It can't figure out if it wants to attack us or not," Frank said. The piece of board came loose in his hands. "See if you can work that lid up a little more, Pete. If you can, I think I can slip this board in there and pry it open."

Grunting with the effort he put into it, Conway struggled with the crate. With a squeal of metal against wood, the nails holding the lid down gave slightly.

Frank wedged the end of the board into the gap. "You pull up on the lid while I press down on this board," he told Conway. "Ready?"

Conway nodded as he cast a nervous glance toward the bear. "I suppose so."

The two men worked together, throwing their remaining strength into the task. The nails screeched loudly this time as muscle power added to the leverage of the board pried the lid up. It came loose suddenly, flying up into the air and nearly hitting Conway, who jumped back, tripped, and sat down down on the beach.

"Oh, hell, Frank, here he comes!" the young man exclaimed.

Frank turned to look at the bear, which had tottered several steps out of the trees. The massive creature stopped short, though, and lifted its head higher as its nose wrinkled. The bear stood there for several tense moments, then turned abruptly, dropped to all fours, and lumbered off into the woods, vanishing into the shadows under the trees.

Conway stared after it uncomprehendingly and muttered, "What . . . what the hell just happened?"

Frank dropped the piece of board he was still holding. It wouldn't have done much good as a weapon against a monster like that bear.

"Like I said, a bear's got a really sensitive sense of smell. I thought all the oilcloth and grease packed around these guns might stink pretty bad to it. If it's ever been around any hunters, it's smelled those scents before and knows they mean trouble. So the bear figured it would be better off somewhere else."

Conway stared at him. "You knew that was going to happen?"

"I hoped it would," Frank said. "But no, I wasn't sure. Just played a hunch."

"It was a good one," Conway said with a nod. He clambered to his feet. "We'd better get some of these guns out, clean 'em up, and get them loaded before we run into any more wild animals."

"That's just what I was thinking," Frank agreed. "Come on, we'll drag what's left of the boat farther up toward the trees and make a camp here. It can be our base while we're searching for the others."

"You really think we'll find any of them still alive?"

"I don't know," Frank said honestly. "But like with that bear, I'm going to play a hunch."

They worked hard for the next hour, dragging the wrecked boat and the supplies up to the edge of the trees. They took rifles and pistols from the crate, cleaned the grease off the weapons, and broke open the cases of ammunition to load them. Frank felt a lot better with the weight of a Colt riding in his holster again, even a .32, and with a fully-loaded Winchester leaning against a nearby tree.

Then, while Conway went back up the beach to retrieve the other two crates of supplies, Frank found enough dry wood and pine needles in the forest to make a good-sized fire. He carried the fuel out onto the edge of the beach and made a pile of it, then knelt and used his knife and the piece of flint to start the fire. By the time Conway got back, Frank had a roaring, leaping blaze going, sending a column of smoke high into the gray sky.

"If they're anywhere along this beach, maybe they'll see that smoke," he told Conway. "We can continue searching for them, too."

"How about if we fire some shots into the air?" Conway suggested. "The others might hear them."

"Good idea." Frank picked up one of the Winchesters and cranked off three rounds. "We don't need to waste ammunition, though, so we'll only try this every so often."

They managed to pry off the lids of the other crates and found salt pork, flour, sugar, and salt. Seawater had gotten into some of the containers and ruined the contents, but quite a few of the provisions were still usable. One crate had axes and hatchets in it, and those tools might well come in handy, too.

The fire warmed them and finished the job of drying their clothes. Conway stood with his hands on his hips, gazing into the flames, and said, "We're a lot better off than we have any right to expect, considering what happened." His voice caught a little as he went on, "I hope . . . I just hope we're not the only ones who survived."

"I'll bet a hat we aren't," Frank said. "Let's get some food in our bellies, and then we'll start searching."

They skewered pieces of salt pork onto the ends of sticks and roasted the meat in the flames. Frank felt sick for a minute when the food hit his stomach, but the feeling soon passed. When the two men had eaten, they added more branches to the fire and then set off down the beach, taking the rifles with them. Behind them, the column of smoke continued to climb into the sky like a beacon.

Frank knew it was possible that there might be men in this wilderness who weren't friendly. The smoke could attract danger. But it was a risk he was willing to run if it meant there was a better chance of reuniting with other survivors from the *Montclair*.

The fog had thinned out, so they were able to look back and see the fire for quite a distance as they followed the curve of the beach. Then they came to an area where jagged rocks thrust up out of the sand, and they had to work their way through them before they came to another open stretch.

As they stepped out onto the sand, Frank caught a

glimpse of movement at the edge of the trees. The sky was still overcast, but enough sunlight filtered through the clouds to show him a golden gleam in the shadows. He stopped in his tracks, his heart pounding. He thought he recognized that sleek, shining hide.

"What is it, Frank?" Conway asked.

Instead of answering, Frank lifted his fingers to his mouth and used them to help him let out a shrill, piercing whistle. In response, Goldy burst out of the trees, followed by the rangy gray stallion called Stormy. Both horses tossed their heads in the air and then galloped along the sand toward Frank and Conway.

Frank ran to meet them, throwing his arms around Stormy's neck and then Goldy's. He had known there was a chance the horses would be able to swim to shore, but he hadn't really expected that hope to come true.

"Son of a gun," Conway said in an awed voice. "They made it."

"They sure did," Frank said. "That means some of the others could have, too."

"Do we ride now?"

Frank shook his head. "We'll keep walking for the time being. These fellas have been through hell, just like we have. They can use some rest."

Leading the horses, Frank and Conway continued down the beach. After another half hour or so, Frank stopped again and listened intently.

"Hear that?" he asked as a smile tugged at the grim lines of his mouth. "That's barking."

Sure enough, it was. Stormy and Goldy heard it, too, and broke loose, tugging their reins out of the hands of Frank and Conway. The horses trotted down the beach with the two men following.

A few moments later, Dog came into sight, bounding along the sand. Frank saw human figures struggling along behind the big cur. Dog reached Stormy and Goldy and capered around them in sheer joy for a few seconds before launching himself at Frank with a madly wagging tail and an eagerly licking tongue. Frank wrestled happily with Dog for a moment, then looked along the beach and felt his spirits lifting as he recognized Fiona Devereaux, Meg Goodwin, Jessica Harpe, and the cheechako from New York named Neville. They were all pale and drawn from their ordeal, and their clothes were still wet, but they were grinning at the sight of Frank and Conway.

Fiona threw her arms around Frank, and Jessica did likewise with Conway. "We thought you were dead, we thought you were dead," Fiona babbled. "We saw you fall off the ship into the water, Frank. My God, how did you survive?"

"You just explained it," Frank said. "El Señor Dios was watching over me, and Pete there gave Him a hand." He looked at the others. "How many of you made it?"

"All of us except . . . except Constance and Gertrude," Fiona said in a grief-wracked voice. "They . . . they fell out of the lifeboat while it was being tossed around so madly. We never saw them again."

Frank nodded. He and Conway had survived going

into the water, but he held out no hope that the two young women had. They wouldn't have been strong enough to stay afloat and fight off the cold.

"Mr. Neville and three of his friends were in the boat as well," Fiona went on. "They made it, too, and we have the supplies we were carrying."

"Pete and I managed to salvage some supplies, too," Frank said, "including the guns. Seen anybody else from the ship?"

Fiona shook her head. "No. No one."

Frank figured that Captain Hoffman and most of the crew had still been on the *Montclair* when it broke up. He doubted if any of them had survived.

Neville said, "We saw that dog of yours swimming for it and pulled him on board the lifeboat with us, Morgan."

Frank kept his left arm around Fiona's shoulders and held out his right hand to the little cheechako. "Then I owe you a big debt, amigo," he said. "Dog and I have been through a lot together. I'd have hated to lose him."

Neville gripped Frank's hand. "Glad we could help. I see your horses made it, too. What now?"

Frank felt Fiona trembling against him. "Now we need to get all of you back up the beach to the camp Pete and I made. We have a fire burning there. You can thaw out and dry your clothes."

Through chattering teeth, Fiona said, "Th-that sounds w-wonderful."

"Pete, show them the way. I'll gather up the rest of the party."

Conway led the women and Neville back up the

beach. Frank sent Stormy and Goldy with the group, but kept Dog with him. He hurried along the sand, calling out the names of the other women. They emerged from the trees, along with the three other gold-hunters. The young women had to hug Frank, and the men had to shake his hand.

"Grab all the supplies you have and let's go," Frank told them. "By nightfall you should all be warm and dry and have some hot food in your bellies."

They all exclaimed with joy at hearing that.

It took an hour to herd everyone up the beach to the camp. Conway had started feeding branches and pine needles into the fire as soon as he and his companions got there, so by the time Frank and the others arrived, the blaze was roaring again, throwing off waves of welcome heat. Everyone gathered around it.

Frank studied the survivors as they basked in the warmth. There were seventeen of them in all, counting him. The *Montclair* had carried between forty and fifty passengers and had a crew of more than twenty men. That meant there had been about seventy souls on board. At least fifty of them had died in the wreck. It was a sobering thought.

But no more sobering than the fact that the ones who had survived were still in great danger, despite the incredible good fortune that had brought them this far. They had supplies, guns, and ammunition, but they were a long way from any outposts of civilization, faced with an overland trek through some of the most hostile country in the world. And if another storm blew up, they would be in even worse shape.

Frank knew all that . . . but he had to smile anyway. They had a fighting chance.

That was all he had ever asked for in life.

Chapter 15

The next morning brought a grim discovery. Frank became aware of it when he heard one of the young women screaming. He was hunkered by the fire, cooking more of the salt pork. He handed the stick to a startled Fiona and stood quickly, reaching for the Winchester on the sand beside him.

"I'll go see what's wrong," he said. "Pete, come with me. Neville, you and the other boys stay here and keep an eye on things."

The cheechakos were all armed with pistols now, as were Fiona, Meg, and several other of the women. That was one of the first things Frank had seen to the day before.

With no blankets, they had all been forced to huddle together, close to the fire, during the night; otherwise some of them might have frozen to death as the temperature plummeted. This morning, the women had wanted some privacy to tend to their needs, so Frank had been letting them go down the beach to the rocks. That was where the screams were coming from now.

He had been sending the women to the rocks two at a time, and one of them had to have a pistol and keep watch while the other took care of her business. Lucy Calvert and Maureen Kincaid were down there now, he recalled.

"What do you reckon's wrong?" Conway asked as they trotted along the beach.

"I don't know," Frank said, "but at least there hasn't been any shooting so far."

They reached the rocks, ducked among them, and came out on the other side to see Lucy and Maureen cringing back against one of the boulders and clinging to each other. A few yards away, a man's body lay facedown on the sand, rising as the waves came in, then sinking as they went back out.

The man wore the blue uniform of one of the ship's officers. Frank wasn't particularly surprised to see the corpse. Not all the bodies would float in to shore, but he'd been certain that some of them would.

"Ladies, go on back to the others," he told Lucy and Maureen. "Pete and I will tend to this."

"Is . . . is he dead?" Lucy asked.

Frank looked at how the body was already beginning to bloat and nodded. "Yes, ma'am, I'm afraid so."

"How terrible," Maureen muttered.

She and Lucy started back up the beach. Frank handed his rifle to Conway, went over to the corpse, and reached down to grab hold of the uniform jacket and haul the body completely out of the water. He rolled the man onto his back.

The bloating distorted the man's features, and fish had been at him, too. Frank was still able to recognize the first mate from the *Montclair.* He had heard the man's name but was unable to recall it, and he felt bad about that. Nobody ought to die without someone knowing who he was. Unfortunately, that was often the case.

"Frank . . ." Conway said.

Frank looked up. Conway was staring along the beach with a bleak expression on his face. Frank followed the direction of the young man's gaze and saw three more corpses bobbing in the water just offshore. As he watched, the waves brought those bodies in and deposited them partially on the sand as well.

"This fella might've been the first, but I knew he wouldn't be the last," Frank said.

By midday, in fact, a dozen more bodies had washed ashore, including those of Captain Rudolph Hoffman, Gertrude Nevins, and Constance Wilson. It was a horrible thing for the young women to see the bodies of their former companions, Frank thought, but at least they had the certainty of knowing that Gertrude and Constance were gone. It would have been harder for them to leave this place if they had harbored even the faintest hope that the two young women might still be alive.

And leaving was exactly what Frank had in mind—the sooner, the better. Winter was making its inexorable way down from the Arctic Circle, and if they didn't reach some sort of haven before it arrived in its full fury, they wouldn't stand a chance. He was willing to let them have this day to rest and recover from the ordeal, but no longer.

Frank and Conway explored into the trees and found a ravine about a quarter of a mile inland. They took the bodies there and lowered them into the defile, then rolled rocks down on top of them. It was a poor excuse for a burial but the best they could do under the circumstances. If more bodies washed ashore, they could bring them here later.

When they returned to the beach, Frank gathered everyone around and told them what he and Conway had done. Some of the women wept for Gertrude and Constance. Frank let them grieve for a while, then said, "Everyone needs to get a good night's sleep tonight, because we'll be leaving first thing in the morning."

Neville looked up in surprise. "Leaving? But we have wood here for the fire and plenty of supplies."

"We don't have enough supplies to last until next spring," Frank said. "We don't have a shelter to protect us during the winter, either."

"Maybe we could build a cabin," one of the men suggested. "We have axes, and there are plenty of trees. There are wild animals around here, too. You said you saw a bear yesterday. We could hunt for fresh meat."

Frank nodded. "All those things are true. But I still think our chances for survival are better if we make it to Skagway or some other settlement."

"Do you have any idea how far we are from Skagway?" Fiona asked.

"Nope." Frank waved a hand toward the sea. "That

may be Glacier Bay out there. If it is, we can follow the shoreline north along the inlet that leads to Skagway. It may not be more than fifty or sixty miles to the settlement."

"You want us to walk fifty or sixty miles, in cold weather like this?" Marie asked, sounding like she could hardly believe it.

Frank smiled. "It's liable to get a lot colder before it gets warmer again, Miss Boulieu. Anyway, we have a couple of horses. You ladies can take turns riding, so you won't have to walk the whole way."

"I think Frank's right," Fiona said. "Besides, have you forgotten that there are husbands waiting for you once you get to Whitehorse?"

"We're still going to Whitehorse?" Meg asked.

"Why not? If we can make it to Skagway, we can buy more supplies and carry on just as we planned. We've just been delayed a little, that's all."

"And there are two less of us," Jessica pointed out.

"And that's a shame, but the rest of us are still alive." Fiona's hoarse voice took on a determined tone as she went on. "I don't intend to give up just because we've had some bad luck along the way."

Bad luck was putting it mildly, Frank thought, but he agreed with the sentiment Fiona expressed. He didn't believe in giving up. If he did, he would have been dead a long time ago.

Anyway, he knew more about the wilderness than any of the others, and he intended to see to it that they got out of this mess, whether they liked it or not.

* * *

By the next morning, the rest of the group had come around to Frank's way of thinking. They didn't want to try to spend the winter on this bleak, isolated beach.

Several more bodies had washed up during the night. Frank and Conway carried them to the ravine and laid them to rest as best they could, then returned to the camp. Frank had stripped the jackets off a number of the corpses, and he used them to make packs for carrying supplies. The women found that distasteful but went along with it. The only supplies they could take with them were what they were able to carry.

Everyone shrugged into their packs, and then the group strung out along the beach and headed north. Frank took the lead, with Dog bounding on out ahead of him. No one was riding at the moment. Frank wanted to save the horses for when their strength was really needed. He put Conway and Neville at the back of the line to bring up the rear and keep an eye on things. The other three cheechakos were spaced out among the women to lend them a hand if necessary.

A cold wind blew in Frank's face and sent thick gray clouds scudding through the sky. It was only a matter of time before the first real blizzard of the season came roaring down out of the north, Frank knew. They were in a race against that blizzard, and the stakes were their lives.

He wanted to make at least five miles a day, preferably more. If they could cover ten miles each day, he felt sure they could reach Skagway in less than a week. That gave them an outside chance of making it while the relatively good weather held.

The first morning went well, but then the women began to flag. They had to take turns riding, and even with that, the pace slowed slightly. By nightfall, Frank wasn't sure how much ground they had covered. But it was a start, and he was going to remain optimistic as long as he could.

The next day, the going was harder. The trees came right down to the edge of the water in places, forcing everyone to wind among the pines rather than striding along the open sand. In other places, boulders blocked the beach and made them go inland as well. Frank kept everyone moving, though, that day and the next and the next.

He felt sure they were more than halfway to Skagway by now. When he looked out across the water, he could see low, tree-covered hills in the distance, proof that they were tramping along beside an inlet now, not Glacier Bay. Every instinct Frank possessed told him that they were heading in the right direction. It was just a matter of time before they sighted the smoke from Skagway.

So far, though, they hadn't seen a single sign of human habitation. Frank had thought they might come across a trapper's cabin, or some sourdough's gold claim. Not along this coast, obviously.

On the fifth day after leaving the camp where they had come ashore, the women were barely able to stagger along. Conway and the other cheechakos were pretty worn out, too. Frank began to consider calling a halt and giving them a day to rest. He squinted at the gray sky. Was there snow up there? He couldn't tell, but he felt a tingle of unease along his spine. Would taking a day to rest just doom them when they were practically at their destination?

He didn't have much choice in the matter. Some of the women collapsed, dropping off their feet and unable to get up again. Frank said, "All right, unsling your packs. We'll stop here for a while."

Maybe after an hour or two, they could go on, he thought. It was worth a try.

All of the women except Meg Goodwin slumped to the ground. Meg had been a real trouper. She had to be as worn out as the others, but she had kept on as if she could go all day. She came over to Frank now and said, "Thank you, Mr. Morgan. Mrs. Devereaux and the other girls are really tired."

"And you're not?" he asked her with a smile.

"I'm fine," she insisted. "I grew up on a farm and did most of the plowing from the time I was ten years old. I must have walked thousands of miles behind an old mule. This . . ." She gestured toward the beach. "This is nothing."

"Farm girl, eh?"

"That's right. So I figured being a sourdough's wife wouldn't be much harder."

"You might be right about that." Frank nodded toward the north. "I was thinking about scouting on ahead with Dog. You want to come with us?"

Meg's quirky smile lit up her face. "I'd like that."

Frank went over to Conway and said, "Miss Goodwin and I are going to scout on up the beach a ways. You mind staying here and keeping an eye on things?"

"Nope, that's fine," the young man replied. He glanced at Jessica Harpe, and Frank figured Conway planned on spending the break talking to the curvy little brunette. If Fiona was able to follow through on her plan and take the women to Whitehorse, Conway was liable to be disappointed when he had to say good-bye to Jessica and let her travel on to the man who had paid to have her brought up here to marry him. But Frank couldn't do anything about that. It was just Conway's bad luck.

He and Meg set off up the beach. Dog ran ahead of them, darting into the woods at times and then running back out onto the sand. As they walked, Meg talked about her life on her family's farm back in Ohio.

"What about you, Mr. Morgan?" she asked after a while. "You must have had a very interesting life, what with being a gunfighter and all."

"A lot of hard, lonely trails," Frank said. "That's what most of it has been."

"Have you ever been married?"

"A couple of times."

Meg frowned. "What happened?"

"I lost them both," Frank said.

She put a hand on his arm. "I'm so sorry. I didn't mean to bring up bad memories. Although I guess I should have known that I would, with questions like that."

"It's all right," Frank told her. "Life goes on and time passes, and after a while, if you're lucky you're left with more good memories than bad ones."

"What about children?"

Frank had to grin. "I've got a boy. Conrad. He had some trouble along the way, but he grew into a fine man." He grew sober again as he thought about what had happened in Conrad's life in recent months. "Then he had some more trouble. But he'll come through it all right. He's strong."

"Like his father," Meg said. Her hand still rested on Frank's arm.

He frowned suddenly as he realized how easy it was to talk to this woman. But she was *young,* he reminded himself. His son's age, or thereabouts, which meant he was old enough to be her father. Somehow, it hadn't seemed like there was quite as big a difference between him and Fiona . . .

He didn't have time to ponder on those troubling thoughts, because at that moment, somewhere behind them, the roar of gunshots suddenly filled the cold air.

Chapter 16

Frank whirled toward the sound and saw to his surprise that he and Meg had walked so far along the beach the others were now out of sight. The shots were definitely coming from that direction, though. He broke into a run along the hard-packed sand, calling over his shoulder to Meg, "Stay here!"

"No!" she said as she hustled after him. "You may need my help!"

Frank knew there was no time to argue with her. He wanted to get back to the rest of the survivors as fast as he could. It was possible that they had just spotted a bear or a moose and were blazing away at it, but he had a bad feeling that this was something worse.

A point of land jutted out into the water ahead of them. Frank and Meg had walked around it without him really noticing it. That point cut off the view down the beach.

Instinct suddenly send Frank veering toward the trees on the point. "Follow me!" he called to Meg. He

didn't want to go charging blindly around there until
he knew what the situation was. He whistled Dog
back beside him, too.

They slowed as they reached the trees. The shooting stopped, and an ominous silence fell over the
beach. Frank crouched and held the Winchester at
the ready as he weaved his way through the trunks.
The thick carpet of decaying pine needles muffled
his footsteps. Meg started to say something, but
Frank made a curt gesture that silenced her. He
didn't want to give away their presence.

As they neared the far edge of the trees, he went to
his belly and motioned for Meg to do likewise. They
crawled forward until they could look along the
beach and see what was happening.

Meg's breath hissed between her teeth in surprise.
Frank didn't make a sound, but his jaw tightened. He
watched as eight roughly dressed, heavily armed
hardcases rounded up Fiona and the nine remaining
young women. Conway, Neville, and the other three
cheechakos were sprawled limply on the sand. Frank
saw blood staining their clothes, and none of them
moved.

"My God," Meg whispered. "Oh, Frank—"

"Shhh."

She cast an anguished look over at him. "But we
have to *help* them!"

"If we do anything to let those varmints know
we're here, they'll just kill me and take you prisoner,
too," Frank whispered, leaning over to put his mouth
close to her ear. "The only way we can help them is
by waiting for a better chance."

"But you're a gunfighter—"

"And there would be eight to one odds against me," he said. "I'd get half of them, maybe more, but they'd get me, too." He shook his head. "I don't like it any more than you do, Meg, but we have to bide our time."

She bit her lip as she thought about what he'd said. Then she nodded. "What do you think happened?" she asked as the men started forcing their prisoners into the trees at gunpoint. The hardcases had picked up all the packs of supplies and were carrying them as well.

"Those hombres ambushed our bunch. Conway and the other men put up a fight, but they didn't stand a chance."

"Who *are* those men?"

"Outlaws, most likely." Frank had been studying the men. They wore fur coats and a mixture of headgear ranging from Stetsons to derbies to fur caps. Each man carried a rifle, and when their coats hung open, he saw holstered six-guns on each man as well, not to mention knives and a couple of hatchets.

"Did they do it to steal our supplies?"

"I'm sure that's part of it."

"Then why are they taking Mrs. Devereaux and the other— Oh. Oh, no."

Frank nodded. "Yeah, they either plan to keep the girls for themselves or maybe sell them. Maybe both, eventually. Sorry to be so plainspoken about it."

"This is no time for worrying about propriety," Meg said. "What are we going to do?"

"Wait until they're gone, then check on Conway

and the other men to see if any of them are still alive. Then we'll figure out some way of getting the prisoners away from those no-good scoundrels."

"Why don't you just call them no-good bastards instead? That's what they are."

Frank couldn't dispute that. He smiled tightly and went on. "Even if we can free the prisoners, we'll have to do something to keep those men from coming after us. Otherwise we're liable to be in pretty much the same fix we are now."

"You mean to kill them?"

"They can't come after us if they're dead," Frank said.

Meg nodded and said, "All right. I'll help you. Just tell me what to do."

Frank motioned for her to be quiet again. He listened intently and heard hoofbeats in the distance. The outlaws had horses with them, and now they were riding away with their prisoners. Frank listened as the hoofbeats faded.

"Come on," he said as he got to his feet.

With Dog following them, he and Meg hurried out of the trees and across the sand toward the bodies of Conway and the other men. Frank reached Neville first and saw that the little New Yorker was shot at least three times through the body. He grimaced in regret. Although there had been friction between the two of them at first, some mutual respect had developed, too.

The other three cheechakos were dead. Frank came to Conway, who lay facedown in a pool of blood. Frank rolled the young man onto his back, expecting to find a bullet hole in the middle of Conway's face.

Instead he saw a deep gash on the side of Conway's forehead with blood still seeping from it. But Conway was breathing, Frank realized. Head wounds always bled like crazy, but from the looks of it, the slug had glanced off Conway's skull, knocking him out but not killing him. The outlaws must have seen all that blood and assumed that he was a goner, though.

"Pete's alive!" Frank called.

Meg exclaimed in surprise and rushed over to him, dropping to her knees beside Conway. "What can I do?"

"Rip a piece of cloth off your dress and use it to try to stop that bleeding from his head. Hold it on there tight. Dog and I will go have a look around."

With Dog's sensitive nose to help him, it didn't take long for Frank to find the place where someone had waited with the horses while the attack took place. That meant there were at least nine of the outlaws. Frank smiled tightly. The odds were already bad enough that one more hombre didn't make all that much difference.

Dog was able to follow the trail without any trouble. He led Frank through the woods to the northeast. After a few minutes, Frank spotted a rocky ridge in the distance as he peered through the trees. The outlaws' trail seemed to lead straight toward it.

They probably had a hideout somewhere over there around that ridge, Frank thought. He was confident that Dog could find it later, so for now he called out to the big cur and turned around to head back to the beach.

He hadn't seen any sign of Stormy and Goldy so far, but he wasn't surprised when he got to the beach and found both horses waiting there with Meg and Conway. They weren't the sort to let themselves be captured. They had probably run off as soon as the shooting started.

Frank was glad to see that Conway was conscious again and sitting up. He held the torn piece of cloth from Meg's dress to his injured head. His face was drawn and haggard with pain, grief, and anger.

"We didn't have a chance, Frank," he said. "They opened up on us from the trees before we even knew they were there. All I remember after that is what felt like the whole world falling on my head."

"That was when a bullet clipped you," Frank said. "Did Meg tell you that Fiona and the rest of the women were taken prisoner?"

"Yeah." Conway looked up at him. "What are we going to do, Frank?"

"What do you think we're going to do?" Frank looked toward the northeast, toward the ridge where he had a hunch they would find the outlaws. "We're going to get them back."

With the thick overcast that clogged the sky nearly every day, the high northern latitudes at which they found themselves, and the time of year it was, darkness came very early these days. It began to settle down over the rugged landscape as Frank, Conway,

Meg, and Dog made their way toward the ridge. Frank and Meg led the two horses. Dog ranged ahead, following the scent left by the outlaws and their prisoners.

As they approached the ridge, Frank saw an orange glow lighting up the sky. "Looks like they've got a big bonfire burning," he said quietly to his companions. "Probably celebrating their good luck."

Carefully, they moved closer until they could peer through some brush toward the foot of the ridge. That was where the fire was located, in a large open area where the trees had been cleared away and all the vegetation had been burned off. The big pile of wood blazed fiercely, with flames jumping up at least ten feet in the air. At the base of the ridge itself stood several log cabins, and off to one side was a corral made of peeled pine poles where the horses were kept.

Most of the outlaws congregated around the fire and passed bottles of whiskey back and forth as they laughed and talked about their good fortune, but a couple of hardcases armed with rifles stood just outside one of the cabins. Frank pointed that out to Conway and Meg and whispered, "I'll bet a hat that's where the prisoners are being held."

"You'll have to make it to Skagway and buy a hat before you have one to bet," Meg whispered back to him, causing Frank to grin. The girl had spunk, and he, for one, admired that.

"How do we get them out of there?" Conway asked.

Frank studied the face of the ridge. It was fairly steep

and dotted with trees, but he saw a few boulders here and there, too. Not enough to cause an avalanche if he started one of them rolling, though. Anyway, a rock slide might crush the cabin where the prisoners were.

An idea began to form in his head. Meg still had her revolver, and Frank had given Conway his Winchester, leaving him armed with one of the .32s he had kept for himself. He was used to a heavier gun, but a .32 slug was enough to kill a man if it hit him in the right place—and nobody was better than Frank Morgan at hitting the places he wanted to hit.

What they needed was a distraction, something to shake the outlaws up so bad they wouldn't know what was going on until Frank, Conway, and Meg had had a chance to cut down some of them and even up the odds a little. Frank thought he saw a way to do that.

But first he had to be sure of his allies. He looked at them in the faint light that reached into the brush from the bonfire and asked, "Meg, can you kill a man?"

"I can kill more than one if I get the chance," she answered without hesitation.

"How good a shot are you? Have you ever used a pistol? I was going to give all of you ladies some tips on gun-handling while we were on the *Montclair,* but the weather was too bad and you were all too sick most of the time."

"I can shoot a pistol," she said. "I used to plink at foxes and other varmints back on the farm."

Frank nodded. "All right. How about you, Pete?"

"I'm a good shot," the young man said.

"Ever kill a man?"

"Well . . . no. But I've been thinking about everything those poor gals have gone through already and how terrified they must be right now." Conway swallowed. "I can pull the trigger when I need to, Frank. Don't worry about that."

"All right, then. Here's what I'm going to do . . ."

Quickly, he explained his plan to them, and when he was sure they understood their part in it, he left them there and started circling wide around the outlaw stronghold, taking Dog with him. Once he was sure they were out of reach of the light from the fire, Frank darted to the base of the ridge and started climbing it. It was steep enough to be tough going, and he was a little out of breath before he got as high as he needed to be.

He began working his way back along the ridge until he was above the fire and the cabins. Once he reached the right spot, he studied the terrain again, just to make sure he had figured things correctly and his plan had a chance of working. After a moment, he nodded to himself, satisfied that what he was about to do was the only chance they had of freeing the prisoners and dealing with the outlaws. He went to the boulder that was the key to everything and turned around so that he could put his back against it. Then he planted his feet against the slope and started to push.

He didn't have to worry about giving a signal to Conway and Meg. If this worked, they would know when to go into action.

Frank groaned with effort as he strained hard against the big rock. At first it didn't want to budge.

Then it rocked a little, no more than an inch or two. Frank redoubled his efforts. Cords of muscle stood out in his neck as he strained. The boulder shifted again, and this time he didn't let it rock back. He was able to keep it moving instead. He heard a scraping sound, and then suddenly the boulder fell away from him as it overbalanced and began to roll down the ridge.

Frank dropped to the ground as the boulder's resistance vanished. He sprang up in time to see the outlaws around the bonfire looking up. They must have heard the rumble of the massive rock coming toward them. Someone down below shouted.

Then, just as it began to build up some speed, the boulder reached the little hummock of ground Frank had spotted earlier. Like it was launched from a ramp, the big rock shot up into the air, arching out away from the face of the ridge. It seemed to hang there for a second, suspended, before its weight sent it plummeting down . . .

To crash right in the middle of the bonfire and send burning brands flying everywhere like a bundle of dynamite had just gone off.

Chapter 17

Some of the outlaws screamed as the red-hot ashes and burning branches pelted them. A couple of the fur coats worn by the men blazed up as they caught on fire. Others ran around waving guns, looking for something to shoot even though it must have seemed to them like the boulder had dropped magically out of the sky into the fire.

Frank lined the sights of the .32 and began to fire, targeting the guards by the cabin. They hadn't been injured when the fire scattered, since they were farther away from it, so they represented the greatest threats. The range was long for a handgun, but The Drifter was a superb marksman. He tried for head-shots, and both of the outlaws went down as Frank's bullets bored through their brains.

At the same time, Conway and Meg opened fire from the brush where they were hidden. Two more of the hardcases stumbled and fell because of that volley. That left five of the outlaws on their feet. Of that five, two were on fire, staggering around and screaming as they slapped at the flames engulfing their clothes, and another man shrieked as he pawed at his eyes, which had evidently been blinded by the spray of hot ashes. The final two fired back at Conway and Meg in the brush. They must not have spotted Frank on the slope behind them. He drew a bead and shot one of the men in the back, the slug driving the outlaw forward onto his face as it ripped through him. That made the other one whirl toward the ridge and fire his rifle wildly. Lead whipped through the trees near Frank.

Then two more shots roared out from the brush. Both of them found their target, knocking the outlaw off his feet.

Less than thirty seconds had passed since the boulder slammed into the fire. Six of the nine outlaws were down. As Frank reloaded swiftly and efficiently, the two men in the burning coats finally succeeded in ripping the garments off themselves. Before they could do anything else, though, Frank snapped the cylinder of his revolver closed, lifted the gun, and fired two more shots—*one, two!* Both men staggered and collapsed.

That left only the blinded man. As the echoes of the shots died away, he fell onto his knees and screamed, "Don't kill me! Please, don't kill me!"

Frank was sure the man wouldn't have shown any mercy if the circumstances had been reversed. But that didn't really matter. He wasn't a cold-blooded killer and never had been. He stood up and called to Conway and Meg, "Hold your fire!"

He kept his gun trained on the remaining outlaw as

he made his way down the steep slope. Conway and Meg emerged from the brush. "Cover the others!" Frank told them. "They might not all be dead!"

He reached level ground and strode over to the blinded man. The outlaw must have heard Frank coming, because he took his hands away from his scorched eyes and held them out in front of him as he pleaded, "Oh, God, don't kill me, mister!"

Frank stopped in front of the man and drew back the Colt's hammer so that the outlaw could hear it being cocked. "Are the women in that cabin where the guards were?" he asked.

"Y-yeah. I swear!"

"Have any of them been molested or hurt in any other way?"

"No! I swear, mister, I swear! Nobody laid a finger on 'em!"

"Yet," Frank said coldly.

"Well . . . yeah. We . . . we were gonna—"

Frank pressed the gun's muzzle against the man's forehead, shutting him up. "Don't tell me what you were going to do," he said. "You don't have to."

"I . . . I'm sorry, mister. We didn't know the women was yours."

"How far are we from Skagway?"

The question seemed to take the outlaw by surprise. "Skagway?"

"That's right." Frank increased the pressure with the gun barrel.

"Don't shoot, don't shoot! It's about five miles on up the coast, that's all! Not far at all, mister!"

Frank had already seen that the door to the cabin

where the women were being held was closed off
with a simple bar, so he wouldn't need a key to
unlock it. There were still a few things he wanted to
know, though.

"What's your name?"

The man licked his lips. "Jennings. B-Bart Jennings."

"Were you the boss of this bunch, Jennings?"

"No, sir. That was Ben Cregar. It was all his idea
to grab them women, I swear!"

"You swear a lot," Frank said. "Are there any more
men in this gang, or were you all here tonight?"

"This is it. This is all of us."

"Got any friends or relatives in these parts who'll
be looking to even the score for you?"

"Nary a one. We . . . we all come up here to Alaska
to look for gold, but—"

"But that was hard work, wasn't it?" Frank said.
"So you turned to being outlaws instead."

"Mister, I'm blind," Jennings moaned. "I can't see
a damned thing. I know why you was askin' them
questions. You're plannin' on killin' me to cover your
trail. But you don't have to. I never saw your face. I
don't know who you are."

"You're bound to hear about a man who brought a
dozen women to Skagway, though."

Jennings began to shake. Clearly, he was convinced that he was only seconds away from death.

Frank leaned closer and said in a low voice, "You
know what I did here tonight, Jennings. You think I
couldn't get to a blind man any time I wanted? You
know what'll happen if you tell anybody about this?"

"I . . . I know! You don't have to worry about me, mister! Nobody'll ever hear about it from me!"

"Is there any law in Skagway?"

"Law?" That question took Jennings by surprise, too. "N-no, none to speak of. A fella by the name of Soapy Smith sort of runs the town, I guess you'd say. You don't have to worry about the law up here, mister."

"That means there's nobody to save you if you go back on your word to me," Frank warned.

"I wouldn't do that! Not ever!"

"Remember that, Jennings," Frank said, then reversed the Colt and slammed the butt against the man's head, knocking him out cold and sending him sprawling on the ground.

Conway said, "Miss Goodwin and I checked the others, Frank. They're all dead." The young man's voice was a little hollow, probably because he wasn't accustomed to the sight of so much death, but he and Meg had handled their part of the chore just fine, Frank thought.

"Let's go get those ladies out of there," he said. "They've been locked up long enough."

The prisoners must have heard the crash of the boulder landing, followed by the shouting and the gunfire, then the silence, and Frank figured that silence must have sounded pretty ominous to them. So as he and Conway and Meg approached the cabin, he called out, "Fiona! Can you hear me? It's all right, ladies!"

"Frank!" Fiona's excited shout came from inside,

muffled somewhat by the thick, log wall and the heavy door. "Oh, Lord, Frank, is it really you?"

"Grab the other end of that bar, Pete, and we'll lift it out of its brackets," Frank told Conway. "Hang on in there! We'll have you out in just a minute!"

They removed the bar and lifted the latch, and the door swung out, revealing that there was no handle for the latch on the inside. Ben Cregar and his gang had used this cabin for locking up prisoners in the past, and Frank didn't want to think about the unfortunate folks who had wound up as prisoners of the outlaws. Chances were, none of them had come to a good end.

Fiona came out first, followed by the nine young women. She threw her arms around Frank, while Jessica cried, "Pete!" and ran to him. The others hugged Meg, who patted them on the back and assured them that everything was going to be all right.

Fiona stepped back a little, looked up at Frank, then raised herself on her toes so that she could kiss him hard on the mouth. She pulled away after a moment and asked, "How in the world did you find us?"

Frank glanced over at Meg, who gave him that crooked grin of hers. She seemed amused by Fiona's demonstration of gratitude. He cleared his throat and said, "Finding you wasn't the problem. Dog took care of that. It was getting the drop on those varmints who took you that was a mite difficult."

"I see that you managed, though," Fiona said as she looked around the clearing. "Are . . . are they all dead?"

"All but one, and he won't cause any trouble for us or anybody else."

"What are we going to do now?" A shudder went through her. "I'd like to get away from here."

"That's what I figured. Those fellas don't need their horses anymore, and we do. So we're taking them, and we'll ride into Skagway first thing tomorrow morning. It's only about five miles from here."

"We made it almost all the way, then."

Frank nodded. "We did. We've come through hell. But it'll be over soon."

With Stormy and Goldy, they now had almost enough horses for everybody. Some of the young women could ride double. They saddled the mounts and led them back to the beach where the bodies of Neville and the other three cheechakos still lay. In the morning, they wrapped those bodies in blankets brought from the cabins, carried them into the woods, and buried them in graves that Frank and Conway dug with shovels they also found at the outlaw camp.

Frank had collected the gang's guns and ammunition as well, along with all the supplies he found. It felt good to have a fine Colt .45 riding in his holster again. The gun was nearly new, so he figured the man he'd taken it from had either bought it or more likely stolen it recently.

They were a well-equipped group now, especially for the short journey to Skagway that they faced. Frank surprised his companions by taking Bart Jennings with them. He had thought it over, and he couldn't leave the blinded man to wander around in the woods alone. That was a sure death sentence. He had bathed Jennings's scorched eyes with fresh water, then tied a rag around the man's head to cover them and protect them from further injury.

"You got a friend for life if you want one, mister," Jennings declared fervently. "I never should've fell in with that bad bunch to start with. The way I see it, you could've killed me and you didn't, so I owe you my life."

Later, Conway told Frank in a quiet voice, "I wouldn't trust him if I was you, Frank. Once an outlaw, always an outlaw."

Frank wasn't sure that was always completely true. He had known some badmen who had reformed and walked the straight and narrow. He himself was considered a badman by some, simply because of his reputation as a fast gun. But he planned to keep a close eye on Jennings anyway. It never hurt to be careful. Because of that, he had Jennings double up with him on Stormy.

They rode up the beach, the young women using the outlaws' saddles, and it was a lot easier and faster than trudging along on foot. As the miles fell behind them, the hills on the other side of the water drew closer. The inlet was getting narrower. Skagway was at the end of it, Frank recalled from Captain Hoffman's maps.

The sky was still thickly overcast, with a cold wind blowing from the north. Jennings licked his lips as he rode in front of Frank on Stormy. He said, "There's snow comin'. I can taste it."

"We'll be in Skagway before it gets here," Frank said. He had spotted several columns of white smoke rising against the gray clouds and knew they came from the settlement.

A short time later, Conway let out a whoop as he spotted the buildings. "There it is!" he said, tightening his arm around Jessica's waist as she rode in front of him. "We made it, by God! We made it!"

The women were excited to be reaching Skagway, too, even though it wasn't their final destination. That was still Whitehorse, Fiona insisted. Frank reckoned she didn't want to lose the fees she had been promised, and after all she had gone through to get here, he didn't suppose he could blame her.

The settlement wasn't very impressive-looking as they came closer. It was a jumble of muddy streets lined with tents, tar-paper shacks, and crude buildings constructed of raw, unplaned lumber. Plank sidewalks ran in front of the buildings and tall pines loomed over them. The waters of the inlet washed against several docks that were probably the sturdiest-looking structures in town.

From the looks on the faces of Fiona and her charges, though, it might as well have been San Francisco or Boston. They were that happy to be here.

Up ahead and to the right, Frank spotted a building with a sign over its door that read CLANCY'S SALOON. Three men leaned against one of the hitch rails in front of it. When they saw Frank and his companions riding into the settlement, they straightened from their casual poses and walked forward to meet

them, the mud sucking at their boots. They had the
look of a semiofficial welcoming committee.

The man in the center, who was slightly in the
lead, was slender, with a close-cropped black beard,
gaunt features, and deep-set, piercing eyes. He wore
a dark suit and broad-brimmed hat. One of his companions was a burly, mustachioed gent in a derby.
The other wore a cloth cap on the back of his head
and had a clean-shaven face that reminded Frank of
a ferret.

The black-bearded man raised a hand in greeting
as Frank and the others reined in. His eyes took in
Fiona and the young women, and his eyebrows rose
in surprise. He had probably never seen this many eligible women in this rugged place before.

"Howdy, folks," he said with a smile that didn't
reach his chilly eyes. "Welcome to Skagway. They
call me Soapy Smith."

Chapter 18

Frank remembered what Jennings had said about Soapy Smith running things in Skagway. During the ride that morning, Frank had asked Jennings to tell him more about Smith, and Jennings had related how the man had shown up not long after Skagway's founding, accompanied by five tough companions, two of whom were probably the men with him now. Even though there was no official law, Soapy had quickly established himself as a force for law and order by stopping a lynch mob from hanging a bartender accused of murder. No one wanted to buck Smith, especially as long as he was surrounded by such obviously dangerous cronies. For that matter, as long as things stayed relatively peaceful, the entrepreneurs who had come to Skagway to set up businesses didn't really care who was running things in the settlement.

"I don't know it for a fact," Jennings had told Frank, "but I figure Soapy must be some sort of crook. I don't know for sure because the boys and me never got into town much. They didn't like us there."

Frank couldn't blame the townspeople for that. Lawless hardcases like Ben Cregar and his gang made it difficult for those who had come to Alaska to make their fortunes legally.

Now, as Frank looked at Soapy Smith with narrowed eyes, he felt an instinctive dislike for the man and agreed with Jennings's hunch that Smith was a crook masquerading as a slick community leader.

"This is Yeah Mow Hopkins," Smith went on, nodding to the burly man in the derby, "and Sid Dixon." That was the ferret-faced man in the cloth cap. "A couple of associates of mine."

Smith paused, obviously waiting for Frank to introduce himself and the others. "My name's Morgan," he said. "This is Mrs. Devereaux, Mr. Conway, and Mr. Jennings. The young ladies are traveling with us."

"I can see that," Smith murmured. "What brings such a bevy of beauties to a backwater burg like this?"

"The ladies and I are bound for Whitehorse," Fiona said stiffly, "where they will be marrying gentlemen who are waiting for them there."

"Oh, ho!" A grin tugged at Smith's mouth. "Mail-order brides! I should have known someone would come up with that idea sooner or later. Now that I think about it, I'm surprised that it's taken this long." He glanced toward the docks. "I'm also surprised that you didn't come in by ship. There's one due any day now. Overdue, in fact."

"The *Montclair*?" Frank asked.

A puzzled frown appeared on Smith's narrow face. Hopkins's expression remained stolid and unreadable. From the way Dixon's eyes darted around nervously and he constantly licked his lips, Frank figured he was some sort of drug addict.

"That's right, the *Montclair*," Smith said. "Do you have news of her?"

"Unfortunately, yes. She sank in a bad storm a couple of days ago." Frank leaned his head toward his companions. "We're the only survivors, as far as I know."

He included Jennings in that group, figuring it was easier to do that than to try to explain the real circumstances that had led to him accompanying them.

Smith's eyebrows went up in surprise. "You survived the ship sinking in rough seas? That's mighty lucky, Mister . . . Morgan, was it?"

"That's right. I won't deny that we had guardian angels watching over us."

"Seems like it," Smith said. "Where'd you get those horses?"

Frank had hoped to avoid having to explain about that, but obviously, he wasn't going to be able to do so.

"We were attacked by a gang of outlaws. When the fight was over, they didn't need their horses anymore."

Sid Dixon let out a low whistle. "You must be a fightin' fool, mister, if you killed a whole gang."

"Never said I killed them by myself," Frank drawled.

Smith chuckled. "Even more impressive. It's not every day you meet a group of mail-order brides who can tangle with outlaws and come out on top."

Frank didn't want to continue this discussion. He asked, "Have you got a hotel here in town?"

"Yeah. It ain't fancy, but you can put up there." Smith turned to point along the curving street. "Go on around the corner, past the general mercantile, and you'll see the Klondike Hotel on the left."

"I thought the Klondike country was in Canada," Conway said.

"It is, but since that's where so many of the gents who come to Skagway are bound, the proprietor thought that would be a good name for the hotel," Smith explained.

Frank nodded. "Much obliged for the information." He lifted Stormy's reins.

"If there's anything else I can help you with, come on back down here to Clancy's place and ask for me," Smith said quickly. "I'm sort of the unofficial mayor of Skagway, I guess you could say, and Clancy's is the unofficial city hall, until I can get a place of my own built."

"We'll remember that," Frank said. In reality, though, he wanted as little as possible to do with Soapy Smith. He didn't trust the man and had been suspicious of him on sight.

In fact, there was something familiar about Smith, both his name and his appearance, and Frank couldn't help but wonder if he had run into the man somewhere before. A memory tickled at the back of his brain, and he knew it would come to him sooner or later.

In the meantime, he led the group around the corner, following Smith's directions, and found the Klondike Hotel. As Smith had said, it wasn't fancy. It was a one-story frame building with a false front, and extending out from each side were a couple of wings with walls made of canvas. In the winter, which was coming soon, it would probably be ice-cold in those rooms, but at least the canvas would block the wind and keep most of the snow out.

A cadaverous man with a smile on his skull-like face stood near the hotel entrance with a Bible in his hands. "Welcome to Skagway, my friends," he said as Frank and the others drew rein in front of the place. "I'm Reverend Bowers, and if you have any spiritual needs to tend to, I'd be happy to help you in coming to the Lord. In the meantime, I'm collecting for our permanent fund for widows and orphans, if you'd care to contribute."

Frank swung down from Stormy's back and shook his head. "Sorry, Reverend. We don't have any spare cash." He didn't add that so far he hadn't seen any children at all in Skagway, and the only woman he had seen other than the ones with him was an Indian whore leaning in the doorway of Clancy's Saloon. Frank wasn't sure there was a single widow or orphan in the whole settlement, not counting Fiona, of course.

"Well, if I can be of assistance to you, don't hesitate to let me know." Still smiling, Reverend Bowers moved off down the muddy street.

As Frank helped Jennings down from the horse, the blinded outlaw asked quietly, "Was that that phony sky pilot talkin' to you, Mr. Morgan?"

"Reverend Bowers? Yeah."

"Don't trust him. He's in with Soapy Smith. I got a feelin' he's a crook, too."

"I wouldn't be a bit surprised."

Frank left Jennings standing there holding on to the hitch rail where he looped Stormy's reins, then moved over to Goldy to help Fiona dismount. He would have tried to help Meg, too, but she swung down with ease on her own. Conway lifted Jessica from the saddle with one hand on either side of her waist, handling her as if she weighed no more than a doll. Then he hurried to help the other young women dismount, too, although he wasn't quite as solicitous of them.

The Klondike had a narrow porch that ran along the front, with a couple of ladderback chairs on it. A bulky bundle of furs was piled on one of the chairs. As Frank started past it, the bundle of furs moved, and he was startled to see a head lift from it. An old man's wizened eyes peered out from under a fur cap and a mop of white hair. Not much of his leathery skin was visible because a bushy white beard covered most of his face.

"I heard the rev'rend put the touch on ye," the old-timer rasped, "so I won't bother. But if ye've ever got a spare crust o' bread or such, I'd be obliged if ye'd remember ol' Salty."

"That's you?" Frank asked.

"Aye. Salty Stevens, by name. And I've fallen on hard times, amigo. Mighty hard times."

Frank heard the soft drawl of the Southwest in the old man's voice and felt an immediate kinship with him. He rested a hand on the man's shoulder for a second, or where he thought the shoulder would be in that pile of furs, and said, "Maybe I'll have something for you later."

"Be much obliged, Tex. That's where you hail from, ain't it?"

Frank smiled. "You've got a good ear, Salty."

"Been all over that country." The old-timer sighed. "Wisht I was down on the Rio right now, listenin' to some Mex play the guitar in a cantina and watchin' the señoritas."

Frank patted his shoulder. "Sounds good. We'll have to get together and talk about old times."

He led the others into the hotel, where a skinny, balding man with spectacles perched on the end of a long nose waited behind a desk. Frank gestured toward his companions and said, "We're going to need some rooms."

The prominent Adam's apple in the clerk's neck bobbed up and down. "I don't have but three rooms empty, mister, and they're in the east wing. No heat over there. Got plenty of blankets, though. You're lucky we have any empties at all."

Frank wasn't so sure about that. The streets of Skagway were less crowded than he had thought they would be. He figured that most of the men who were headed for the gold fields around Whitehorse had already set out, hoping to reach their destination and get situated before winter closed everything down. Most of the people in Skagway now were either gold-hunters who planned to wait out the winter here or folks who worked in the settlement.

He and his companions couldn't afford to be too particular about their accommodations, though. He nodded and said, "We'll take them. You ladies can have the rooms. Pete and Bart and I will find some-place else to bunk down."

"I hate for you to have to do that," Fiona said. "For one thing, I was hoping to have you close by in case of trouble, Frank."

"Don't worry, we won't be far off," Frank assured her. "I think I spotted a livery stable across the street. We can bed down with the horses." He smiled. "After all we've been through, I reckon that'll seem almost like the lap of luxury."

"Yes, but there's one more thing . . ." Fiona tugged him aside and whispered, "How are we going to pay for this? All my traveling funds went down with the *Montclair*."

"Don't worry about that," Frank told her. He reached under his coat and shirt and took out a thin leather wallet. The greenbacks in there had gotten soaked in the various drenchings they had taken, but they hadn't fallen apart and were dry by now. He slipped a couple of bills out of the wallet.

Fiona smiled. "I thought you told that preacher you didn't have any money."

"I don't have any money for a crooked sky pilot, and I had a hunch that's what he was. Bart confirmed it." Frank turned back to the desk and slapped the bills down on it. "That cover the rooms for a few days?"

The clerk scooped them up. "Yes, sir!" He pointed. "Go right through that door over there. They'll be the third, fourth, and fifth rooms on the left."

Frank nodded. "Much obliged."

The next ten minutes were spent carrying in their supplies and arranging for the horses to be stabled across the street. The liveryman was agreeable to letting Frank, Conway, Jennings, and Dog stay with the horses, for an extra price, of course.

The hotel rooms were crude and primitive, with dirt floors, no windows, and only a flap of canvas for a door. The flap could be tied closed, but that wouldn't keep anybody out who wanted to get in.

"Tell the ladies to keep their pistols handy," Frank advised Fiona as they stood in the dirt-floored corridor of the hotel's east wing, just outside the rented rooms. "And if there's trouble, let out a holler. We'll be just across the street, so I reckon we'll be able to hear it."

"Thank you, Frank." She put a hand on his arm and rubbed her fingers back and forth on the sleeve of his sheepskin coat. "And thank you for getting us this far. I don't think there's another man in the world who could have pulled us through all that trouble."

"I don't know about that," Frank said. "I'm just trying to keep my word to Jacob. As soon as we can figure out what we'll need, we'll round up an outfit and set out for Whitehorse."

"You think we can still make it before winter sets

in? Captain Hoffman was wrong about how much time we had left to get here to Skagway."

"Maybe that storm was just a fluke and there's still some time. Jennings has been up here for a while. I'll talk to him about it."

Fiona frowned at him. "You'd trust that man? He's an outlaw! He kidnapped us!"

"Yeah, but he seems genuinely grateful that I didn't kill him. Don't worry, he's not the only one I plan to talk to. If we have to, we can wait out the winter here, I suppose."

"My clients in Whitehorse won't like that."

"Better to have a warm wife next spring than a frozen fiancée this winter."

She looked at him for a second, then laughed. "You do have a way with words, Frank Morgan." With a sigh and a shake of her head, she went on. "I was hoping we might be able to spend some time together here, just you and me."

"Maybe when we get back from Whitehorse," Frank said. "We won't be able to return to Seattle until spring, so we'll be spending all winter in Skagway."

"A long, cold winter . . ." Fiona mused. "We'll have to come up with some way to keep warm."

Frank smiled. "I reckon we'll manage," he said.

Chapter 19

Frank had noticed when he went across the street with Conway and Jennings to stable the horses that Salty Stevens was no longer huddled in his furs on the front porch of the hotel. He asked the clerk, "That old-timer who was outside earlier, where can I find him?"

The clerk frowned. "You mean Salty? Did that old beggar bother you, mister? I try to run him off whenever I see him out there. The boss doesn't like him hanging around the hotel."

Frank wondered if the boss was Soapy Smith. Smith had been quick to direct them here to the Klondike and might well be the owner of the place.

"No, the old man didn't bother us," Frank said in reply to the clerk's question. "I just want to talk to him. I think we may be from the same part of the country."

"Oh. In that case . . . there's a saloon down the street called Ike's. I think Salty hangs around there a lot, too, trying to cadge drinks." The clerk shook his head. "I warn you, though, mister, it's a pretty squalid place."

From what Frank had seen so far, most of Skagway fit that description. But he just nodded and said, "All right, thanks."

As he came out of the hotel, Conway and Jennings emerged from the stable across the street. They had been tending to the horses, or rather Conway had, since Jennings couldn't see. He was able to stand and hold a saddle, though, if somebody handed it to him.

Frank told them, "I want to talk to that old-timer who was at the hotel earlier. I figure he can tell us something about what the weather's going to do. The clerk says that if he's not here, he's probably at a saloon called Ike's."

"I know the place," Jennings said. "I can show— Well, no, I reckon I can't show you where it is, after all."

"We'll find it. Come on."

Jennings looked surprised. "You still want me to come with you? I figured once we got to Skagway, I'd be on my own."

Frank lowered his voice and asked, "How long would you last in this town without being able to see? From what I can tell, there are as many dangerous critters around here as there are in the woods."

Jennings sighed. "Maybe more."

"So you're one of us now, at least for the time being."

Conway frowned, visibly upset by Frank's words. "No offense, Frank," he said, "but this fellow is an outlaw. As far as we know, he may be the one who killed Neville."

Jennings shook his head emphatically. "I didn't kill nobody, Mr. Conway. I was holdin' the horses while the rest of the boys jumped your camp and grabbed them ladies. I swear it."

"Yeah, you'd say that whether it was true or not," Conway said with a disdainful grunt.

Jennings held up a hand like he was being sworn in to testify in court. "Word of honor, sir. I . . . I stole plenty of things in my life, but I never killed nobody, at least not that I know of."

"You can travel with us as long as you behave yourself," Frank said. "Get out of line, though, especially with the women, and you're on your own."

"You can count on me, Mr. Morgan."

The three of them walked along the street, Frank resting a hand on Jennings's shoulder to guide him. Ike's was a tent saloon with a couple of stumps in front of it where pine trees had been cut down. When Frank pushed aside the canvas flap over the entrance and stepped inside, he saw several more stumps sticking up from the dirt floor. Men sat on them to drink, using them as makeshift chairs. The bar was to the right. It consisted of rough planks laid across the tops of several whiskey barrels. As a saloon, Ike's was about as crude as it could be.

It was doing good business, though. More than a dozen men stood around nursing drinks from tin cups, and all the stumps were occupied. Frank looked around and spotted a familiar pile of furs shuffling along the bar, stopping next to each of the customers to ask something. Each of the men shook his head, and some of them barked angrily at the desolate old-timer.

In fact, one of the drinkers seemed to take offense at being approached like that. He turned toward Salty and said loudly, "Get away from me, you damned bum." He drew his arm across his body, as if he were about to backhand the old-timer.

Frank's left hand fell hard on the man's shoulder. "I wouldn't do that if I was you, mister," he said.

The man jerked around with a furious glare on his face. He started to say, "Who the hell do you think you—" Then he stopped short as he saw the menace glittering in The Drifter's eyes. He said, "You know that old tramp?"

"We're amigos," Frank said.

"You ought to keep him from bothering people, then."

Frank took his hand off the man's shoulder, reached into his pocket, and found a coin. He tossed it on the bar and said coldly, "Next drink's on me. Just take it down to the other end of the bar."

"Sure, sure," the man muttered. He held out his tin cup to the moon-faced bartender for a refill, then moved away toward the other end of the bar.

"Thanks, Tex," Salty said, "but you didn't have to do that. I'm sorta used to gettin' walloped."

"Well, you shouldn't be. We want to talk to you, Salty. Is there someplace better than this?"

Salty licked his lips, which were barely visible under the bushy white mustache and beard. "I reckon we could go to my shack."

"How about if we take a bottle with us?"

Salty cackled. "Now you're talkin'! Damned if you ain't!"

Frank bought a bottle from the bartender, who looked like a half-breed. The bottle had no label on it, and he was sure that what was inside had been brewed up in one of those barrels. It was probably raw stuff, but if they were lucky, it wouldn't give them the blind staggers.

The four men went outside. Salty led the way to the edge of the settlement, stopping at something that was more shed than shack, a haphazard arrangement of broken boards, tarpaper, tin, and canvas. It looked almost like the various parts of it had been thrown up in the air, and however they came down was the way Salty had left it.

The place had a door, though, and when they went inside, Frank saw that it had a rickety table as well, and a tangle of blankets in a corner that served as a bunk. The only places to sit down were a wobbly stool and an empty nail keg. Frank told Salty and Jennings to take those seats, and then placed the bottle in the center of the table.

Salty licked his lips again and obviously ached to grab the bottle, but he resisted its lure for the moment. "How come you're bein' so nice to me, Tex?" he asked.

"I told you, we're from the same part of the country. And the name's Frank Morgan, by the way, not Tex."

Salty's head jerked up. "Frank Morgan!" he repeated. "You mean The Drifter?"

"Heard of me, have you?"

"Damn straight I have! You might not know it to look at me, but there was a time I worked as a range detective with a cousin o' mine and his pardner, and I was friends for a while with a deputy U.S. marshal, too. I weren't never an official lawman, mind you, but I was next thing to it." The old-timer sighed. "Them was better days, that's for damn' sure. Anyway, I heard of you, sure enough, Mr. Morgan. And the way I heard it, you're one o' the fastest fellas ever to slap leather. If anybody'd asked me, though, I'd've had to say that I didn't know whether you was still alive."

Frank grinned. "I'm still kicking, all right. Tell me, Salty, where are you from?"

"Well, I was born in Arizony. Or was it New Mexico Territory? Been so long ago, I don't rightly remember. But I growed up all over the whole Southwest, a-huntin' and a-trappin'. Met one o' the last o' the old-time mountain men once, a contrary ol' critter called Preacher. When I got a few more years on me, I done a mite of scoutin' for the army and drove a stagecoach for a while out Californy way. It was a while later I met that marshal fella and then went to range detectin'. Been a good life, a mighty full life."

Conway said, "A man your age ought to be sitting in a rocking chair somewhere, enjoying his old age."

Salty got a truculent look on his bushy face. "Old age, is it? I'll have you know, young fella, that I can still mush all day on a pair o' snowshoes if I have to, and I can grab a gee-pole and handle a team o' sled dogs just fine, too."

"What brought you to Alaska in the first place?" Frank asked.

"Gold, o' course, same thing as brought all these other cheechakos and stampeders up here!" Salty paused, and when he went on, there was a wistful note in his voice. "And I, uh, got a mite tired o' sittin' on my granddaughter's front porch in that rockin' chair the young fella just mentioned. Figured I might have one last grand adventure in me, so I took off for the Klondike! Found me a nice gold claim, too, and worked it for a while. Had me a poke full o' nuggets when I got back here."

"And then what happened?"

"Soapy Smith and his gang o' thieves and swindlers and murderers happened," Salty said. "Soapy claimed I was breakin' a local ord'nance when I got drunk, and he got his pet judge to sock a big fine against me. One o' his pickpockets finished cleanin' me out. I couldn't go home, couldn't go back across the passes to Whitehorse, couldn't do nothin' but stay here and become a bum." The old-timer spread his hands. "And that's what you see before you now, gents. A plumb worthless excuse for an old fool."

"I wouldn't be so sure about that," Frank said. "You say you've been to Whitehorse, so you must have been over Chilkoot Pass."

"Yeah, and White Pass, too. You got to go over it before you get to Chilkoot."

"What do you think? If a party left Skagway in the next day or two, could they get over the passes and make it to Whitehorse before winter sets in?"

Salty frowned, but the only way to tell it was by

the way the scraggly curtain of white hair lowered over his brow. "Well, I don't rightly know. I'd have to think on it . . . and I think a mite better when my thinkin' apparatus is lubricated."

Frank pushed the bottle of rotgut toward him. "Oil it up, old-timer."

Salty pulled the cork with his teeth, spit it out, and lifted the bottle to his mouth. The whiskey gurgled as he took a long swallow of it.

"I hear that," Jennings said. "It's a pretty sound."

Salty reached out, took Jennings's hand, and pressed the bottle into it. "Have a slug, old son. It might not restore your sight, but it can't hurt to try."

While Jennings took a drink, Salty looked up at Frank and went on. "If folks was to leave right now and had good sleds and dogs, I reckon they could make it through the passes to Whitehorse."

"You couldn't go on horseback?"

Salty shook his head. "No, there's already snow-pack up there. You could go part of the way on horses, but you'd have to break out the dogs to get over the passes and on down to Whitehorse."

"How about getting back here?"

"That'd be riskier. Still, a fella might could do it, if he knew the quickest way there and back."

"Someone like you, you mean?" Frank said.

"Well, come to think of it . . . yeah. I know all the trails."

Frank didn't hesitate. "How'd you like to go to Whitehorse with us?"

Before Salty could answer, Conway stepped

forward and lifted a hand. "Wait a minute, Frank. We've already picked up a blind outlaw—"

"You're an outlaw?" Salty said to Jennings.

"I was," Jennings replied with a sober nod. "I've given up banditry. I'm a changed man because of Mr. Morgan."

As if he hadn't been interrupted, Conway went on. "Now you're going to add a drunken old man to our party? You'd put the safety of those ladies in the hands of a—"

"A former range detective, army scout, and unofficial deputy U.S. marshal?" Frank said. "I reckon I would."

Salty reached for the bottle again. "Now, the young galoot may have a point there, Mr. Morgan. I ain't all that dependable these days, not since I got a taste for this Who-hit-John."

Frank picked up the bottle before Salty could. "Then maybe it's time to put this away. How about you have the rest of it when we get back to Skagway from Whitehorse?"

"But . . . we might not make it back till spring. That's a long time!"

"You'll be all right, Salty. You'll have a job to do."

The old-timer ran gnarled fingers through his tangled beard. "That *would* be nice," he said in a half-whisper. "Folks used to depend on me, and I never let 'em down."

"You won't now, either."

Salty gave an abrupt nod. "Count me in," he declared. "Put the cork in the bottle, and we'll have it when we get back."

"Maybe," Frank said, "or maybe we'll have something better."

Conway looked like he thought they were making a big mistake.

The young man would really feel that way, Frank thought, if he knew that before they left Skagway, he intended to have a talk with Soapy Smith about an old man's stolen gold.

Chapter 20

Before leaving the shack, Frank asked Salty if he had any more bottles of whiskey stashed there. The old-timer insisted that he didn't. "I ain't never had enough money to buy a whole bottle since Smith and his varmints cleaned me out," Salty declared. "Most I could ever beg was enough for a shot or two."

Frank believed him. "You can stay here for now, but tomorrow you're going to help me pick out some sleds and dogs and everything else we'll need for the trip."

"Why're you so bound and determined to go to Whitehorse? This got somethin' to do with them pretty young gals who come into town with you?"

"It has everything to do with them," Frank explained. "They're mail-order brides, and they have husbands-to-be waiting for them in the Klondike."

Salty let out a little whistle of surprise. "Doggone! No wonder you're anxious to get through. I reckon some o' them prospectors who've found good claims would pay a mighty handsome price to have a comely gal keep 'em warm all winter."

"That's the idea," Frank said with a grin.

"Makes me feel like I'll be doin' some good for the world by helpin' you get 'em there."

"That's one way to look at it," Frank said.

"One thing you got to remember, though . . . this late in the season, the best dogs is prob'ly already gone. You'll be gettin' the runts of the litter."

Frank nodded. "We'll do the best we can." He wondered how Dog would take to being hitched to a sled. They might find out before the journey was over.

He and Conway and Jennings went back to the hotel to check on Fiona and the rest of the women. They had split up among the three rooms and were resting, some on the bunks, some on blankets spread on the floor. After everything they had been through, even such primitive accommodations seemed almost like the lap of luxury. Frank didn't disturb them, but left them sleeping instead.

"I'm going down to Clancy's," he told Conway and Jennings. "I want to have a talk with Soapy Smith."

Jennings shook his head. "I ain't sure that's a good idea. You'd do well to stay as far away from him as you can, Mr. Morgan. He's a bad man, and he's got those toughs workin' for him."

"You heard what Salty said. Smith stole his poke, or was responsible for stealing it, anyway."

"You can't prove that, and you can't hope to get the old man's gold back after all this time."

"We'll see about that," Frank said with grim determination.

Conway sighed. "Then we're coming with you. I am, at least."

Frank shook his head and said, "I'd rather you didn't, Pete. I want you and Bart to stay here and keep an eye on the ladies in the hotel and the horses in the stable. We can't afford to have anything happen to any of them. And I'm sorry about the way I put that, Bart. I shouldn't have told you to keep an eye on them."

Jennings waved a hand. "Don't worry about that, Mr. Morgan. I know what you meant. You can't change the way you talk just on account of me."

Conway said, "I don't like the idea of you going to see Smith in his den by yourself. Although, I guess if anybody can handle something like that, it'd be you, Frank."

"Don't worry, I won't be looking for trouble. I just want to see if I can talk Smith into doing the right thing."

"Pretty long odds against that," Jennings said glumly.

Frank grinned. "I've beaten 'em before."

He left the two men at the livery stable and followed the plank sidewalk around the corner, avoiding the worst of the mud in the street. As he approached Clancy's Saloon, he saw a man stagger out of the place, vomit in the street, and then collapse on the plank sidewalk. By the time Frank got there, the man had started to snore.

Two men in derby hats came out of the saloon.

From the looks of them, Frank wondered if they worked for Soapy Smith. That was confirmed when one of them said, "Grab that bum's feet, Big Ed. Soapy wouldn't want him blockin' the sidewalk."

The man called Big Ed got the drunk's feet while the other one took hold of his shoulders. They lifted the man and threw him into the street. He rolled over a couple of times and came to a stop facedown in the mud without waking up. The two men turned to go back into the saloon.

"Hey!" Frank called to them. "Are you going to leave him like that? He'll suffocate!"

They stopped and looked at Frank in surprise. "That fella a friend of yours, mister?" Big Ed asked.

"No, I never saw him before."

"Then why do you give a damn whether he suffocates or not?"

"Because I wasn't raised to stand by and let a man die when there was something I could do about it," Frank snapped.

The other man shrugged. "Then do something about it. You go out there and turn him over. I ain't gettin' my boots muddy doin' it."

"Yeah," Frank said, "you are."

Both men stiffened in anger. "Do you know who we are?" Big Ed demanded.

"A couple of no-accounts, as far as I'm concerned," Frank said.

"I'm Big Ed Burns, and this is Joe Palmer. Maybe you heard of him."

Frank shook his head. "Can't say as I have."

Big Ed sneered. "He's the fastest gun in Skagway, maybe in all of Alaska, that's all."

Slowly, Frank shook his head. "I've got my doubts about that."

He knew from the rage that appeared on Palmer's face that the gunman was going to rise to that challenge. Palmer stepped forward and pushed his coat back so that his hand hovered near the butt of his gun, fingers curled, ready to hook and draw. Frank was ready, too, although he didn't make such a production out of it.

"Hold on, hold on," Soapy Smith said as he stepped out the front door of Clancy's. "What's going on here, Joe?"

Palmer nodded toward Frank. "Me and Big Ed threw that drunk in the street to get him off the sidewalk, and this fella took exception to it."

"I don't want the man to suffocate," Frank said.

"Well, of course not," Smith said with a nod. "Look how he landed. You boys go get him out of the mud."

Palmer and Burns looked at their boss in surprise. "What'd you say, Soapy?" Big Ed asked.

"I said go get that fella out of the mud," Smith repeated. He gestured toward the drunk. "Prop him up against the wall so he can sleep it off safely."

"But—"

"Do what I say now," Soapy went on softly, but with a tone of menace in his voice.

Palmer and Burns looked at each other. Big Ed shrugged. They turned and went out into the street, slogging through the mud until they reached the drunk. They lifted him and carried him back to the sidewalk, where they propped him against the wall as Smith had told them.

"Sorry about the misunderstanding, mister," Smith said to Frank with a friendly smile. "My boys and I sort of look out for the well-being of everybody in Skagway. Come on in and I'll buy you a drink."

Frank didn't believe for a second that Smith's jovial attitude was genuine, but he wanted to talk to the man anyway, so he said, "Don't mind if I do."

He walked past Palmer and Burns, well aware that they were giving him hard looks. He had made a couple of enemies there, not that he particularly cared.

Frank followed Smith into the saloon and saw that it was a notch or two above Ike's. The place had plank floors instead of dirt and real tables and chairs instead of tree stumps. The bar had been nailed together out of planks, but at least they had been planed a little and weren't just lying on top of whiskey barrels. There was no mirror on the wall behind the bar, but the shelves there held bottles with actual labels on them, although Frank would have been willing to bet that they no longer contained their original contents.

Smith led Frank to a large round table in the rear of the room. This was undoubtedly where the unofficial mayor of Skagway held court, so to speak. According to what Salty Stevens had said, Smith had a tame judge in his pocket, so actual court might be held here, too, although it would be mostly of the kangaroo variety. Smith waved Frank into one of the chairs and asked, "What's your pleasure, friend? Beer or whiskey?"

"Beer's fine," Frank said as he took a seat.

"Two beers, Claude," Smith called to the bartender. Still smiling, he sat down across from Frank. "Well, I never expected to see the famous Frank Morgan in my town."

Before Frank could say anything, the Indian whore he had seen earlier came over to the table, carrying a tray with two mugs of beer on it. Obviously she doubled as a waitress, as well as a soiled dove. Frank waited until she set the mugs on the table and returned to the bar before he said, "I don't recall telling you my first name when we rode into town."

"You didn't," Smith said, "but you looked familiar to me and the name Morgan finally jogged my memory. You're The Drifter. You rode through a town in Colorado where I was a few years ago."

"Creede," Frank said suddenly. "I remember."

Smith inclined his head to acknowledge that Frank was right.

"You had a pretty shady reputation there, as I recall." Frank didn't preface the statement with the words "No offense," because he didn't really care whether or not he offended Smith.

"That was due to another series of misunderstandings," Smith said without hesitation.

"Like the ones in Leadville and Denver?" The memories had come back to Frank in a flash once Smith's mention of Colorado triggered them. Smith had been well known in those places as a swindler and thief and a suspected killer. Clearly, he hadn't changed his stripes when he came to Alaska.

Smith picked up his beer and drank from it. He set the mug down and licked his lips. "If anyone would know about how a man's reputation follows him, whether it's deserved or not, it would be you, Frank," he said. "I seem to recall that you've been run out of a few towns yourself."

"If I was asked to leave by the local law, I went along with it because I didn't want to cause trouble," Frank said stiffly.

Smith gave a lazy shrug and smiled as if Frank's answer proved his point. "I didn't ask you in here to argue with you," he said. "I really am glad to make your acquaintance. It's not every day that Skagway gets such a famous visitor. When word gets around that Frank Morgan has been here, it'll just attract more people to the settlement. I'm for anything that helps Skagway to grow and prosper."

"So you'll have more people to fleece?"

For a second, anger danced in Smith's eyes before he banished it. "Think whatever you want about me. I'm just trying to help this town."

"Like you helped yourself to all the gold in Salty Stevens's poke?"

Smith frowned. "Who?"

His puzzlement seemed genuine, Frank thought. Then he realized that it probably was. Smith had had so many victims, he couldn't be expected to remember them all.

"The old-timer who hangs around the hotel and

Ike's Saloon, begging for drinks and food because he's broke."

"You mean that sourdough who looks like a walking pile of furs?" Smith chuckled. "He's still alive? I thought the booze would have killed him by now."

"Nope. He's alive, and he's going to help me and my friends take those ladies to Whitehorse."

Smith's eyebrows went up in surprise. "Really?"

"That's right. And I'd appreciate it if you'd return what you stole from him."

"Now, I didn't steal anything from the man. As I recall, he was in violation of one of the local ordinances, and Judge Van Horn had to levy a heavy fine on him. After that, someone stole the rest of his gold, but I didn't have anything to do with it. And I don't really appreciate anybody saying that I did." Smith waved his hand above his beer mug. "But that's not really important. I'm used to people telling lies about me by now. What matters is the two of us."

Frank was taken aback and couldn't help repeating it. "What do you mean, the two of us?"

Smith leaned forward with a wolfish grin on his face. "You know where the real gold mine is, Frank? It's not across the line in the Klondike. It's right here!" He slapped the table. "Skagway is the gold mine. It's where I'm making my fortune, and it's where you can make your fortune, too. All you have to do is throw in with me!"

Frank stared. "You want me to work for you?"

"No, I want you to be my partner, fifty-fifty. And all you have to do to seal the deal is give me those women."

Chapter 21

For a long moment, Frank battled the impulse to stand up and smash his fist into the middle of Smith's face. When he had it under control, he said steadily, "You want me to give you those mail-order brides."

"I know, I know, they're promised to prospectors over in Whitehorse. But just think about it. Why should you collect just one time on each of them, when you can collect again and again and again?"

"You want to make soiled doves out of them."

Smith leaned back languidly in his chair. "They're reasonably young and healthy, and they look unspoiled, whether they really are or not. They'll stay innocent-looking for a while, too. Men up here will pay through the nose for something like that, maybe a whole poke full of nuggets or dust." He laughed. "A poke for a poke, eh? And even once the bloom is off the rose, so to speak, they can still generate a lot of money for us. A man spends five or six months holed up alone in an eight-by-ten cabin, he'll fork over most of his worldly goods for a few minutes with a woman, especially one who ain't an Indian." Smith took another swallow of beer. "The women aren't the only reasons I want to come to an agreement with you, though."

"Go on," Frank said flatly.

"You saw Joe Palmer and Big Ed outside, and you met Yeah Mow and Sid earlier. They're good men, all of 'em. Tough as nails, and they do what they're told. Big Ed and Yeah Mow can bust a man in half with their bare hands, and Sid's real handy with a knife when he ain't been on the nod too much. Joe handles the gun work, and he's slick at it. But he's nowhere near as slick as The Drifter, and none of those boys will strike fear in a man's heart like the name Frank Morgan will."

"So you want me to handle your dirty work for you."

"I want you to earn your share," Smith snapped. "Fifty-fifty, like I said. Of course, expenses come off the top before we divvy up."

Frank nodded. "Of course."

Smith took that as an encouraging sign. He leaned forward again. "Well, what do you say?"

Frank picked his beer up and took a sip from the mug for the first time. The brew was sour and bitter, as he had figured it would be. He wouldn't expect anything else from a snake like Smith.

"First of all," he said as he replaced the mug on the table, "those women aren't mine to give you, and I wouldn't even if they were. I'm taking them to Whitehorse like I promised I would. Second, when we leave tomorrow, Salty Stevens is going with us, and I expect you to return his gold before we leave."

Smith stared across the table at him, eyes narrowing until they were slits of evil. "You son of a bitch," he breathed.

"Talk like that can get a man killed."

"Yeah, you! Take a look at that table to your right. Yeah Mow's over there with a gun pointed at you, Morgan, and all I have to do is say the word for him to pull the trigger."

"You see my right hand?" Frank asked quietly.

"What?" Smith looked at the table. Frank's left hand was still wrapped around the handle of the beer mug, but his right was nowhere to be seen.

"I've had a .45 lined up on your belly pretty much from the moment we sat down," Frank went on. "My thumb's over the hammer, and that's all that's holding it back. You can have your boy Yeah Mow shoot me, but you'll get a bullet in the guts at the same time. I've got a hunch there's not a doctor up here who could pull a man through with a wound like that. You'd be a long, slow, hard time dying, too."

Smith's lips writhed with hate. "You . . . you . . ."

"Don't call me a son of a bitch again," Frank said. "Get out."

"Have Hopkins put his gun on the table first, then stand up and move away from it."

Smith hesitated, and for a second Frank thought the man was going to call his bluff . . . although it really wasn't a bluff at all. Frank was prepared to shoot his way out of here if necessary. Then Smith made a curt gesture to Yeah Mow and said, "Put your gun on the table and get out."

"But, Boss—" the man started to protest.

"Just do it!"

Hopkins laid a heavy revolver on the table and stood up. He glared at Frank as he moved toward the doorway.

Frank got to his feet, keeping his Colt in his hand. The men drinking in Clancy's must have sensed that something was going on, and at the sight of Yeah Mow's gun and now Frank's, they knew it. Most of them headed for the door, eager to get out of the line of fire if gunplay broke out.

"You're going to walk me back to the hotel, Soapy," Frank said.

"The hell I will," Smith snarled.

"It's that or I gun you down right here and now and take my chances."

Their eyes dueled for a second; then Smith muttered a curse and stood up. "All right. But you're gonna regret this, Morgan."

"Now, you see, that's another mistake."

"Another?"

"Your first was thinking that I'd ever throw in with a polecat like you," Frank said. "It'll be your second if you don't let this go. You see, I didn't come to Skagway to clean up the town or anything like that, Smith. I don't like you, and somebody ought to put a stop to what you're doing here, but I have another chore I need to take care of, namely keeping a promise to an old friend and getting those women to Whitehorse. We'll be leaving tomorrow, and if you and your boys don't bother us in the meantime, we won't bother you. But if anything *does* happen . . . I'll be coming for you, Soapy. And that's a promise, too."

"You always act so high-handed with folks, Morgan?"

"Only those who deserve it."

Muttering under his breath, Smith turned toward the door. Frank followed closely behind him, gun still drawn. As they stepped out onto the plank sidewalk, Frank glanced in both directions. He saw Yeah Mow Hopkins standing nearby, along with Big Ed Burns and the opium addict, Sid Dixon. There was no sign of Joe Palmer.

"If Palmer tries to bushwhack me, my thumb's going to slip off this hammer, sure as hell," Frank told Smith. "At this range, the slug will blow your spine clean in two. I'd speak up if I was you."

"You're trying to make a fool of me in front of the whole town," Smith said between clenched teeth.

"You made a fool of yourself when you asked me to help you turn those women into whores."

Smith took a deep breath, then said in a loud voice, "I'm gonna walk over to the hotel with Morgan. Nobody better bother us."

Frank nodded. "Go ahead."

With Smith in front, the two of them walked around the corner toward the hotel. As they approached, Pete Conway stepped out of the livery stable across the street, holding a rifle. "Are you all right, Frank?" he called.

"Yeah, fine," Frank replied. Dog stepped out of the

stable as well and stood there stiff-legged, the fur on his back ruffled with anger. Frank knew that at a word from him, the big cur would bound across the street in the blink of an eye and rip Smith's throat out before anyone could stop him.

The two of them came to a stop on the hotel porch. Frank said, "You can send Salty's gold over here to the hotel. I'll see that it gets to him, and I'll expect it before ten o'clock tomorrow morning."

"You believe in pushing your luck, don't you?" Smith said.

"It's not luck if you can back it up. And I can, Soapy. Don't doubt that for a second. I've been through all sorts of hell getting here with those women, and I'm not going to let a second-rate crook like you stop us now. So take my advice. Return the old man's gold, let us go on about our business, and you go on about yours. Just forget we ever came to Skagway."

"Yeah. Sure."

From the hollow sound of Smith's voice, Frank knew that was unlikely.

"Go on back to Clancy's. I don't expect to see you again."

Smith stalked off without a word. As soon as he was gone, Conway hurried across the street, along with Jennings and Dog.

"What the hell happened?" Conway wanted to know. "How come you marched Smith over here at gunpoint?"

"He did something that bothered me," Frank said.

"He suggested that I partner up with him so we could put the ladies to work as soiled doves."

"You mean he wanted to turn Jessica into—" Conway's hands tightened on his rifle. "I ought to go down to that saloon and—"

"It's already taken care of." Quickly, Frank related the highlights of the conversation in Clancy's and its outcome.

Jennings said, "Do you really think he'll return the old man's gold and leave us alone?"

"That would be the smart thing to do. We're not trying to drive him out of power here in Skagway. He can go on fleecing the citizens until they decide they've had enough of him . . . or he can try to stop us from leaving and wind up with a war on his hands. So tell me, Bart . . . how smart is he?"

"He's smart, all right," Jennings said, "smart as he is crooked. But he's loco, too, and he may lean more on his pride than his brain when he goes to makin' up his mind what to do."

"In that case," Frank said with a slight smile, "we may have to fight our way out of here."

Now that Smith knew Salty was one of Frank's allies, Frank didn't think it was safe for the old-timer to stay at the shack alone. He sent Conway to fetch him and left Dog at the stable to guard the horses. Then he called the women together in the hotel to explain the situation to them.

"Why, that . . . that scoundrel!" Fiona exclaimed

when she heard what Smith had proposed to do. "You should have shot him, Frank!"

"I thought about it," Frank admitted wryly. "I figured that might just shake things up even worse, though. At least Smith has some control over what happens around here. If he was dead, all hell might break loose. The important thing is that we get out of Skagway and get started toward Whitehorse as soon as possible. Until we do, I want all of you to be alert. Keep your guns handy, and don't be afraid to use them."

Meg pushed her blond hair back off her forehead. "We should set up some sort of schedule for standing guard, and maybe we should all be in the same room."

Frank nodded and said, "I was thinking the same thing. It'll be crowded, but at least you can keep an eye on each other that way."

"What are you going to do?" Fiona asked.

"As soon as Conway gets back with Salty, we're going to start getting ready to leave early tomorrow morning. I want to line up our dogs and sleds and supplies today, if I can."

"We have to go by dogsled?" Marie asked.

"Part of the way, according to Salty. We'll take the horses as far as we can." Frank paused. "It'll be a rough trip, make no mistake about that. But we'll get through, and once we get to Whitehorse, you'll have your new husbands to rely on. It'll be all right."

They seemed to take some comfort from his encouraging words, but a sense of worry still hung over the group. Frank understood that well enough. He was worried himself.

He became more so when he stepped outside and saw that the leaden sky had started spitting down snowflakes. The snow was falling only lightly now, but as he gazed up at the clouds, he had a hunch it was going to get worse. If a blizzard blew in tonight, they might not be able to take the horses at all and would have to leave Skagway by dogsled.

They had come too far to turn back now, he told himself, and besides, with Soapy Smith as an enemy, it wouldn't be safe to try to spend the winter in Skagway. They had to make the run to Whitehorse.

Conway came along a few minutes later with Salty Stevens. The old-timer said to Frank, "The young fella tells me you had a big fallin'-out with Soapy on account o' me."

"That wasn't all of it, by any means," Frank said.

"Well, no matter what caused it, you don't want to hang around Skagway if Soapy's got blood in his eye for ye."

"That's why I want us to leave as soon as we can. First thing tomorrow morning, if possible."

Salty cast an eye toward the sky. "With this snow fallin', that's a good idea. Come on. I'll take you to see a feller who's got some dogs."

They were going to need at least four sleds and teams, according to Salty. The sleds wouldn't be a problem, as there were still plenty to be had in the settlement. Coming up with twenty-four good dogs would be.

"Most folks use huskies or malamutes," Salty told

Frank, Conway, and Jennings. "You may have to settle for mostly mutts, though."

"As long as they can pull the sleds," Frank said, "that's all that matters."

"Oh, they'll be able to pull, but they won't have the stamina or the experience a good team would. We'll have to teach 'em and toughen 'em up as we go along."

The man Salty took them to see had such a thick Swedish accent Frank understood only about half of what he had to say. Salty could converse with him, though, and after some haggling, they went behind the man's cabin to look into a long kennel made of posts and wire. A couple of dozen dogs were behind the fence. They were all big and shaggy and looked strong enough to Frank, but Salty shook his head in dismay. "This is the best we can do," he told Frank, "but it ain't good."

"Like you said, maybe they'll get better as they go along."

The Swede agreed to have the dogs in front of the hotel at eight o'clock the next morning. That was well before dawn at this time of the year.

From there Frank and the others went to the general store to make arrangements for their supplies. While they were in the store, Frank spotted some Stetsons hanging on pegs driven into one of the log walls, and went over to take down one very similar to the hat he had lost in the Pacific. He had been hatless since the shipwreck, and he was tired of his head feeling naked. He bought the hat as well, and felt better when he had settled it on his head. He got a fur cap for Conway and better coats for everyone, along with blankets, furs, more ammunition, food, and plenty of dried fish for the dogs. Sled dogs, Salty explained, lived on fish, not beef.

They also bought four sleds at the store. The supplies would be divided among them, leaving room for the young women to ride. Settling up with the storekeeper took most of the cash Frank had left.

As they stepped outside, Frank saw that the snow was still coming down and that there was already a thin layer of the white stuff on the ground. Salty looked at that and nodded.

"Yeah, we might as well start off on the sleds," he said. "Ain't no need to bring all them hosses. You'd just have to leave 'em somewheres along the way."

"My two are coming with me." Frank wasn't going to abandon Stormy and Goldy to Soapy Smith. He didn't care about the horses they had taken from the gang of outlaws.

"That's fine, you can prob'ly get a couple o' horses through the passes. There's a chance you won't be able to, but it's your decision to make, I reckon. We'll need men to handle the dog teams, though."

"You can handle one, can't you?"

"Yep." Salty jerked a thumb at Conway. "I figure I can teach this big fella how to, as well. But that still leaves two teams."

"What about me?" Jennings asked. "What would I have to do?"

Salty squinted skeptically at him. "A blind man, drivin' a sled team? I don't see how it's rightly possible."

"I can hear just fine," Jennings insisted. "Put my

sled in the middle and shout a lot. I can steer by sound."

Salty scratched at his beard. "Well . . . it might work. Them dogs got a natural tendency to foller each other, anyway. I reckon we can give it a try. If it don't work, maybe one o' them gals can take over. Looks like we're gonna need one of 'em for the fourth team, anyway."

"I have an idea one of them will volunteer," Frank said, thinking of Meg Goodwin. Following a dog team might not be too different from following a plow mule.

"Well, then, it seems to me like you're 'most ready to go."

Frank looked up at the sky. The light had already faded from it, and the snowflakes continued to swirl down.

"All we have to do is make it through the night," he said.

Chapter 22

Salty had long since traded his guns for whiskey, so Frank saw to it that the old man was armed with a pistol and rifle from their supplies. Then he told Conway, Salty, and Jennings to stay with the horses in the livery stable. Even though they weren't going to use the mounts, Soapy Smith and his men didn't know that. Frank thought they might be tempted to try to steal the horses in order to strike back at him.

"Aren't you staying in the stable?" Conway asked.

Frank shook his head. "I'll be around," he said cryptically. "It's possible Smith might try to grab the ladies. I want to be able to stop that if it happens."

As Meg had suggested, the women had worked out a guard schedule. At least two of them would be awake at all times during the night, watching out for trouble.

With that settled, they all ate supper in the hotel dining room. The fare at the Klondike was simple but filling: moose steaks, potatoes, and beans. The women were all still tired and turned in as soon as they had eaten, except for Ruth Donnelly and Wilma Keller, who had drawn the first shift on guard.

Before he left them, Frank spoke to Fiona in the corridor just outside the canvas-walled room that all the women were crowded into now. "Ought to be warmer with all of you sleeping in such close quarters," he said wryly.

"Is Smith going to try something tonight, Frank?" she asked.

He shook his head. "I don't know. I reckon he's got spies all over town, so he's bound to know that we're pulling out first thing in the morning. If he's going to make a move against us, it'll have to be tonight. So I wouldn't be surprised either way."

"I'll be glad when we get to Whitehorse and all of this is behind us."

"Just keep thinking about that," Frank told her.

Fiona acted like she wanted a kiss, but Frank just brushed his lips across her forehead before leaving the hotel. He stepped back out into the snowy night. The crystals crunched under his boots as he walked along the planks.

He started around the hotel, intending to make sure no one was lurking behind the wing where the women were staying. He had just rounded the front corner when he heard snow crunch under someone else's boots in the shadows ahead of him. Instinct made his hand flash toward his Colt as he threw himself to the ground.

A huge orange flash lit up the night, accompanied by a thunderous roar. Frank knew that someone had just unleashed both barrels of a shotgun at him.

The would-be killer had made two mistakes, though. He had gotten too close before firing, so the loads of buckshot didn't have time to spread out much and Frank was able to avoid them by diving to the ground. The other mistake was triggering both barrels at once. Now the weapon was empty.

As he sprawled on the thin layer of snow, Frank tilted his revolver's barrel up and fired at the spot where the muzzle flashes had ripped through the night. The Colt blasted just once, but the shot was rewarded by a cry of pain. Even though Frank was a little deafened by the shotgun going off, he heard the thud as the weapon hit the ground.

Before he could get to his feet and investigate, a woman screamed somewhere nearby. Knowing the cry had to come from either Fiona or one of the brides, he leaped up and whipped around the east wing of the hotel. A smaller-caliber pistol cracked several times. The gunfire had a panicky sound to it, as if the wielder of the pistol had simply pointed it and started pulling the trigger as fast as she could.

As Frank approached the back of the room where the women were staying, he saw lantern light from inside spilling out through a huge rent in the canvas. Knowing that one swipe of a knife could open up a big hole in the wall, he had been afraid that Soapy might try something like that. Some of Smith's henchmen could try to grab the women at the same time as the shotgunner attempted to dispose of Frank.

Not surprisingly, shots blasted from across the street, too, as Smith and his men tried to make a clean sweep of it by attacking Conway and the other two men at the livery stable as well. Frank couldn't go to their aid right now, so they would have to fight off their assailants alone. He had to make sure the women were safe before he did anything else.

A man reeled into the light between Frank and the hole in the canvas wall. He moved like he was injured, but he wasn't hurt so bad that he couldn't jerk up a revolver and fire. Frank dropped to a knee as he heard a slug whistle past his head. The Colt roared and bucked in his hand. The man doubled over as the slug from Frank's gun punched into his belly.

Frank sprang up and clubbed the man in the head to get him out of the way. "Fiona!" he shouted. "Meg!"

More muzzle flame spurted from the shadows. Frank returned the fire, then a second later heard running footsteps slapping against the ground. The second gunman had lost his stomach for the fight. Was he the only one left, or were there more of Smith's men lurking in the shadows?

"Frank!" That was Fiona's voice, coming from inside. "Frank, are you all right?"

"Blow out that light!" Frank called to her. "Get down and stay down!"

As the room went dark, Frank weaved to the side in case anybody in the shadows tried to aim at the sound of his voice. Knowing that they might be able to spot the dark shape of his body against the light-colored canvas, even without a lantern burning inside, he moved away from the hotel, stepping as quietly as he could in the snow.

A man loomed up beside him and whispered, "Where'd that bastard go?"

Frank just grunted.

"Soapy's gonna be mad as hell if he gets away. He wants that son of a bitch dead!"

Frank didn't wait to hear any more. His hand rose and fell, and the Colt crashed against the man's head. Smith's henchman folded up without a sound.

Pouching his iron, Frank bent over and yanked the man's belt off, then used it to tie his hands behind his back. He left the man there and resumed stalking any more of Smith's men who might be hanging around the rear of the hotel.

He didn't find anyone, though. A considerable uproar had started in the street. No more shots came from the area of the livery stable, and now that the trouble seemed to be over, men were coming out of hiding and demanding to know what was going on.

What Frank wanted to know was whether Fiona, Meg, and the other women were all right, as well as Conway, Jennings, and Salty. He moved along the back of the hotel's east wing, and as he approached the slit-open canvas wall, he called softly, "Ladies, it's me, Frank Morgan." He didn't want any of them getting trigger-happy and blasting him when he stuck his head through that opening.

Fiona stepped out through the flapping canvas. "Frank!" she said as she flung her arms around his neck. "Are you all right?"

"I'm fine," he assured her. "Didn't even pick up a nick, even with all that lead flying around. What about you and the rest of the ladies?"

"None of us are hurt," she said, and a wave of relief went through him when he heard that. "We're just scared. Most of us had dozed off when there was a sound like cloth ripping, really loud."

Frank nodded, even though she probably couldn't see him in the dark. "That was Smith's men cutting through the canvas."

"Smith?"

"Who else would try to grab you like that? They sliced open the wall and were probably planning to drag you off and lock you up somewhere. They came after me at the same time, and from the sound of it, Pete and Salty and Bart over in the livery stable, too."

Jessica must have heard that inside the room, because she rushed out through the opening. "Pete!" she exclaimed. "You say Pete was attacked, too?"

"I'm about to go find out," Frank replied grimly. "You ladies stay here. Keep your guns handy."

"I'm coming with you," Jessica insisted.

"Better not."

Meg stepped out and put an arm around her smaller friend's shoulders. "Stay here and let Frank check it out, Jess. That would be best."

Fiona still had hold of Frank. He stepped away from her and said, "I'll be back in a minute."

"Be careful," she told him.

"I intend to."

The three-pronged attack didn't surprise him. He'd had a hunch Smith would try something tonight, while they were still in Skagway. The man's pride had been wounded too deeply to let Frank get away with showing him up in front of the whole settlement. Plus

Smith's greed meant that he really wanted to get his hands on the women and use them to turn a big profit.

The street was full of men who had emerged from the saloons to see what all the shooting and yelling was about. They got out of Frank's way as he strode toward the livery stable. He felt relief go through him again as he saw Conway and Salty emerge from the barn, carrying rifles. Jennings followed them.

"Frank!" Conway called. "Are you all right?"

"Yeah. How about the three of you?"

"I got a little scratch on my side from a bullet, but that's all. What about the ladies?"

"None of them are hurt," Frank said, leading Conway to exclaim, "Thank God!"

Frank went on. "Some of Smith's men tried to get into the hotel by cutting through that canvas wall, but the ladies held them off until I got there."

Salty said, "I thought I heard a Greener go off. You know anything about that?"

Frank chuckled. "Yeah, it was pointed at me when it made that racket. I was able to duck under the buckshot, though."

Conway let out an impressed whistle. "That was lucky. They came at us with pistols, front and back, and it was a hornet's nest in there for a while. That dog of yours got hold of one of them, though, and tore him up. We must've winged a couple of others, because they yelped and ran."

"Took off for the tall and uncut, they did," Salty added. "Reckon we put up more of a fight than they was expectin'."

"How about the horses?" Frank asked. "Any of them hurt?"

Conway shook his head. "No. The walls of those stalls are pretty thick. They stopped all the bullets that came their way."

"Did you manage to grab any of the varmints?" Frank hoped to have at least one prisoner who could testify that the attackers had been acting on Soapy Smith's orders. There might not be any official law here, but faced with solid proof of Smith's villainy, the community might rise up against him.

Conway replied, "No, I'm afraid not. The only one who was left behind was the fellow your dog got hold of, and . . . well, he won't be talking anymore."

Frank knew what the young man meant. Dog had probably torn the attacker's throat out. The big cur didn't take it easy when it came to fighting.

"I knocked one man out and tied him up, and there may be some others behind the hotel who are wounded," Frank said. "I'd better go see."

"We'll come with you," Salty said.

"No, Salty, you and Bart stay here. Pete, go across to the hotel and get the ladies."

Conway sounded confused as he said, "And do what with them?"

"Bring them back over here with you. Everybody's staying in the barn tonight. If Smith tries anything else, he'll find us all forted up together."

Conway nodded. "That sounds like a mighty good idea." He headed toward the front of the hotel while Frank began circling the canvas-walled east wing again.

He drew his gun as he moved along the wall. His foot struck something soft, and he knew he had found the man he'd left tied up. Frank figured the man might have regained consciousness by now, but he didn't react to the inadvertent kick. Reaching down to grab the man's shoulder, Frank said, "Wake up, mister. You're going to tell everybody in Skagway that Soapy Smith ordered this attack tonight."

The man simply sagged back and forth limply when Frank shook him. Frank knelt, fished a lucifer from his coat pocket, and snapped it into life with his thumbnail.

The sudden flare of light revealed a grisly picture. The man lay there with his hands still tied behind his back with his own belt. His throat had been cut from ear to ear. Blood stained the snow crimson in a big circle around his head.

Frank muttered a curse under his breath as he dropped the match, letting it hiss out in the snow. He came to his feet and turned in a half circle, ready to fire if the murderer was still nearby and came at him. Everything was quiet back here, though.

He had gotten a pretty good look at the man's face and hadn't recognized him. That wasn't surprising. Smith probably had dozens of henchmen working for him. He had probably recruited some of them to come along on tonight's raid, although Frank suspected that one of Smith's cronies, like Joe Palmer or Big Ed Burns, had been in charge of the attacks.

During their conversation in Clancy's, Smith had mentioned that the little opium addict, Sid Dixon, was good with a knife. Frank had a hunch that Dixon had been responsible for slitting this man's throat so that he couldn't tie Smith to what had happened. Frank knew he couldn't prove that, though.

He struck another match and looked around quickly, finding more splashes of blood on the snow but no dead or wounded men. The others must have taken the man he shot in the belly with them. That hombre would be dead soon, too, if he wasn't already, and unable to testify against Smith.

Soapy's try for the women had failed, but he was going to get away with making the attempt, Frank thought.

The question now was, would he try again before they could leave Skagway?

Chapter 23

By the time Frank got back to the livery stable, Conway had brought all the women across the street. They were gathered in the big center aisle of the barn, fully dressed, with blankets wrapped around them. The stable's feisty little proprietor was there as well, and he greeted Frank by saying, "Mr. Morgan, this here is a livery stable, not a danged hotel!"

"It's only for one night, Clem, and we'll pay you extra," Frank told him. "But the ladies are staying here. Soapy Smith's men just tried to kidnap them."

The stableman's eyes widened. "You know that for a fact?"

"I can't prove it, but I'm sure Smith was behind what happened."

The man rubbed his beard-bristly jaw. "Well, I got to admit, I wouldn't be surprised. Soapy's friendly, but sometimes he seems like a mite of a shady character, too. I wouldn't go spreadin' stories about him that I couldn't prove, though. Those fellas who work for him can be mighty rough." The stable man lowered his voice and went on. "I don't reckon you need to pay me any extra. It ain't costin' me nothin' to have these ladies here, and it'll be good for business when word gets around that nigh on to a dozen honest-to-God women spent the night in my stable!"

Frank grinned and clapped a hand on the man's shoulder. "Thanks, Clem." He turned to the women. "Ladies, right up that ladder is the hayloft. I think you can take your blankets and make yourselves comfortable up there. We'll stay down here to make sure no one bothers you again tonight."

"All right," Meg said with a smile, "but you should have seen Ruth and Wilma blazing away at those men who tried to get into our room. They were a couple of real Annie Oakleys!"

The two young woman blushed, but they looked pleased by the praise.

Frank asked the proprietor, "Is there an outside door into that loft?"

"Yeah, but it's closed and bolted from the inside. Nobody can get in that way. Only way is up the ladder."

Frank nodded. "Good. One man can guard it, then. Pete, Salty, we'll take turns doing that, along with Dog. Bart, you find yourself a place and get some sleep."

"Dadgum it, I wish I could help more," Jennings protested. "I still feel like I owe you folks for what I helped Ben and those other fellas try to do."

"Maybe the time will come," Frank said. "Your sight might come back when your eyes heal up some more."

"I sure hope that's true."

The women climbed up into the hayloft, taking their blankets with them. The proprietor retired to his quarters in the rear. Only one lantern was burning, and Frank turned the flame on it down so that it cast only a faint glow. The doors were all closed and fastened, and he didn't see any way that Smith's men could get at them easily. He should have brought the women in here earlier, he told himself, but he'd been trying to give them as much comfort as possible before they started the long, arduous journey to Whitehorse.

Of course, if Smith was angry enough over what had happened, he could order his men to set the barn on fire. Frank was convinced Soapy wouldn't do that, though. For one thing, if the barn burned down and the women were killed in the blaze, then Smith would lose any chance of getting his hands on them. For another, the inhabitants of most frontier communities lived in fear of fire, and Frank figured Skagway was no different. With so many frame and canvas buildings, out-of-control flames might spread rapidly, and the whole settlement could burn to the ground. It had happened many times before in the West. Frank had even witnessed such an inferno firsthand, a number of years earlier.

So as far as Frank could tell, this was the safest place for all of them tonight.

Salty came over to him and volunteered to take the first watch while Frank and Conway got some sleep. Frank studied the old-timer intently and said, "Are you all right? The thirst isn't too bad?"

Salty licked his lips. "That's one reason I figured it might be best for me to take the first turn," he said. "Right now, I ain't got the fantods yet, but I ain't sure how long that'll last. Without some Who-hit-John to ease me through the night, the bugs're liable to be crawlin' all over me 'fore mornin'. I'm hopin' that ain't the way it is . . . but it might be."

"All right, then it's a good idea for you to take the first watch, like you said," Frank agreed. "Let out a shout if there's any trouble, though."

"Don't you worry. If anything bad starts to happen, I'll holler so loud they'll hear it clear down on the Rio Grande."

Nothing bad happened, though. The night passed peacefully except for a brief commotion when the young women discovered that they were sharing the hayloft with a few rats. Frank shooed the varmints away, and the ladies settled down after that and got some more sleep.

The snow had stopped by morning, but the storm had left about six inches on the ground with deeper drifts in places. The Swede delivered the dogs at eight o'clock, as promised. By that time Frank and Conway had the sleds ready in front of the livery stable, with the supplies already loaded on them. Salty supervised the hitching of the dogs to the sleds, trying to pick out the best animals and split them up among the teams. While that was going on, Frank saddled Stormy and Goldy, using saddles and tack that had been on a couple of the outlaws' horses, then told everyone else to go over to the hotel and have a good breakfast before they left.

"I'll stay here to keep an eye on our outfit," he added.

Salty shook his head. "Let me do that, Frank," the old-timer insisted. "I never have much of an appetite of a mornin', and I sure as shootin' don't today."

"How are you doing?" Frank asked.

Salty lifted a slighty shaking hand and stroked his beard. "Not as bad as I figured I would be. I reckon I'm in plenty good enough shape to stand guard over our belongin's, but I don't figure I could stomach any food. Maybe later I can gnaw some jerky on the trail, and if we stop in the middle o' the day to brew up some coffee, I might give that a try."

"All right, if that's the way you want it," Frank said with a nod. "Pete and I will go over to the hotel with the women, to make sure Smith doesn't try anything again over there. Dog, stay here with Salty."

The old man grinned under his beard. "You might as well be leavin' a regiment with me. That critter's worth a heap o' fightin' men in a ruckus."

Frank and Conway escorted the women across the street to the hotel. It was frozen solid now under the snow, so they didn't have to worry about the mud. Frank scanned the street carefully for any sign of Soapy Smith and his minions. He didn't see anybody he recognized, but he realized Smith could have plenty of men working for him that Frank didn't know about. Still, no one made a move that was out of line.

The women's entrance into the hotel dining room

caused quite a stir among the men having breakfast. The news of what had happened the night before had gotten around town, and men who would have craned their necks anyway to get a glimpse of the mail-order brides were even more interested because the women were accompanied by the notorious gunfighter known as The Drifter.

Frank ignored the curious stares, as he always did, and ushered the women to a big, empty table. They were the only females in the place. A waiter brought coffee for everybody, and Frank ordered hotcakes and bacon all around. This would clean out the last of his cash. From here on, though, they would be living on the supplies he had already bought, plus whatever fresh meat they could kill along the trail.

"Eat as much as you can," Frank told the women as the platters of food arrived at the table. "You won't be getting another meal like this for a while. Not until you get to Whitehorse, anyway."

The women followed his advice and ate heartily, finishing off several platters of hotcakes and bacon and washing the food down with three pots of coffee. When they were finished, Lucy Calvert moaned and said, "Oh, I don't think I'll need to eat again for a month!"

"You'd better remember that," Meg told her with a grin. "The rest of us will split your share of the supplies."

"Now, hold on—" Lucy said before realizing that Meg was joking. She smiled and laughed then, too.

Frank settled the hotel bill, including the breakfast, and then he and Conway took the women outside again. Fiona said quietly to him, "I owe you more than I can ever repay, Frank, and I'm not just talking about money. Although I intend to make things right with you on that account, too."

"Wait and see how things go when we get to White-horse," he told her.

"All right, but just don't forget . . . you can have anything you want from me. That's how much I'm in your debt."

Before he could think about what Fiona meant by that, he heard Conway say in a warning tone, "Frank . . ." and looked up to see Soapy Smith standing near the sleds, along with Yeah Mow Hopkins, Joe Palmer, Sid Dixon, and Big Ed Burns. Salty Stevens was on the other side of the sleds, clutching a Winchester tightly in his gnarled hands. Dog was at his side, growling softly.

Smith grinned and waved a hand toward the old-timer and the big cur, saying, "Call off your dogs, Morgan . . . both of 'em."

Frank didn't respond to Smith right away. He said to Conway, "Take the women into the livery stable, Pete. Keep them there until I tell you it's clear."

"Right, Frank," the young man said. He glared at Smith and kept his rifle pointing in the man's general direction as he went with the women into the stable.

Still smiling, Smith said, "All this caution isn't necessary, Morgan. We may have had our differences yesterday, but that's all in the past. I'm not the sort of man who believes in holding a grudge."

Frank didn't believe that for a second. "What about last night?" he snapped.

"Last night?" Smith said, raising his eyebrows in apparent innocence. "I heard that there was some sort of ruckus at the hotel, but it didn't have anything to do with me. What was that all about, anyway?"

"Somebody tried to kidnap the women and kill the rest of us." Frank paused, then added meaningfully, "I figured you knew all about it."

Smith shook his head. "No, this is the first I've heard exactly what happened."

That was a bald-faced lie, and all of them knew it, but Frank didn't have any proof to the contrary. He thought about the man whose throat had been cut and glanced at Sid Dixon. The little opium addict gave him a sly grin that caused anger to well up inside Frank. Dixon could have untied the man and helped him to escape. Instead, he had taken the quick, easy way out and used his knife, probably because he enjoyed it. As far as Frank was concerned, a man like Dixon was lower than a snake's belly.

"Anyway, I'd heard that you were leaving this morning," Smith went on, "and I just wanted to come over and wish you good luck on your journey. I'm sorry we couldn't come to an agreement on a business arrangement," he shrugged, "but I respect your decision on that."

"You came to wish us good luck," Frank said, allowing a tone of skepticism into his voice.

"Sure. It's a long way to Whitehorse. A long, hard way." Smith was still smiling, but hatred burned in his dark, deep-set eyes. "And I figure that you'll be able to use all the luck you can get."

Chapter 24

Smith and his men left, but the veiled threat in the man's words stayed with Frank as he called the women out of the stable and got them loaded onto the sleds. They were bundled up in parkas, fur hats, and blankets. Fiona, Elizabeth, and Lucy rode on the first sled, the one that would be handled by Salty, with bundles of supplies lashed on in front of them. The arrangement was the same on the other sleds: supplies in front, passengers in back.

As Frank had expected, Meg had volunteered when she found out that one of the women would have to handle a sled. She took the second sled, with Marie, Ruth, and Ginnie. Lizzie and Maureen were on the third sled, with Bart Jennings standing at the gee-pole. Jessica and Elizabeth settled in on the fourth sled, the one that was Pete Conway's responsibility.

Frank wasn't surprised that Jessica wanted to be close to Conway. The budding romance between them was obvious, and Frank still thought that might cause trouble once they got to Whitehorse. That problem could be dealt with later, though.

Jennings told Salty and Meg, "If the two of you will sing out pretty often, I should be able to follow you without much trouble. I can still hear just fine. In fact, I think I hear a little better now than I did before I lost my sight."

Meg patted him on the shoulder and said, "Don't worry, Mr. Jennings. We won't let you go astray."

He shook his head in obvious amazement. "I still can't get over the way you folks have accepted me, even after all the bad things I done."

"Yes, but since then you've tried to help us as much as you can," Meg pointed out. "I think most people could use a second chance, don't you?"

"Some of 'em might even need a third or a fourth chance before it takes," Jennings said with a smile under the cloth tied around his eyes.

When everything was squared away and ready to go, Frank led Stormy and Goldy out of the stable. He shook hands with Clem, the proprietor, and then swung up into the saddle on Goldy's back. The street was crowded by now, even though it was still dark. The sun wouldn't make its brief appearance until later in the day. Many of the citizens of Skagway had turned out to say good-bye to the women who had brought some femininity and excitement to the raw frontier settlement, even if only for a short time.

"You know the trails, Salty," Frank called to the old-timer. "Lead off whenever you're ready."

"All right." Salty's beard bristled in the cold air as he stood on the runners at the rear of the sled and looked around at the others. "Ever'body ready at the gee-poles?"

Meg, Jennings, and Conway called out that they were, and Salty lifted a hand over his head and swept it forward.

"Mush, yuh danged hairy varmints!" he called to the sled dogs. "Mush!"

With a noisy chorus of barking, the dogs strained against their traces and pulled ahead, drawing the harnesses taut. The sled's polished runners began to glide over the snow. The other teams followed the example of the leaders, and with a big racket, including cheers of encouragement from some of the onlookers, all four sleds departed from Skagway.

Frank rode ahead, and Dog bounded even farther in front. The barking of the sled dogs seemed to excite him, and he turned from time to time to bark back at them.

Even though the sun wasn't up, gray light filled the eastern sky. It would stay that way for hours yet, but during that time, the glow was enough for the travelers to see where they were going. Frank could tell from the light that they were headed almost due north.

He rode ahead of the sleds at times, alongside them at others, and every now and then he dropped well behind them to check on their back trail. Soapy Smith had all but said that he was coming after the women, or at least sending men to run them down and capture them. Frank had a hunch that Smith would let them get away from Skagway before he tried anything else, but not too far. He would want to kill Frank and the other men and take the women prisoner while it would still be fairly easy to get them back to the settlement.

Because of that, Frank knew he would have to be on guard nearly twenty-four hours a day.

Which was a shame in a way because his vigilance didn't allow him to just ride along and appreciate the magnificent scenery around him. Vast, snow-covered slopes; majestic stands of pine, fir, and spruce trees with their branches also decorated with the white, powdery snow; rugged mountains that were studies in black and white and gray looming over everything . . . Frank had seen some mighty pretty places in his life, but Alaska was right up there with the best of them.

It was too bad that like most of the other places Frank had been, lurking in all that beauty were scores of dangers, dozens of ways a man could get himself dead in a hurry.

One time when Goldy was trotting alongside Salty's sled and Frank was leading Stormy, the old-timer pointed into the distance and said, "See that little notch where them two mountains come together?"

"Yeah. Is that where we're going?"

"That's White Pass, where we're headed first. 'Bout thirty miles from here. Chilkoot's only about ten miles beyond it, but it's a mighty brutal ten miles. You'll feel like you're goin' straight up a sheet o' ice durin' some of it. It'll be hard goin' for them horses of yours."

"They can make it," Frank said. He had every confidence in the world in Stormy and Goldy.

"The ladies'll have to get off and walk when we

get there. The dogs can't pull the loads on the sleds and their weight, too, not at that angle. That's why I told you to get hobnailed boots for all of 'em. Otherwise they won't be able to make it on the ice. If we're lucky, there'll be a little snowpack. It ain't as slippery. Then, once we get past Chilkoot, things don't get much easier for a while. The goin's still slick, it's just downhill instead of up. We'll tie the sleds together and put all the dogs behind 'em, instead of in front, until we get down from the pass."

"What's the terrain like after that?"

"A mite better. Hills instead o' mountains. We'll have to cross some cricks, but they'll be froze over already and shouldn't be a problem, long as the ice ain't too thin."

"Where's the border?"

"White Pass. By the time we get to the glacier that runs along there and turn northwest along it toward Chilkoot, we'll be in Canada."

Frank nodded. He figured that Smith would make his move before they reached White Pass, not because that landmark was the borderline between Alaska and Canada, but because Smith wouldn't want to go to the trouble of having to bring the women back that far, over such rugged ground.

"How long will it take us to reach White Pass?"

"At least three days, more likely four or five, dependin' on the dogs and what we run into betwixt here and there. It looks a lot closer'n it really is."

So for the next five days, he couldn't let down his guard, Frank thought, and he couldn't once they passed that point, either, because Soapy Smith was hardly the only threat out here. The wilderness itself was an even bigger danger.

"How about from White Pass to Chilkoot?"

"Count on two days, at least. 'Taint far, but like I said, it's slow goin'."

"And then on to White Horse?"

"Another week, if we're lucky and these brutes do better'n I think they will." Salty waved a mittened hand toward the dogs pulling his sled. "Could be ten or eleven days."

Frank thought it over. "So it'll take us at least two weeks to get to Whitehorse, maybe longer."

"It'll be longer," Salty declared. "I'd bet this fur hat o' mine on that."

Fiona must have been listening to the conversation. She turned around to look at the old-timer. "Will it be this cold all the way, Mr. Stevens?"

"Cold?" Salty repeated. "Beggin' yer pardon, ma'am, but this ain't cold. This here's a nice balmy day compared to what it'll be once we get up around them high passes. Problem is, it'll be even worse a month from now."

"You think winter will hold off that long?" Frank asked.

"I durned sure hope so. If a real storm comes in whilst we're up there betwixt White and Chilkoot . . ."

Salty's voice trailed off, but the old-timer didn't have to finish the sentence for Frank to know what he meant. A blizzard striking at the wrong time could easily mean death for all of them.

* * *

The first day's travel went well, although some of the women complained bitterly of the cold and their muscles were stiff and sore from riding all day on the sleds.

Meg really took to it, though. She had taken Bart Jennings literally when he told her to sing out so he could follow her voice, because a lot of the day she sang songs as she stood on the back of the sled and steered it with the gee-pole. She tried, without much success, to get the other women to sing with her.

When they stopped at midday, while watery sunlight filled the sky, Meg came over to Frank and asked, "How am I doing?"

"You'd have to ask Salty," Frank said. "He knows a lot more about handling sleds than I do. Matter of fact, I don't know a blasted thing about it."

The old-timer came over, slapping his mittened hands together. He grinned and said, "I heard what you asked, girlie, and I don't mind tellin' you, you're doin' a top-notch job. You sure you're really a cheechako and not an ol' sourdough like me?"

Meg laughed and pushed the hood of her parka back off her blond hair. Her cheeks were bright red from the cold, and at that moment, Frank thought she was one of the prettiest women he had ever seen.

"Maybe it just comes naturally to me," she said. "I don't know if Frank told you or not, but I used to do a lot of plowing."

"I reckon that experience comes in handy." Salty moved on to Jennings and put a hand on his shoulder. "You're doin' a fine job, too, Bart. Never would'a figured a blind man could steer a sled, but you're managin'."

"Thanks, Mr. Stevens."

"Shoot, call me Salty. That's all anybody's called me for nigh on to fifty years."

"What's your given name?" Frank asked curiously.

Salty frowned. "Well, now . . . I wish you hadn't asked me that . . . I'm tryin' to recollect. Been so long since I heard it. Seems like it's George. Yeah, that's what it is. George. Maybe."

They set up one of the Primus stoves Frank had bought at the store back in Skagway, melted snow and heated water for coffee, then set off again with Frank riding Stormy this time instead of Goldy. Most of the travelers were gnawing jerky so their bodies would constantly have fuel to burn. Hunger just increased the effects of the cold. During the long, gray afternoon, they stopped several more times to rest the dogs, pushing on each time after only a short halt.

They had to find a place to camp for the night before darkness fell. Salty led them to a spot where a scattering of boulders formed an irregular ring. The big rocks blocked the wind to a certain extent, and so the snow hadn't drifted as deeply in the space between them. Salty pointed out that they could clear off a spot and build a decent-sized fire.

"I reckon the ladies'll like that," he said. "It'll help 'em thaw out a mite."

"I'm all f-for th-that," Fiona said through chattering teeth. "This is a h-hellish country."

Frank wondered what she had thought it would be like when she came up with the idea of delivering mail-order brides to the miners all the way in Whitehorse. She probably hadn't thought much about the hardships involved, only the money she could make.

Salty started showing Bart Jennings how to un-hitch the dogs, working by feel. While they were doing that, Frank and Conway walked into the trees and found enough dry wood for the fire. When they got back, they found that Meg and Jessica had swept an area clean with their mittens. They piled the wood on the hard-packed dirt. Frank picked out some of the branches and arranged them so that they would burn properly. He had a plentiful supply of matches and tinder now, so he didn't have to rely on flint and steel this time. Within a few minutes, he had a nice little blaze going, and the women made grateful noises as they gathered around the flames.

Fiona stood close beside Frank and said, "It was a good start today, don't you think?"

"Yeah, a good start," Frank agreed.

But they still had a long way to go, he reminded himself. As Soapy Smith had said that morning before they left the settlement, a long, *hard* way.

And as Frank looked out across the wilderness in the fading light, he couldn't help but wonder what the night would hold.

Chapter 25

Before everyone went to sleep, Frank set up shifts for guard duty. He wanted two people awake at all times, and of course he relied heavily on the senses of Dog, Stormy, and Goldy to alert them if any danger came around, too. The women would have to take their turns, but it wouldn't be necessary for all of them to stand guard every night. They could rotate the duty among them, so that some of them would get a full night's sleep each night.

Somewhat to his surprise, the first night passed quietly except for some wolves howling in the distance. The sound spooked the women for a while, until Salty explained that the wolves wouldn't come near the fire.

"If it was after a hard winter and they was starvin'," the old-timer said. "Right now, though, we don't have to worry about them varmints."

At one point during the night, while the guard shifts were changing, Frank and Salty were both awake and had a brief conversation by the fire while the others slept in the tents that had been set up. Salty nodded toward the flames and commented, "When I was a young feller growin' up, I didn't dare have a fire like that whilst I was on the trail. It'd be too likely to draw attention from some Comanch' or Apaches lookin' to lift my hair."

"I know what you mean," Frank said with a nod. "It goes against the grain for me to have a fire that big at night, too. Drawing attention's never a good thing."

"You ain't as old as me, Frank, but you been around long enough to've seen the elephant a time or two. I'll bet you've rid some hard, lonely trails."

Frank had a cup of coffee in his hand. He took a sip from it and said, "I've heard the owl hoot a time or two, if that's what you're asking."

"No, sir. Ain't none o' my business."

"I figured that since you'd worked with that deputy marshal and those range detectives, you were still a badge-toter at heart. Once a lawman, always a lawman, they say."

Salty chuckled. "Tell that to all the fellers who wore a star and then turned crooked, or the ones that rode the owlhoot and then went straight. You can't tell what a feller will be by lookin' at what he was. Folks change all the time."

"That they do," Frank agreed with a solemn nod. "Look at you. You haven't had a drink in more than two days."

"And I'm feelin' it, too," Salty muttered. "But it's gettin' better, slowly but surely."

"Go ahead and turn in and get some sleep. You'll feel even better in the morning."

"I hope so."

Salty was up again when the first hints of gray began to appear in the eastern sky, and he woke all the others, too. "Ever'body up!" he called. "We got ground to cover today!"

They set off about an hour later, after everyone had had breakfast, including the sled teams. Dog didn't care for the dried fish that the sled dogs ate, so he went bounding off into the trees and came back with a rabbit's bloody carcass in his jaws. When the other dogs showed an interest in it, a deep-throated growl from the big cur made them think twice about trying to take his prize away from him.

With only a day's experience behind them, Conway, Jennings, and the women were hardly seasoned veterans of the far north, but at least they had some idea what to expect now. The sleds moved smoothly over the snow, with the others following Salty's lead. Frank rode alongside most of the time, since he didn't know exactly where the trails were and Salty had a tendency of weaving in and out of hills and stands of trees, following the easiest route over the terrain. The snow was a little deeper the farther north they went, but it was still less than a foot except in the drifts, and the horses had no trouble with it.

By Frank's estimation, they covered more ground that day than they had the day before. Whenever he looked toward White Pass in the distance, though, it didn't appear to be any closer. Salty noticed him doing that one time and chuckled.

"You been in the high country enough to know what it's like, Frank," the old-timer said. "The air's so clear it seems like you can see forever. It's like crossin' the Great Plains toward the Rockies. They look like they're so close you can reach right out and touch 'em, but it still takes you days or even weeks to get there."

"I know. If anything, the air is even clearer up here."

"Yeah, especially when it's cold. Alaska's a great place, Frank. I don't know that I want to spend the rest of my borned days up here, but I'm mighty glad I came. Yes, sir, even with all the bad things that've happened, I wouldn't have missed it for the world."

Frank knew exactly what the old-timer meant. Life held a lot of pain and trouble, as he knew better than most, but those things were just the price folks had to pay for all the moments of beauty and joy. If a person was lucky, they would experience more of the latter than the former.

The women must have been getting used to the cold. There were fewer complaints today. They all seemed quite happy to gather around the fire Frank built at that night's camp, though. Again, the men—except for Jennings—took turns standing guard all night, each of them paired up with one of the women. As it happened, Meg had the same shift as Frank.

They spoke briefly before splitting up to go to opposite sides of the camp. "You won't be able to see much, so I'm sending Dog with you," Frank told her. "He'll know it if anybody comes around. If he starts growling, get ready for trouble."

Meg hefted the Winchester in her hands. "Do I shoot?"

"Not unless you're sure of what you're shooting at. Could be some innocent pilgrim who saw our fire wandering up, looking for some hot food and coffee."

"Or it could be Soapy Smith and his men coming to get us."

Frank nodded. "Yeah, it could be. If you recognize any of that bunch, don't hesitate to shoot. They're not going to be up to anything good, that's for sure."

Meg started to turn away, then paused. "Doesn't it ever get old, Frank? Constantly knowing that there's somebody out there who wants to kill you?"

"I've been living with that almost ever since I got back from the war," he said. "All I wanted to do was come home, marry the girl I loved, maybe someday have a ranch of my own. It didn't work out that way, but I didn't have much choice in the matter, so I try not to lose any sleep over it. I figure it was meant to be."

"You didn't choose the life you've led. It chose you."

"Something like that."

"But doesn't that seem awfully . . . random? Don't we have any control over what happens to us?"

"Sure we do," Frank said, thinking that this was a mighty odd conversation to be having in the middle of the Alaskan wilderness, with wolves howling in the distance. But then, Meg Goodwin was sort of an odd young woman. "Life pushes us one way, then another, and sometimes we push back. When we do, sometimes we win and sometimes we don't. It's all part of the game."

"That's what life is? A game?"

"The biggest one of all," Frank said.

Meg stepped closer to him, reached up, and rested a mittened hand on his cheek. She brought her mouth to his and kissed him. When she stepped back, she said, "Then I'm all in."

Then she grinned at him and turned to walk to the other side of the camp and stand her watch on guard duty. Frank stood there for a second, wondering what the hell had just happened, before he said, "Dog, go with her. Guard."

The big cur loped off into the darkness.

In the morning, Meg didn't say anything about what had happened, and neither did Frank. The group got started early again, heading toward White Pass. Frank hoped they would reach it today. Once they did, they wouldn't be beyond the reach of Soapy Smith, but Frank figured the odds of an attack would go down.

Around midday, they came to a valley with a long, tree-dotted slope on each side. Salty brought his team to a halt and the others followed suit, with Meg calling to Jennings, "We're stopping, Bart!"

Frank had been at the rear of the little convoy, talking to Pete Conway. As the sleds came to a halt, he rode forward to see why Salty had stopped.

The old-timer pointed at the bottom of the valley. "Down yonder is Eight Mile Creek."

"I don't even see a creek," Frank said with a shake of his head.

"That's 'cause it's froze over and covered with snow." Salty stepped off the runners at the rear of the sled and went to the piles of supplies. He started unstrapping a pair of snowshoes that were lashed to one of the bundles. "I'm gonna have to go down there and check the ice 'fore we can drive these sleds over it."

"I'll come with you," Frank said.

Salty shook his head as he started fastening the snowshoes on his feet. "No, you stay here with the others. This here's a one-man job."

When the bulky snowshoes were fastened securely to his feet, he started tramping down the hill toward the creek. The snow wasn't so deep that Salty really needed the shoes, Frank thought. The old-timer could have handled it just in his boots. But it was quicker and easier with the snowshoes, Frank saw as he watched Salty moving down the hill in a peculiar, gliding stride.

Several of the women got off the sleds to move around, and they came up to the lip of the hill to watch Salty's progress, as well. Meg stood beside Stormy and asked Frank, "Will we just drive right over the ice?"

"If it's thick enough to support the weight of the sleds and everything on them," he replied. "The ladies probably ought to get off and walk across, just as a precaution." Salty hadn't said anything about that, but it just made sense to Frank.

The dogs sat there watching as well, tongues lolling from their mouths and their breath fogging the air in front of their faces. Dog had followed Salty down the hill, and the old-timer hadn't sent him back.

Frank took off his mittens and rubbed his hands together, trying to get some warmth back in them. He could handle the reins just fine wearing the mittens, but he couldn't hope to draw and fire a gun with them on, so he left them off part of the time and wore them at others. His knuckles had begun to chap from the cold, but that was a small price to pay to be able to slap leather if he needed to.

Fiona walked up on the other side of Frank's horse. "Will we reach White Pass today?" she asked.

"I don't know. Maybe. Salty said that's called Eight Mile Creek, and I've got a hunch it got the name because it's eight miles from here to the pass. That's the way things like that usually work. If I had to guess, we won't be able to cover that much ground in the time we have left today before it starts getting dark, but maybe we'll be there by the middle of the day tomorrow."

Fiona shook her head. "I'm not sure why I'm anxious to get there. From what Mr. Stevens said, it's just going to get worse on the other side of the pass."

Frank was about to nod when he saw that Salty had reached the creek. He moved out carefully onto the snow-covered ice, pausing for long seconds between each step with his head cocked slightly. Frank knew that Salty was listening for the tiny telltale noises that meant the ice was cracking underneath him. If he heard them, he would have to pull back to the bank.

That would also mean that they couldn't risk driving the sleds across the ice. They would have to find a way around the creek, or a section where the ice was thicker and sturdier. Either alternative meant adding more time to the trip, and with every minute that went by, they were that much closer to the first real storm of the winter.

Salty kept moving slowly until Frank was sure he must be getting close to the other side of the creek. Suddenly, he lunged ahead, snowshoes flashing now instead of moving deliberately. Frank leaned forward in the saddle in alarm, knowing that Salty's frantic reaction meant the ice was giving way underneath him. The old-timer had known better than to turn and try to come back, though. He was closer to the other bank, and reaching it was his only chance.

With a crack so loud that Frank could hear it even at this distance, the ice abruptly went out from under Salty's feet, and he was plunged into the frigid waters of Eight Mile Creek.

Chapter 26

Salty fell through the ice so quickly he didn't even have a chance to let out a yell before he disappeared under the creek's surface. Meg screamed, though, as she saw him disappear, and so did some of the other women. Conway yelled, "What the hell!" and started floundering forward through the snow.

Frank was already in motion, pounding down the hill on Goldy. As he leaned forward in the saddle, he saw Dog bunching his muscles to leap into the creek in an attempt to save Salty. The big cur ran out onto the ice and splashed into the stream before Frank could call out to stop him.

None of the saddles used by the outlaws had had lariats with them. This wasn't cattle country, so folks didn't have much call to use a rope. But Frank had picked one up in Skagway simply because, like any good Texan, he was used to carrying a lariat with him. Now he was glad he had thought of it. With any luck, it would come in mighty handy.

In all that white expanse of snow covering the valley,

he wasn't sure exactly where the creek began. He reined in about where he thought the right spot was, swung down from the saddle, and found himself still on solid ground. He took the rope and swiftly tied one end to the saddle horn, then started out onto the ice, holding on to the rope and paying it out behind him.

"Stand, Goldy!" he called to the horse. He knew that Goldy wouldn't move now.

A glance up the hill told him that Conway was making his way down the slope on foot. The women were still standing at the top, watching anxiously.

Frank felt his boots sliding a little on the surface under the snow and knew that he was on the ice now. The place where Salty had broken through was about twenty yards in front of him. Frank scanned the water, which was clogged with chunks of broken ice, but didn't see Salty or Dog anywhere. His heart pounded in his chest with fear for them.

He heard another crack and knew the fissures in the ice must be spreading. He wrapped the rope around his left wrist and then lay down on the ice, sprawling on his stomach. That spread out his weight without concentrating too much of it in any one spot, he knew. Using his toes and elbows, he began to pull himself forward.

The soaked forms of Dog and Salty suddenly broke the surface. The big cur's teeth were fastened in Salty's fur coat. The old-timer flailed around and gasped for breath.

Frank was only about ten yards from the water now. He called out, "Hang on, Salty, hang on! I'm almost there!" He crawled closer and saw that Salty, helped by Dog, was trying to swim closer to the spot where the ice ended.

From the bank, Conway shouted, "Frank, what can I do to help?"

Frank twisted his head around to call to the young man, "Stay there! We don't need anybody else on this ice!"

He turned his attention back to Salty. The old-timer was trying to scramble up onto the unbroken ice, but he kept slipping. He wasn't strong enough to pull himself out of the water, and the ice was too slick.

Frank pushed himself forward again. He was within a couple of feet now. He reached out with his right hand, stretching his arm as far as it would go. As he did so, he felt the ice move a little underneath him. Not much, but enough to send a tingle of alarm through him.

"Salty! Grab my hand!"

The sourdough was sputtering and choking, and Frank didn't know if he'd heard him. He called again, "Salty!" and stretched a little farther.

Salty's fingers brushed his, and Frank grabbed hold. He pulled the old man closer and shifted his fingers so that he had a solid grip on Salty's wrist. Then he looked at the shore and shouted, "Goldy, back up!"

The horse began to move backward. The rope pulled taut as Frank held it with his left hand. He felt himself revolving ninety degrees on the ice, so that he lay parallel to the jagged edge where it had broken. Both arms were stretched out, the left one toward Goldy, the right toward Salty.

"Hang on, Dog!" he told the big cur. Dog probably couldn't climb out on the slippery ice, either. Goldy was going to have to pull both of them out of the creek.

Conway saw what Frank was trying to do and grabbed the rope to help pull. Frank felt the strain in his muscles and bones and ligaments and hoped that one or both of his shoulders wouldn't pop out of their sockets.

Thankfully, the pain lasted only a moment. With Goldy and Conway hauling on the rope, Salty and Dog were lifted out of the creek and onto the ice. Frank didn't try to get up, though. Still lying on his belly, he called, "Pull us to shore!"

Goldy continued backing. The two men and the dog plowed a wide furrow through the snow as they slid across the ice. It took only a moment for them to reach the bank. Conway was there waiting for them. Frank scrambled to his feet without any assistance as Dog finally let go of Salty's coat and shook himself so that water flew everywhere off his thick pelt. Conway started to help Salty.

"Wood!" Frank said urgently. "Find some wood! We've got to have a fire!" The water in that stream was even colder than the Pacific had been when they plunged into it from the sinking *Montclair.* They had to get Salty warm and dry as quickly as possible, or he might not survive.

Conway whirled toward the trees, and as he did so, Frank heard another sharp crack. For a second he thought that the ice on the creek was continuing to break up, but then he realized that the sound came from the top of the hill. It was followed by more

cracks and pops and a woman's scream. What sounded
like a giant bee buzzed past Frank's ear.

Somebody was shooting at them.

"Pete! Grab some cover! Dog! Hunt!"

As he shouted the orders, Frank lunged toward
Goldy. He jerked the Winchester out of the saddle
boot. He heard another slug whistle through the air
nearby as he sprang back to Salty's side and reached
down to grab the old-timer's coat with his other hand.
With a grunt of effort, Frank dragged Salty behind a
nearby tree. Salty sat up and leaned against it, clutching himself and shivering.

"Th-that'll b-be Sm-Smith's m-men!" Salty managed to say.

Frank nodded. He had figured that out as soon as
he heard the first shot and realized what it was. Smith's
men had waited for their chance to strike, and Salty's
mishap had given it to them. With Frank and Conway
busy trying to rescue the old-timer, the women had no
one to defend them except themselves. From the sounds
of the small-caliber rounds that had been fired, they
had tried to put up a fight, but that had ended quickly
and now the only shots being fired were from rifles.
They were directed at Frank and his companions.

He looked around the trunk of the tree and saw
Dog bounding up the slope. Even soaked and freezing, the cur's fighting spirit knew no limits. Dog disappeared over the crest, and a second later Frank
heard snarling and screeching. Dog had gotten hold
of one of the bushwhackers.

But he couldn't take all of them on alone. Frank

called to Conway, who had drawn his pistol, "We'll trade off giving each other covering fire! Go!"

With that, he started squeezing off rounds toward the top of the hill. None of the women were visible now, so he wasn't worried about hitting them. He just wanted to force Smith's men to keep their heads down. Spotting several spurts of powder smoke, Frank aimed his fire at them while Conway dashed forward through the trees.

The young man stopped behind a thick-trunked spruce to catch his breath, which wreathed his head with coils of fog. After a few seconds, he called, "All right, Frank, you go!"

Conway stuck his pistol around the tree and started blazing away. Frank leaped out into the open as bark flew from the trunk behind him, chewed off by slugs hitting it. He raced as fast as he could through the snow, leaving the trees behind and heading for a rocky outcropping about halfway up the slope.

Conway's gun fell silent before Frank got there. The young man's revolver was empty. As bullets whipped around him, Frank left his feet in a dive that carried him into the cover of the outcropping. The snow softened the impact of his landing a little, but it still jolted him.

As soon as he had grabbed a deep breath, he raised himself enough to fire over the rocks with the Winchester. Conway was off and running again, this time heading for some trees about twenty yards to Frank's right. He made it and knelt behind one of the trunks, waving his gun to indicate that it was reloaded and he was ready to cover Frank again.

As Conway began firing, Frank started running again, veering toward some trees to his left. This stand of pines ran all the way to the top of the hill. If he could reach them, they could give him all the cover he needed to make it the rest of the way. A bullet tugged at the tail of his sheepskin coat, but that was as close as any of Smith's men came with their shots before Frank ran into the trees.

They kept trying for him anyway. He heard slugs thudding into the trunks and rattling through the branches. Moving fast in a crouching run, he ignored the danger.

Before he reached the top of the hill, the shooting stopped and he heard shouts. He thought he caught the word "Go!" and realized that the bushwhackers might be withdrawing . . . and taking the women with them. That made his lips draw back from his teeth in an angry grimace. Once again, the women he had promised to protect were being kidnapped.

Somebody was going to pay for this.

When he reached the top of the hill, he could see that he was right. Five sleds were drawing off into the distance, three of theirs plus two more. One sled had been left behind, but the team had been cut loose and the dogs were following the other sleds, barking crazily. He didn't see Dog anywhere, or any of the women.

Bart Jennings, though, lay facedown in the snow next to what appeared to be the body of another man.

Frank stepped out of the trees and shouted to Conway, "Pete, they're gone! Get back down there and build that fire for Salty! Now!"

They had to save the old man's life. Chances were,

they would need his help if they were going to rescue the women.

Holding the Winchester ready in case the bush-whackers had left anybody behind to make a try for him, Frank hurried to Jennings's side. He dropped to a knee, grabbed the man's shoulder, and rolled him onto his back.

There was a large crimson stain on the snow where Jennings had been lying.

After seeing how much blood Jennings had lost, Frank wouldn't have been surprised if the outlaw was dead. Jennings's breath rasped in his throat, though, and his chest rose and fell raggedly. Frank moved the parka aside and saw that Jennings had what appeared to be three or four knife wounds in his belly.

Dixon again, Frank thought bitterly. He wished he had shot the little opium addict on sight.

Jennings clutched at his arm. "Who . . . who . . ."

"Take it easy, Bart. It's me, Frank."

"Oh, my God . . . I . . . I'm so sorry, Frank. I tried to fight 'em . . . When the girls started screamin', I ran to them as best I could . . . Meg hollered that she had one of them and for me to help her . . . I didn't have to see . . . I got hold of a man's throat . . . I could feel his beard against my hands . . . I swore to myself I wasn't gonna let go until . . . until he was dead . . ."

Frank glanced at the man who lay nearby on his side. The man had a beard, and his eyes looked like they had popped halfway from their sockets. His face was blue, and his tongue protruded from his mouth.

"You got him, all right, Bart," Frank said softly. "He's right here close by, and he's dead."

Jennings's face contorted with pain and grief. "It wasn't enough," he choked out. "Meg screamed again . . . and then I felt this terrible pain in my stomach . . . again and again . . . The bastard . . . cut me to pieces . . . didn't he?"

"I'm afraid so."

"Ah . . . hell. Now I . . . can't go with you . . . help you save those girls . . . You're gonna save 'em . . . aren't you, Frank?"

"You can count on it," Frank promised.

"I know you will . . . Frank, pull that rag . . . off my eyes . . . would you?"

"Sure." Gently, Frank worked the strip of cloth up onto Jennings's forehead, uncovering his injured eyes. "Can you see anything, Bart?"

A smile suddenly wreathed the dying outlaw's face. "Yeah!" he said. "I can see . . . my ma . . . and my brothers . . . and . . . and . . . my wife . . ."

His final breath came out of him in a long sigh. His eyes continued to stare sightlessly at the blue Alaskan sky. With a grim look on his face, Frank reached out and closed those dead eyes.

Then he stood and looked down the hill, seeing a thin column of smoke rising from somewhere along the creek bank. Conway had gotten a fire going to thaw out Salty, as Frank had told him to do. Leaving Jennings where he was, Frank started down the slope toward the others.

They had some planning to do.

Chapter 27

"Here's the thing," Salty was saying an hour later. "They didn't head back toward Skagway. It looks to me like they're headin' for an old sourdough's cabin a couple o' miles or so east o' here. It's the only thing in that direction 'cept some mountains that you can't get through."

Conway frowned in confusion. "If they're Smith's men, why aren't they taking the women back to Skagway? That's why he sent them after us, isn't it? To get the women?"

The three men were standing near the spot of the brief battle. A mound of rocks marked the place where Bart Jennings's body lay, wrapped in a blanket that had been tied securely around him. It was the best they could do in the way of a burial, at least right now. Salty had suggested that someone could come back in the spring, when the ground had thawed out, and see to it that Jennings was laid to rest properly. Jennings might not have redeemed himself completely from the life he had led as an outlaw, but at least he had made a good start on it. That was more than some men ever did, Frank thought.

There were two more bodies still lying in the open: the man Jennings had choked to death and another of the bushwhackers, who had been mauled by Dog. They had found that one in the edge of the trees. The bodies would be left for the wolves. It was a hard fate, but they had brought it on themselves by going to work for a murderous snake like Soapy Smith.

Frank was still convinced that Smith was behind the attack, even though the bushwhackers hadn't started straight back to Skagway with their prisoners. In reply to Conway's question, he said, "Smith didn't send them *after* us. He sent them *ahead* of us."

Salty was wrapped up tightly in a thick fur robe to help ward off a chill. He looked at Frank and exclaimed, "Doggone it if you ain't right! That's how come you never spotted 'em when you checked our back trail."

Conway shook his head. "I don't understand."

"Smith had those men leave Skagway the night before we did, after the attacks at the hotel and the livery stable didn't pan out," Frank explained. "Most of them, anyway. I'm convinced that Dixon was with them, but he could have circled around us and caught up to them later with more orders from Smith. Smith knew where we were going and knew the route we'd be taking, so he put his men in front of us to watch for a good opportunity to jump us and grab the women. They must have been hidden in the trees. When they saw Salty fall through the ice and Pete and I rushed down there to help him, they figured that was their chance."

"Then it's my fault, gol-durn it," Salty said bitterly. "I knowed it was early in the season for Eight Mile to be froze over solid, but I figured it'd save us some time if we could cross here, instead o' havin' to side-track a couple o' miles. And the ice was good an' sturdy on this side, too. It played out 'fore I got across, though. If it wasn't for Dog, I don't reckon I'd've ever come up." Salty shook his head. "Hope the critter's all right."

Dog hadn't returned after the fight. Frank believed that the big cur had pursued the bushwhackers. He was a little surprised that Dog hadn't come back by now, though.

Salty was right about Dog saving his life. As it was, things had been touch and go for a while. Salty's face had been blue when Frank went down the hill to the fire Conway had built, and the old-timer had been shaking so hard that it seemed like the few teeth he had remaining might come flying out of his head. The sled that had been left behind by the bushwhackers had some fur robes on it, so Frank had grabbed a couple of them before starting down, as well as a blanket.

He and Conway had worked the soaked clothes off Salty. They were already frozen and crackling. They dried him as best they could with the blanket, then wrapped the robes around his spindly shanks. Combined with the heat from the fire, that gradually eased the chill that gripped the old-timer. They used branches to rig a framework next to the fire so that his clothes could be draped on it and dry out while Salty was warming up.

Now, dressed again and studying the trail left by the bushwhackers, the old man was still cold but no longer in any danger of freezing. As long as he didn't come down with the grippe, he would recover from his plunge through the ice.

"At least since there's not much wind and no fresh snow falling, we shouldn't have any trouble following their trail," Conway commented.

"Yeah, and that's exactly what they're counting on," Frank said.

"What do you mean?"

"Smith didn't send those men just to bring the women back. They were supposed to kill the rest of us."

Salty grunted. "They ain't too good at their jobs. The only one they managed to send across the divide was a blind man."

"I'm sure they thought you'd drown in the creek and that they could gun down Pete and me. When it didn't work out that way, I reckon they must've panicked a mite. That's why they grabbed the women and lit a shuck out of here. But then they started thinking again. They don't want to go back to Skagway and have to tell Soapy Smith that we're still alive. So they headed for that old cabin you mentioned, Salty, instead of the settlement."

"You mean they're settin' a trap for us."

"And the women are the bait," Conway added.

Frank nodded. "That's the only thing that makes any sense."

Salty scratched his beard. "So if we go after 'em, we'll be doin' 'zackly what they want us to do."

"Yep."

"But we're gonna do it anyway."

"Damn straight," Frank said. "Just maybe not the way they're expecting."

They couldn't formulate any plans until they had gotten a look at the situation facing them. What Salty remembered about the cabin wasn't encouraging. According to him, it sat out in the open, with no cover around it, so it would be impossible to approach without being seen.

They were getting ready to set out on the trail, with Frank riding Stormy and Conway and Salty doubling up on Goldy, when Frank suddenly spotted something moving across the snow in the distance to the east. His heart leaped as he thought he recognized Dog.

A moment later he knew for sure that was his old friend and trail partner bounding toward them. Dog's barks floated to their ears through the vast Alaskan sky.

"Thank God!" Salty exclaimed. "I was afraid the critter might've froze after bein' dunked in the creek like that."

"Dog's coat sheds water pretty well, and it's thick," Frank said. "Plus he never stays still long enough to get cold."

Dog ran up to them, and Frank greeted the big cur by wrestling with him for a moment. There was a shallow wound on Dog's hip where it looked like a bullet had grazed him, but that was the only injury Frank could find.

"The fella he jumped got a shot off, but that was all," Frank said. "You're like Salty and me, Dog. You're slowing down a mite."

Salty snorted. "Speak for yourself, mister! Now that I ain't froze half to death no more, I'm as spry as ever."

"Maybe we should hitch Dog to that sled," Conway suggested. "We might need some of those supplies before we get the women back."

Frank nodded. "I was thinking the same thing. Salty can ride on the sled."

"You're gonna ask the big feller to pull me after he done saved my life once today already?" the old-timer said.

"I don't reckon he'll mind. Let's get to work mending that harness they cut."

The repairs didn't take long. They hitched Dog into the harness, and Salty climbed onto the runners and grasped the gee-pole.

"You followed those varmints before and then came back for us, Dog," Frank said. "You lead the way. Trail!"

Dog seemed a little confused by the harness and the weight attached to him, but he threw his muscles into the effort and ran along through the snow, pulling the sled behind him. Frank and Conway flanked the sled on the horses as Dog followed the trail left by the bushwhackers.

The marks left in the snow by the sleds weaved

around hills and through valleys. A range of jagged peaks loomed over the spectacular scenery. Farther to the north, White Pass cut a gap through that range, and on the other side of the pass was the glacial ribbon of ice that led to Chilkoot Pass.

For now, though, Frank could only be concerned about rescuing the women, not the rest of the journey to Whitehorse. Without the women, there was no reason to keep going.

Salty had said that the cabin was about two miles east of the place where they had attempted to cross the creek. But that was as the crow flies, and the trail weaved back and forth so much that they actually had to cover at least twice that much ground. It was late in the afternoon, with the light beginning to fade, when they reached the top of a wooded ridge that overlooked a wide flat. In the middle of that flat, as Salty had said, stood a ramshackle old log cabin.

White smoke curled from the cabin's stone chimney.

"Well, I reckon they're in there," Frank said as the three men came to a halt. He pointed to the five sleds and the large gang of dogs outside the cabin. That was more proof the men they sought were here.

"What do they think we're going to do?" Conway asked. "Just walk right up and demand that they give us the women, so they can shoot us?"

"They won't expect us to do anything that stupid," Frank said. His eyes narrowed as they studied the terrain around the cabin. About a hundred yards behind it, there was a long, irregular line where the snow had drifted several feet deep, forming a snakelike hump that eventually ran within twenty feet of the cabin's rear corner. He pointed it out to Salty. "I thought you said there wasn't any cover around the cabin. What's that?"

"There's a old fence along there, most of it fallen down. It ain't enough to give a man any cover when there's no snow. And when the snow's deeper, it ain't drifted up like that. That hump's completely covered. Reckon when the snow's like this is about the only time a feller could hide behind it to sneak up."

"Is that what we're going to do?" Conway asked.

"You and Salty are," Frank said. "We'll wait until dark, though."

"It won't make much difference," Salty pointed out. "Sky's clear. There'll be enough starlight they can see us almost plain as day against that snow when we stand up and try to make it to the cabin."

Frank shook his head. "No, they won't, because I'll be distracting them."

"How you gonna do that?" Salty wanted to know.

Frank didn't answer immediately. He dismounted and went to the sled, where he started pawing through the bundles of supplies that were packed onto it.

"Frank?" Conway prodded. "What are you going to do?"

"Come at them from the direction they least expect, right straight in front."

"But they'll spot you and fill you full o' lead!" Salty protested.

Frank found what he was looking for in the supplies and straightened from the sled with a grin, holding up something so that the other two men could see what he had.

"They can't shoot me if they can't see me," he said as a breeze fluttered the pair of long underwear he held in his hands.

Chapter 28

Frank was already wearing long underwear, of course. They all were. But after the sun had set, he stripped off his outer clothes and donned the second pair. He pulled on two extra pairs of socks to protect his feet and cut holes in another pair for his fingers so that he could use them as makeshift gloves. He found a spare shirt in the supplies that was white and put it on over the long underwear, but only after cutting a piece off the tail that he tied around his head to cover his dark hair.

"It'll never work," Conway said. "They'll still see you."

"Not to mention you're gonna freeze to death in that getup," Salty added.

"They'd see me in the daytime, but not at night. And I can stand the cold for that long," Frank insisted. He took his .45 and one of the .32s and stowed them under the long underwear, next to his body where they would stay warm. Guns had a tendency to freeze up in this weather. "You fellas are going to be colder. You'll have to circle wide around the cabin and crawl a ways through the snow to get to that hump where they can't see you. If you stay as low as you can, you should be able to work your way pretty close to the cabin. Then, when the shooting starts, it'll probably be best if you split up and come around the cabin from different sides."

"How you gonna get the varmints out?" Salty asked.

"With this." Frank took one of the cans of kerosene used as fuel in the Primus stoves from the supplies. He cut another piece of material from the white shirt to wrap around it. The can already had a wick attached to it, so it could be set in the stove's burner and lit just the way it was.

"You're going to set the cabin on fire," Conway said.

"That's the only way I know of to get them out of there in a hurry."

"What if the women are trapped inside?" Conway's voice was hard and angry. "You're taking a chance with their lives."

"Letting them be taken back to Soapy Smith in Skagway would be worse," Frank said. "We don't know how many of Smith's men are in there, and we can't get at them as long as they're holed up. This is the only way to get them out where we can kill them."

Salty scratched at his beard. "It's a risk, all right," he said, "but I reckon Frank's got a point."

"Well, I don't like it," Conway said. "But I can't think of anything else, either. Just be careful when the fire forces them out of the cabin. They're liable to be holding the women in front of them as hostages."

Frank nodded. "I thought of that, too. We may have to take on some of them hand to hand."

Conway thumped his big right fist into the palm of his left hand. "I don't reckon I'd mind that too much."

Frank took the little waterproof tin container of matches he usually carried and tucked it under the long underwear, too. The light had faded from the sky, and he was ready to go. What seemed like a million stars burned in the heavens above, casting silvery illumination over the snow-covered ground.

He draped one of the fur robes around his shoulders and said, "I'll wait twenty minutes for you fellas to get in position, then start my approach to the cabin. That'll probably take another ten minutes or so. I'll need to move pretty slowly, so they'll be less likely to notice me."

"We'll be ready when you are," Salty promised.

He and Conway set off along the ridge. They would have to get out of sight of the cabin before they began to circle behind it. Frank waited in the trees with Dog, Stormy, and Goldy. He rubbed the cur's ears and said, "You wait here until I call you, big fella. But when I do, you come a-running."

Dog whined softly. He was as anxious for the action to start as Frank was.

When Frank judged that enough time had passed, he tossed the robe back onto the sled. He picked up another strip of cloth he had cut from the shirt and tied it around the lower half of his face, covering his mouth and nose so that only his eyes were visible. If anyone had been there to watch, they would have seen how the outfit made him blend into the snow as he left the trees, dropped to his hands and knees, and then stretched out on his belly to begin crawling toward the cabin with the cloth-wrapped can of kerosene in one hand.

He moved slowly, because fast movement drew the eye. Keeping his arms and legs drawn in so that he would leave as narrow a trail in the snow as possible, he inched toward the cabin. His progress seemed agonizingly slow. He couldn't really judge it because he kept his head down most of the time, so that the white cloth wrapped around his head was pointed toward the cabin. Smith's men had to be watching from in there. Frank knew that if they spotted him out in the open like this, they could fill him full of lead before there was anything he could do.

From time to time he glanced up and saw that he was getting closer to the cabin. The warmth from the stove inside had melted the snow on the roof, causing it to run down and form long icicles that glittered in the starlight. Under other circumstances, the scene would have been pretty, or at least picturesque.

Finally, he was about twenty feet from the front door. No one had shot at him yet, which meant they hadn't spotted him. He lifted his head and studied the cabin. The chimney was at the left end of the roof. He figured everyone inside would be gathered at that end, closest to the fireplace. He angled the other way, toward the right end.

Now he was right under the eyes of any watchers inside, so he moved a fraction of an inch at a time. It had been long enough so that Salty and Conway had to be in position and ready. Unless something had happened to delay them, Frank reminded himself . . . but he wasn't going to think about that. Just like he wasn't going to think about the possibility that one of the kidnappers could be drawing a bead on him right now . . .

He reached the corner of the cabin and brushed some snow away to reveal the logs that had been used as its foundation. He pushed the can of kerosene up against them and shoved some snow under the back side of it to tilt it a little toward the wood. Then he got the matches out, struck one, and lit the wick.

A blue flame sprang up, and with it the smell of the fuel burning. Frank hoped the scent of the wood burning in the fireplace inside would mask the kerosene odor. Since the can was sitting at an angle, the flame licked directly at the log foundation. Frank watched until he saw smoke start to curl up from the wood; then he began to back away.

The cabin was old and the wood was dry. Once the logs caught fire, the flames started to spread rapidly, clawing their way up the side of the wall. Frank slid his hands under the long underwear and wrapped them around the grips of the revolvers. More than half the wall on this end of the cabin was on fire. The men inside the place had to notice it soon.

Sure enough, a moment later shouts of alarm rose inside the cabin, and the door flew open. Men began to rush out, and just as Frank had thought might happen, each of them held a struggling woman as a human shield.

But when he sprang to his feet, he was right there among them, taking them completely by surprise. He thrust both arms to the sides, the Colt in his right hand, the .32 in his left, and fired simultaneously. Each barrel was almost touching the head of a kidnapper, and both men probably never knew what hit them as bullets slammed through their skulls and into their brains. They collapsed, letting go of the screaming women they had been holding.

Frank shouted, "Dog! Hunt!" Then he whirled and fired both guns again. Two more men fell. It was chaos in front of the burning cabin now, and Frank was like a phantom gliding through it, the guns in his hands spitting death. Men dropped with slugs in their heads or blood fountaining from bullet-torn throats. The close range allowed him to place his shots perfectly without hitting the women. Frank heard the heavier crash of rifles, along with growling and snarling, and knew that Salty, Conway, and Dog were getting into the fight, too. The sled dogs, tied up a short distance from the cabin, barked and yelped crazily, adding to the noise.

"Shoot the women!" one of the men yelled. Frank put a bullet in his mouth while it was still open from that shouted order. He bulled to the side, barreling into another kidnapper and knocking him away from the hostage he'd been holding. As the man fell, Frank snapped two shots from the smaller revolver into his face.

"Frank!"

That was Fiona's voice. Frank whipped around and saw her trying to run as one of the kidnappers drew a bead on her with a pistol. Frank fired both guns without hesitation. The bullets punched into the man's body and drove him backward over the threshold into the burning cabin, which was fully ablaze by now. The flames engulfed the man, filling the air with the stench of roasting human flesh.

The rest of the gunfire had died away, but as Frank turned from the cabin, he heard the sounds of struggle still going on. He saw Pete Conway and one of the kidnappers trading punches, slugging away at each other. A few yards away on the ground, Salty Stevens was wrestling with one of the men. Salty was on the bottom, doing his best to hold off the hatchet that the kidnapper was trying to bring down in his face. Salty's hand was locked around the man's wrist, but the kidnapper was younger, bigger, and stronger, and Frank knew the old-timer couldn't hold out much longer.

Both revolvers clicked as the hammers fell on empty chambers when Frank tried to shoot the man, though. Frank dropped the guns and launched himself in a diving tackle that knocked the man off of Salty. They rolled through the snow, grappling desperately.

Frank saw starlight wink off the head of the hatchet as it slashed toward his face. He jerked his head aside so the hatchet hit the ground instead and bounced back up. With a grunt of effort, Frank stuck a foot in the man's belly and heaved him up and over his head. The kidnapper howled in surprise as he found himself flying through the air. He lost his grip on the hatchet as he crashed down on his back.

Frank was there to snatch up the weapon. He brought it up and over in a looping strike that buried the razor-sharp head in the center of the kidnapper's forehead. The man spasmed as the keen, cold steel sunk deep into his brain, then went limp. Frank left the hatchet where it was and stood up.

When he looked around, he saw that the fight was over. The bodies of the kidnappers lay sprawled around the area in front of the burning cabin. The light from the flames turned the snow a garish red, but it was a deeper crimson where blood had been splashed. He tugged the white cloth off his head and stood there with his chest heaving and his breath pluming in front of his face.

Meg ran up to him and threw her arms around him. "Frank!" she cried. "Frank, I knew you'd come for us!"

He held her and looked over her shoulder at the other women. Some of them seemed to be disoriented. They were wandering around crying. But as he counted them, including Meg and Jessica Harpe, who was being embraced by Conway, he saw that all eleven of them were there, on their feet and apparently unhurt. Salty was all right, too. He picked up his rifle and started checking on the bodies of the kidnappers, making sure that all of them were dead.

"How many men were there?" Frank asked Meg. He wanted to be certain that none of them had gotten away.

"T-ten, I think," she replied. "Not counting that awful little man Dixon. He already went back to Skagway to tell Smith that they had captured us and were laying a trap for you." She smiled at him. "But I knew you wouldn't fall for it, Frank. I knew you'd figure out some way to save us." She paused. "I just didn't know it would involve running around in your underwear."

Frank glanced down at himself and chuckled. Before, he had been so caught up in carrying out the plan that he hadn't really thought about how cold it was. Now he realized that he was frozen clear through. At least, he would have been if not for the heat coming from the burning cabin.

Salty came over to him and said, "They're all dead."

"Ten of them?"

"Yep, countin' the feller just inside the door of the cabin. Ain't much o' him left, though."

Frank nodded in satisfaction. They had wiped out Smith's men. By the time Smith figured out that the kidnappers wouldn't be returning to Skagway with the women, Frank and his companions would be well on their way to Whitehorse and it would be too late for Smith to do anything about it.

Even though they had ruined Smith's plans, it had come at the cost of Bart Jennings's life, as well as with considerable pain and terror for the women. Those scores would have to be settled, although it might be spring or even summer before Frank got a chance to do so.

But one thing he was sure of: Soapy Smith would be seeing him again.

Chapter 29

Conway and Salty moved the sleds and the dogs well away from the burning cabin while Frank retrieved his clothes from the woods and got dressed again. It felt mighty good to shrug into his thick coat, but even better to buckle on his gun belt and settle his hat on his head. He was The Drifter again, not some hombre who crawled around in the snow.

Fiona seemed awfully quiet. Frank went over to her and asked, "Are you all right? Did any of those varmints hurt you?"

"No, I'm fine, Frank," she told him. "Thank you for saving us. It seems like you're always saving us."

He shrugged. "I set out to get you where you're going, safe and sound."

"Because of that promise you made to Jacob Trench."

"Yeah, that's right."

"Well, we should reach Whitehorse in, what, about two more weeks?"

He nodded. "If we're lucky."

"Then you can wash your hands of us."

"I wouldn't look at it like that," Frank said with a frown. "Anyway, I've got a hunch we'll both be staying there until spring. I don't think we'll be able to get back through those passes to Skagway. I'm not sure I want to, right away. If there's somewhere else you'd like to go, back to Seattle, maybe, we'll find another way, and then I can go back by myself."

It was Fiona's turn to frown in puzzlement. "Why would you go back to Skagway if you didn't have to? It was a terrible place."

"Smith's there," Frank said flatly. "He and I have some business to take care of."

"In other words, you're going back to kill him."

"He needs killing."

"With all his hired guns, the odds may be twenty to one against you," she pointed out.

"Bad odds never stopped me before, when a thing needed doing."

"No," Fiona said with a faint smile and a shake of her head, "I don't expect that they did."

They made camp in the woods, not far from the cabin, which continued to burn until it was a pile of ashes and charred logs. They had two extra sleds and dog teams now, along with the supplies Smith's men had brought with them. That would make the rest of the journey to Whitehorse easier. Not surprisingly, Smith's dog teams were made up of excellent animals. Salty planned to split the animals up the next morning while hitching them to the sleds, so that each team would have several strong, experienced dogs on it.

During the night, wolves came and dragged off the bodies of the kidnappers. None of them were anywhere to be seen when the gray light began to fill the sky. The howling had disturbed the women, but there was nothing that could be done about that. Nature was taking its course.

Frank told Salty that they would get everything ready to go as quickly as they could. The old-timer nodded and said, "Yeah, I know why, too. We're already pushin' it where the weather's concerned. Winter's gonna be right on our tail when we get to Whitehorse, if it ain't overtook us by then."

Salty knew a detour around Eight Mile Creek, but it took them several miles out of their way that morning. Once they were back on the main trail, they were able to make better time.

By late in the day, they had begun the ascent to White Pass. The snow was deeper now, and Goldy and Stormy had more trouble making their way through it. Frank wished there had been a way to leave them behind and reclaim them later, but he knew he couldn't have abandoned them to Soapy Smith. They had been through too much together.

The group made camp on the approach to the pass, and despite the fire and the tents, it was a cold, miserable night. When they got ready to push on the next morning, everyone was quiet, conserving their energy for keeping warm, instead of talking.

Frank didn't like the looks of the sky, and neither did Salty. "If it comes another storm whilst we're still on this side o' Chilkoot, we're gonna be in trouble, Frank."

"We can't turn back. All we can do is keep going and hope for the best."

"Well, there's at least one thing to be thankful for, I reckon." The old-timer grinned. "The cold's done froze the need for a drink right outta me. I don't crave it no more, not even a little nip to warm my belly."

Frank returned the grin and slapped Salty on the shoulder. The old man had sure lived up to his name. He was plenty salty. He had plenty of sand, too.

They reached White Pass at midday. It seemed like the top of the world to Frank as he stood there looking around at the vast, empty, snow-covered terrain falling away on all sides in a landscape filled with bleak beauty. But he knew that Chilkoot was even higher and would be more difficult to reach.

The glacier leading to it was like a river of ice running through the mountains. Enough snow had fallen so that they weren't traveling on bare ice, and Salty told them to be grateful for that. The hard snow was slick enough itself. It was frozen solid enough so that the horses' hooves didn't break through it except occasionally, but it still made for slippery footing.

As Salty had warned them, the slope was steep in places. The women had to get off the sleds and walk, their hobnailed boots crunching in the snow as they helped push the sleds along. Frank led the horses instead of riding. The going was slow, and while they weren't above the timberline, they were high enough so that only a few trees grew here and there. It was an almost colorless world, filled with the white of the snow and ice, the gray of rocks matched by the color of the threatening sky.

Frank could see Chilkoot Pass ahead of them and a little to the right, but it didn't seem to come any closer during the day. He wasn't the sort of man to be discouraged, but as they made camp that night under some sparse trees, he wondered if they were ever going to make it. He wondered, too, if he would ever be warm again. He wore one of the thick parkas now, like all the rest of the travelers, but all it did was blunt the force of the frigid winds that always seemed to blow up here.

Hundreds, maybe even thousands of men had traveled through this frozen hell in search of gold. He wouldn't have done it for that, Frank knew. He had spent a lot of years being poor, so his attitude wasn't the result of knowing that he had more money now than he could ever spend. He remembered quite vividly being hungry and penniless and not knowing where his next meal was coming from, if it came at all. And even knowing that, he thought that the gold just wasn't worth it. He was here because he had given his word, that was all.

But everyone was different, he reminded himself. These young women were willing to travel thousands of miles and endure all these hardships so they could marry men they had never met. Men they didn't know and didn't love. Maybe they would grow to love their new husbands, but they couldn't be sure of that. Why would they do such a thing?

There would be as many different answers to that question as there were women, he realized. And he supposed that was true of the men who came here to hunt for gold, too.

The next day was even colder and grayer as they trudged on toward Chilkoot Pass. Salty kept a wary eye on the sky, and so did Frank. But except for a few flakes that spit down briefly, no more snow fell.

The trail became even steeper, and their pace slowed to a crawl. The dogs were exhausted but continued to pull valiantly. As Salty put it, "Them mutts got more heart than I thought they would. A whole heap more!"

Frank harnessed Dog to the lead team so that the big cur could add his strength to that of the others. With maddening slowness, they climbed toward Chilkoot Pass. Stormy and Goldy struggled even more than the dogs, and several times, Frank thought that the horses weren't going to make it. The bleak prospect occurred to him that he might have to shoot them to put them out of their misery if they couldn't go on, rather than leaving them behind to freeze to death.

When the trail leveled off somewhat, they camped for a second night on the glacier. "Don't think it gets any easier from here on," Salty warned them. "The worst stretch is still up ahead, betwixt here and the pass."

Frank didn't see how the going could get any tougher than it already was, but he refrained from saying that. There was no point in tempting fate.

No one slept much anymore. It was too cold for that. They simply lay in their robes and blankets and shivered. As a result, everyone was exhausted. When they gathered around the stove for coffee in the morning, their faces were gaunt and haggard. They looked like corpses, Frank thought, and he knew he looked the same. He felt like he had aged a year in the past few days.

When the time came to push on, Marie sank down in the snow and said, "I cannot. I simply cannot go another step. Leave me here."

"We're not going to do that," Fiona told her. "We're not going to leave without you or anybody else." Anger suddenly made her voice even hoarser than usual. "It's bad enough I lost the two in the shipwreck. You're all going to Whitehorse so I can collect my money! Get on your feet, damn it!"

Her mittened hands clenched into fists, as if she were about to spring forward and club Marie back to her feet. Frank put his hands on her shoulders and said, "Take it easy, Fiona," while Meg went over to Marie and bent down to take hold of her arm.

"Let me help you, honey," she said. "We can make it. We'll just work together."

Fiona turned and pressed her face against the front of Frank's parka as she began to sob. "It's just so *cold*," she said. "So cold. And I'm so tired."

Nobody could argue with that. They all felt exactly the same way.

After a few minutes, though, Fiona calmed down and stopped crying, and Meg was able to convince Marie not to give up. They resumed their trek through the somber light.

Salty was right, of course: The approach to Chilkoot Pass was the worst of all. Frank hung on grimly to the reins and did what he could to help the horses struggle up the slope. The dogs strained against their traces. The women clung to the sleds and pushed them along. An icy wind rushed down the glacier and pummeled them.

Frank had faced death more times than he could remember, had heard bullets whistle past his ears probably hundreds of times, and yet he had never felt as close to the grave as he did during that long, gray morning as they climbed toward the pass. He was numb in body, mind, and soul, and his brain had slowed to the point that all he could think about was holding on to the reins and putting one foot in front of the other.

He was in such bad shape that he didn't even notice at first when the slope underneath him changed. He had taken several steps before he realized that he was going *down,* not up.

"Salty!" he shouted over the wind as he came to a sudden stop. "Salty!"

"Yeah, I know!" the old-timer's voice came back to him. "I know, Frank! We're there!"

They had reached the top of Chilkoot Pass.

Chapter 30

The ordeal wasn't over, of course. Far from it. But the pass represented a milestone to Frank and to the others. They had more reason to hope now that they could actually make it to Whitehorse and find the destinies that awaited them there.

But first they had to get down from this frozen, windswept pass.

Frank, Salty, and Pete Conway unhitched the dogs from the sleds and tied ropes from each sled to the next in line. Then Salty used the harnesses to attach about half the dogs to the last sled.

"That's just for the first part, 'cause it's the steepest and slickest," the old-timer explained. "When we get lower, we'll hitch the teams back on normal-like and put chains on the runners to slow 'em down, so they won't overrun the dogs."

That made sense to Frank. He said, "You'd better let me go down first with the horses. If they slip and start to fall, they won't take anybody else with them."

"Nobody but you," Meg protested.

"I'll be all right," he assured her. "Salty, how far are we talking about?"

"Worst of it's about a quarter of a mile," the old sourdough said. "Be mighty careful, Frank. I'd hate to think about havin' to go the rest o' the way to Whitehorse without ye."

Frank looked around at everyone, nodded, and then tightly grasped the reins, Stormy's in his left hand, Goldy's in his right. He stepped out onto the slope again. The horses hesitated, clearly uncertain whether they wanted to try it, but they had gone into danger and battle so many times with Frank, their gallant hearts wouldn't let them quit now. They stepped onto the hard-packed snow.

It took Frank close to an hour to lead the two horses down the worst of the slope, one careful step at a time. But at the end of that time, they moved onto relatively level ground and he felt relief flood through him. Looking up at the pass, he pushed back the hood of his parka, took off his hat, and waved it over his head to let the others know that he had made it all right. A few minutes later, he saw the sleds begin to make the descent, followed by the dogs and the other members of the party.

Getting everybody down took awhile, but by late in the afternoon, they were all together again. Salty suggested that they make camp and wait for morning to continue on toward Whitehorse.

"It'll be dark soon," he said, "and we still got some tricky slopes in front of us. We'll need to be able to see where we're goin'."

No one complained, and while they were all still

exhausted, the air of gloom and despair that had hung over the previous camp seemed to have evaporated. Frank thought that Fiona was still a little out of sorts, but everyone else seemed to have at least a trace of optimism about them again. Some of the young women chattered amongst themselves, Conway and Jessica sat near the fire with her head resting on his shoulder, Salty tossed dried fish to the dogs, and Meg came over to Frank to ask, "Are we going to start standing guard at night again?"

He smiled. "Salty and I never stopped. We've been switching off. We just didn't tell anybody. We figured y'all could use all the rest you could get."

"That's not fair! I would have taken my turn."

"We'll probably start doing it again like we were on the other side of the pass, even though I don't think we have to worry about Smith anymore. We're too far from Skagway now. It wouldn't be worth his time and trouble to come after us."

"You can't be sure of that, though," Meg said.

"Nope. That's why we'll keep on standing guard until we get to Whitehorse and get you ladies matched up with your husbands."

"Oh. Yeah, there's still that to do, isn't there?"

Frank said, "You don't sound very happy about the prospect."

· A forlorn note crept into Meg's voice as she said, "I guess I never really thought about what it would mean. I agreed to spend the rest of my life with a man I don't even know. What if he's awful, Frank?"

"That's a chance you take with any marriage, I reckon. Spending time with somebody when you're courting isn't like spending the rest of your life with 'em. You may think you know what's in another person's heart and mind, but chances are, you don't. Not all of it, anyway."

"I know you," she said softly.

"You know I'm good with a gun and I can fight. I don't spook easy. That's about it."

"Not really. I know you love Dog and those horses of yours. You were kind to Mr. Jennings, you respect Salty, and you've tried to help Pete. You've risked your life to save ours over and over again. You're brave, and you're a man of your word."

He laughed. "You'd have me blushing, I reckon, if I was that sort of fella."

"But you're not. And I knew that, too."

"There's something else about me you didn't mention . . . I'm more than twice your age."

"Some people are born old," she said with a smile. "I think I'm one of them."

Frank recalled Diana Woodford, back in Buckskin, Nevada. She had shown some romantic interest in him, too, not long after he had pinned on the badge as Buckskin's marshal, and she was about Meg's age. Frank had nipped that in the bud and had never even thought about doing otherwise.

There was something about Meg Goodwin, though . . . some quality of maturity that Diana had never possessed. Maybe she was right. Maybe some people were older than their actual years.

But it didn't matter, because Meg was promised to somebody else. And like she had said, Frank was a man of his word and believed that other people should honor their promises, too.

"I'm sure everything will be fine once you get to Whitehorse and get to know the fella who sent for you," he said. "You're just a mite nervous because it's all going to be strange to you."

She looked at him for a long moment, then said, "Yes, I'm sure that's all it is. Just nerves."

She didn't sound like she believed it, though.

For the next few days, Meg seemed to be avoiding him, and Frank found himself regretting that. He enjoyed her company and admired her. She was better on the trail than most women he had known. She handled her sled and team better than Conway did his, in fact, and she was a lot more confident than Lucy or Ginnie, who had been drafted to steer the other two sleds.

Fiona warmed up to Frank again now that Meg wasn't spending so much time with him. Fiona had been jealous of Meg, Frank realized, even though she hadn't had any real reason to feel that way. Frank knew he wasn't ever going to settle down with either of them. But Fiona found some excuse to talk to him nearly every time they stopped to rest the dogs.

As Salty had said, once they made several more rather steep descents, the terrain got much easier. There were still hills to either climb or avoid, depending on how big they were, but the dogs could handle them and seemed to have a new lease on life, running effortlessly for hours at a time with the sleds gliding over the snow behind them. It would still take days to reach Whitehorse simply because of the distances involved, but now Frank felt that they had a good chance to make it . . . if only the weather cooperated.

But then, when Salty said they were only two more days from the Canadian settlement, the wind began to pick up during the night and by morning was blowing fiercely out of the north. It brought snow with it, a thick, blinding white cloud. The wind was blowing so hard that it seemed to be snowing sideways, Frank thought as he struggled to help the women take the tents down before they blew away.

"Should we try to wait it out?" he asked Salty, raising his voice to be heard over the wind.

The old-timer gave a vehement shake of his head. "No, we gotta keep movin', at least until it gets worse! The dogs can handle this, and we'll just have to put up with it, too. Whitehorse ain't but about twenty miles from here, and there's a cave about halfway there where we can hole up if we have to. I'm hopin' this storm ain't the real thing, though, and it'll blow over 'fore noon."

That hope proved to be futile. The blizzard continued to rage, filling the air with fresh snow. Frank let Salty lead the way, since the old-timer was the only one among them who had the vaguest notion where he was going. At Salty's suggestion, they ran ropes from each sled to the one behind it, so they wouldn't get separated in the storm, and Frank tied both horses to the rear sled and trudged along beside Conway. Once again, the weather and their surroundings had forced them to slow almost to a crawl.

Salty had to be relying on instinct, Frank thought

on more than one occasion. He couldn't possibly see well enough to know where they were or where they needed to go. The countryside was a blur of white, broken only occasionally by stands of pine or frozen creeks. These streams were covered with thick, solid sheets of ice, and there was no danger of falling through them. The temperature had been well below freezing for more than a week and dipped below zero most nights, according to Salty.

Frank wasn't all that surprised when Salty led them straight to the cave he had mentioned. The instincts that the old-timer had developed as a hunter, scout, stagecoach driver, unofficial lawman, and range detective came in handy now. Frank didn't even see the cave at first, just a big mound of rocks. They had to approach at an angle before the gap between two boulders that led to the black mouth of the cave became visible.

Salty turned to wave the others ahead. "In here!" he shouted over the wind.

At the rear sled, Conway asked Frank, "What if there's a bear or two hibernating in there?"

Frank smiled. "Then I hope they don't mind having some company for the night."

Conway just shook his head.

Still, the young man had a good point, Frank thought. He took his Winchester and strode forward through the piled-up snow, past the other sleds, until he reached Salty's sled.

"Pete wanted to know what we'll do if there are some bears asleep in there!"

Salty shook his head. "There won't be! The

Injuns been usin' this cave for years and years, maybe centuries. Bears don't like the smell o' wood-smoke and men."

Frank went into the cave with him and saw that Salty was right. He lit a match and saw in the glow that the cave's relatively narrow entrance opened out into a roomy chamber with an arched ceiling and rings of soot on the floor where campfires had burned in the past. Salty pointed to the ceiling and said, "There are enough cracks up there to let the smoke out. Shoot, we'll have all the comforts o' home in here. There's just one thing I'm worried about."

"What's that?" Frank asked when the old-timer didn't go on.

"Bein' able to get outta here in the mornin'," Salty said. "If that storm dumps enough snow, it'll drift up over the entrance, and we'll have to dig our way out. That can be dangerous. I've heard tell about fellers who tried to tunnel through deep drifts gettin' turned around so they didn't know which way they was goin'. They just kept diggin' and diggin' until they froze to death or the snow collapsed on 'em and suffocated 'em."

"We're not alone, and we have ropes," Frank pointed out. "If something like that happens, we can tie a rope onto whoever tries to tunnel out and pull them back in if they get into trouble."

Salty nodded slowly. "Yeah, that could work, I reckon. Well, let's get the rest o' those folks in here. I'd planned to stop here tonight anyway, even before this storm blew up. This'll be the first night in more'n two weeks we'll really be warm."

Frank was looking forward to that, and he knew the others were, too.

They left the sleds and the horses outside. The cave was rather crowded anyway with fourteen people and three dozen dogs in it, and the smell got a mite thick, too, Frank thought. But as Salty had promised, after they built a fire in the center of the chamber, the heat from the flames reflected back from the rock walls and ceiling and filled the place with warmth. They were able to take off their parkas, and after a while, everyone shed their coats, too. They had coffee and hot food, and Frank discovered to his amazement that he was actually starting to feel human again. He wasn't the only one, either. The women began to talk and laugh. Color came back into their cheeks. Life sparkled in their eyes. Frank even saw Conway and Jessica steal off into a corner to share a few kisses.

Exhaustion was quick to catch up with everyone, though. The women spread their bedrolls and crawled into the blankets, and within minutes they were all asleep. So were Salty and Conway. Snores came from both men. Frank remained awake for a while, taking the first guard shift. Under the circumstances, he figured one sentry at a time was enough. There was only one way into the cave. Salty and Conway could take the other two shifts, and as always, Dog was the best sentry of all.

The fire had burned down to embers but was still giving off a pleasing warmth when Fiona got out of her blankets and came over to the rock near the entrance where Frank was sitting. He moved over to give her some room, and she sat down beside him.

"Can't sleep?" he asked her quietly.

"We're almost there, Frank," she whispered. "We've almost made it."

He nodded. "I know. Sort of hard to believe, isn't it?"

"You don't really think anything else could possibly go wrong when we're this close, do you?"

"I wouldn't go saying that. You'll jinx us."

She looked worried, so he chuckled and went on. "No, I'm just joshing you. I think we'll be fine."

"Then . . . I have a proposition for you."

His smile went away. "You're not talking again about me being your partner, are you? I told you, I'm not interested in being in the mail-order bride business."

"After everything that's happened on this trip, I'm not sure I am, either," Fiona said. "But whatever happens in the future, we're going to be stuck in White-horse for the next few months, Frank. We might as well enjoy them . . . and while we're at it, maybe we could think of some new business venture that *would* interest you."

The offer was tempting in a way, but as Frank sat there in silence for a moment, he knew his heart wouldn't be in it. Despite what had happened between them in Seattle, Frank knew that he and Fiona Devereaux weren't meant to be together, even for a winter in Whitehorse. And he wasn't going to lead Fiona on and allow her to think anything different.

"That's mighty nice of you," he said, "but I don't reckon it'd work out."

Her face hardened in the faint glow from the fire. "You're sure about that?" she said.

"Yeah. I'm sure."

"Is it because of Meg? I saw you kissing her that night, you know. Blast it, Frank, she's not *that* much younger than I am."

He shook his head, remembering the night Meg had kissed him. "No, Meg's got nothing to do with it. She's got a husband waiting for her, remember?"

"Yes, of course," Fiona said, her voice flat. "All right. I understand. I won't bother you again." She stood up. "I appreciate everything you've done for me, Frank . . . even if it *was* just out of a sense of duty."

"That's not—" he began, but she turned and walked back to her bedroll, not letting him finish.

Just as well, he thought. There was nothing he could tell her that she would want to hear.

Chapter 31

Salty's worries proved to be well founded. The storm piled so much snow in front of the cave's entrance that by the next morning it was completely blocked by the white stuff.

Frank and Salty stood there looking at it for a few moments before Salty said, "Well, I reckon somebody's gonna have to burrow out through there. You feel like bein' a mole, Frank?"

Conway stepped up behind them. "Let me do it," he said. "I'm the biggest. I can make a good tunnel for us."

Frank turned toward him. "Are you sure you want to risk it, Pete? The tunnel could collapse on you."

"Well, you'll have a rope tied to me, right? Just pull me back out, and I'll try again."

Frank thought it might not be that simple, but Conway had a point about being the largest member of the group. He nodded and said, "All right, we'll give it a try. I'll get my rope."

Everyone gathered around as Conway got ready to

try to dig out. Jessica threw her arms around him in a hug that contained a hint of desperation. "Don't let anything happen to you," she told him as she embraced him.

Conway patted her awkwardly on the back. "Don't worry about me," he said. "I'll be fine."

He started the tunnel by digging a hole out as far as he could reach without leaving the cave. Then he stretched out on his belly, and Frank tied the rope around both his ankles, so they could pull him straight out of the tunnel if they needed to. Then Conway looked back over his shoulder, grinned at them for a second, and started using his mittened hands to shovel snow behind him as he crawled forward. He packed it on both sides as best he could, to strengthen the walls of the tunnel.

It was slow going, and it took a long time before Conway's feet and legs disappeared completely into the tunnel. Salty had warned him not to shout back to them unless it was an emergency, because loud noises could cause the snow to fall, collapsing the tunnel. So a tense silence filled the cave as minutes stretched out into an hour or more since Conway had started digging out.

Frank knelt by the entrance to the tunnel, letting the rope slide through his hands. They had worked out signals before Conway went into the hole. Two tugs meant they should pull him back as quickly as they could. Three meant that he had made it through the drift safely.

He didn't really need to feel the three tugs that came on the rope, though. A shaft of light shot through the tunnel, and Frank knew that Conway had reached the outside world. A moment later he felt the rope go slack and pulled it back through.

"Who's next?" he asked.

"I'll go," Jessica said.

Frank knew she didn't want to be separated from Conway any longer than she had to, but they all had to crawl out sooner or later, so Jessica might as well go as any of them. He nodded and said, "All right, lie down here and I'll fasten the rope to you. When you get out, untie it and tug on it three times."

Jessica was able to make it through the tunnel a lot faster than Conway had, of course, since she didn't have to dig her way out. Frank sent the women through one by one; then Salty enticed the dogs to follow him with some dried fish. That just left Frank in the cave. He was glad to be leaving, because that meant they were on the last leg of the trip to Whitehorse, but he was sorry to lose the warmth from the fire, which was burning down to nothing behind him as he crawled out.

The sun wasn't up yet, but the sky appeared to be clear. The storm had passed, leaving several more feet of snow on the ground. That wouldn't slow them down, though, Salty declared. They would be in Whitehorse before nightfall.

Frank had been worried about Stormy and Goldy, but they had made it through the night just fine and tossed their heads in greeting, happy to see him and Dog, as always. He saddled them up while Salty and Conway hitched the dog teams to the sleds. Everyone had already eaten breakfast in the cave, so it didn't take long before they were on the move again.

They left the range of hills where the cave was located and entered a long, broad valley flanked by white-capped mountains. Whitehorse was at the other end of the valley, Salty informed Frank, in a great bend of the Yukon River near that stream's headwaters.

It was a beautiful day and they were able to make good time. Everyone's spirits rose even higher. Frank rode alongside Salty's sled and asked, "What are the chances of getting back to Skagway?"

"None at all," the old-timer said, confirming what Frank had suspected all along. They were doing good to beat the worst of the weather to Whitehorse. "That last storm probably dumped a good fifteen or twenty feet o' snow in the passes. Nobody'll get through there until it melts off in the spring. If you ain't willin' to spend the winter in Whitehorse, you might be able to make it out by goin' down through Canada, but I wouldn't recommend it. That'd be a hell of a hard trek at this time o' year."

Frank smiled. "I suppose I can be a Canadian and stay in Whitehorse for a few months."

"That's what I'm gonna do." A wistful note entered the old-timer's voice. "Next spring, though, I think I'm gonna head south. I got me a hankerin' to see the Rio Grande again."

That sounded good to Frank, too. But before that would be possible, he had to settle accounts with Soapy Smith. And before *that,* he had a few awkward months to look forward to, spending time in the same town with Fiona Devereaux, who was still angry with him. With luck, Meg would be out at her new husband's claim, and he wouldn't have to see her and think too much about what might have been.

It took most of the day to cover the length of the valley. The light had begun to fade by the time they reached the settlement. The sight of smoke rising from numerous chimneys was a welcome one. It represented civilization.

Whitehorse was a bigger town than Skagway, but it was a similar mix of tents, log buildings, and frame structures made of raw, unplaned planks. As the sleds approached, the young women grew more solemn. Maybe they were thinking about the fact that they would soon be meeting their new husbands, Frank mused. Those had to be sobering thoughts.

The dogs were yapping noisily as they entered the settlement, and that drew plenty of attention. Men stepped out of the buildings to see what was happening. Frank expected some cheers of excitement, but the town was strangely quiet.

"Over there," Fiona said, pointing to a large, two-story building with a sign over its entrance that read HARGETT'S. "That's where we're supposed to go."

"Looks like a saloon," Frank said with a puzzled frown.

"Well, it may be, but it's also a hotel. I have rooms booked there for everyone. I lost the letter I got from Mr. Hargett in the shipwreck, but I'm sure he'll honor our arrangement."

Frank hoped so. From what he had heard about

Whitehorse, the place was as full up with gold-hunters as Skagway had been, maybe more so.

The sleds came to a stop in front of Hargett's. The snow in the street was deep enough that it was level with the porch. The women were able to step from the sleds right onto the porch, where they congregated nervously. Frank dismounted and tied Stormy's and Goldy's reins to one of the posts that supported the awning, since the hitch rails were covered up.

Fiona pushed back the hood of her parka and said, "All right, ladies, let's go inside." She turned to Frank and went on. "Would you come with us, Frank? You've been with us all the way, so I'd like for you to see the end of this."

"Well, sure, I suppose I can do that," he said with a smile. "Be nice to be there for the finish."

Meg turned and gave him a sad smile as the group started to file into the place. He sensed that she was saying good-bye to him.

Hargett's looked even more like a saloon when Frank stepped inside. He saw a long hardwood bar on the right, poker tables and faro layouts to the left and rear, and some stairs at the end of the room leading up to a second-floor balcony with rooms opening off it. The main room was full of men, most of them hard-faced hombres in thick coats. A couple of pot-bellied stoves in the corners gave off some heat, but the room still held a chill.

Alarm bells suddenly went off in Frank's brain. Something wasn't right here. His hand had started to move toward his gun when boot leather scuffed on the floor behind him. Even with all the speed he could muster, he wasn't fast enough. The blow was already falling. Just as his fingers touched the Colt, something crashed against the back of head, driving him forward off his feet. He heard screams as he landed on his face, scraping it on the rough floor. Blackness swirled around him, trying to close in and carry him away.

But he was still aware enough to hear Fiona say, "You really should have taken me up on my offer, Frank."

That was the last thing he knew for a while.

As he had told Conway after the shipwreck, pain meant life. Pain was a good thing, because the absence of it was death.

So Frank knew he was alive, because his head hurt like hell.

He had been knocked out before, and the experience hadn't improved any. Now he was cold, too, he realized as awareness seeped back into his brain, and lying in darkness on what felt like cold, rocky ground. He got his hands underneath him and tried to push himself up. As he did, he bumped into something beside him. He heard a groan and then a muttered, "What in tarnation . . . ?"

"Salty?" Frank rasped. "Salty, is that you?"

"Yeah. Frank? What . . . what the hell happened?"

Frank struggled to a sitting position and reached out to explore around him. His fingers brushed what felt like a log wall. He leaned against it to steady himself and ease the pounding in his skull.

"We got double-crossed, that's what happened," he said grimly.

"Double-crossed? By who?"

"Fiona."

"Miz Devereaux? But that don't make no sense!"

It was starting to, Frank thought. It was all starting to make sense now, and he didn't like the picture that it formed in his head.

"There were men waiting for us when we went inside," he said, "but they weren't miners who sent off for mail-order brides. I don't reckon those ladies were ever intended to have husbands. Fiona made a deal with this fella Hargett to bring them up here and turn them into whores."

Salty cursed bitterly. "That's the most low-down, despicable thing I ever heard. Why would anybody take advantage o' innocent gals that way when there's already soiled doves up here?"

"You just said it yourself. They're innocent. Hargett can charge a premium price for them, and he can keep on charging higher prices for a while, just like Soapy Smith intended to do."

"Shoot, if that's what's goin' on, why didn't Miz Devereaux just throw in with Smith whilst we was in Skagway, 'stead o' comin' all the way through that snow and ice to Whitehorse?"

"Maybe Hargett promised her a bigger cut than she thought she could get from Smith," Frank guessed. "I don't know, and I don't reckon it matters. Did they bushwhack you, too?"

"They durned sure did. Some fellers came up and started talkin' to Pete and me, and the next thing we knowed, they walloped us over the head with their guns. Then I reckon they dragged us off and locked us up in . . . what is this place, anyway?"

"A smokehouse would be my guess," Frank said. "Is Pete in here, too?"

"Danged if I know. Lemme feel around . . . Yeah! I got him, Frank. He's here. Got a big, sticky goose egg on his head where they clouted him, too. He's breathin', though."

Conway regained consciousness a few minutes later. After he let out a few groans, his senses returned enough for him to ask where he was and what was going on. Frank and Salty filled the young man in, and he then exclaimed, "Jessica! You mean they're going to turn Jessica into . . . into a . . ."

"Not if we have anything to say about it," Frank said.

"But what *are* we gonna do?" Salty asked. "They bushwhacked us 'cause they knew we wouldn't stand for what they're plannin' to do. They got our guns and locked us up in here."

"How come they didn't just kill us?" Conway wanted to know.

Frank said, "I reckon they had their reasons. As for what we're going to do . . . well, I haven't figured that out yet, but since we're still alive, I don't see any point in giving up."

Salty chuckled. "You sound like that big galoot of a lawman I used to know. Mighty stubborn cuss, he was."

"So am I," Frank said.

The rattle of a chain somewhere outside made them

fall silent. Frank spotted an orange glow filtering into the sturdy shack through cracks around what appeared to be a door. A key turned in a lock, and the door swung open. Light from a lantern spilled into the square room, making the prisoners squint against its glare for a few seconds before their eyes adjusted. Frank saw a man standing outside the doorway, holding the lantern. He was flanked by two more men carrying shotguns.

The man with the lantern wore a suit instead of a parka, but didn't seem to be cold. He was a narrow-faced hombre with dark hair under a flat-crowned hat. The lantern was in his left hand, a Smith & Wesson .38 revolver in his right. He covered Frank, Salty, and Conway with the gun as he grinned and said, "Welcome to Whitehorse, gentlemen. Come on out."

Chapter 32

"My name is Jack Hargett," the man went on by way of introduction as the three prisoners filed out of what proved to be a smokehouse, as Frank had suspected. "You're already acquainted with my partner, Mrs. Devereaux."

"If that's the case, you ought to know that she's been looking for a new partner," Frank said. He didn't think it would do any harm to try to drive a wedge between Fiona and Hargett. "She wanted me to throw in with her. I reckon I would've been taking your place if I'd said yes."

"Oh, I doubt that," Hargett said, evidently untroubled by Frank's accusation. "You would have wound up working for us. Fiona told me all about you. It would have been good to have The Drifter backing us. Nobody would have dared to give us any trouble then. But we'll make do without you, Morgan. We've been getting along just fine."

Night had fallen, but light from the buildings showed Frank that the smokehouse was located behind Hargett's saloon. Hargett and his shotgun-toting henchmen marched them inside through a rear door. The place was cleared out now except for Fiona, who stood at the bar with a drink in her hand.

"Sorry, Frank," she said. "I wish things had worked out better between us."

"Hell will be as cold as Chilkoot Pass before that would have happened," Frank grated.

Fiona's face hardened. "Fine," she snapped. "You had your chance. The three of you are lucky to still be alive. But after tonight, Jack and I won't need you anymore. The only reason we kept you around was so that the ladies would be a little more cooperative. You see, we promised them that we'd let you go if they went along with what we wanted."

"What happens tonight?" Frank asked, although he had a sinking feeling that he already knew the answer.

Fiona lifted her glass in a little salute. "The auction."

Conway started to curse. Hargett slapped him on the side of the head with the Smith & Wesson and said, "Shut up."

Fiona went on. "In a little while we'll open the doors, and men who haven't seen a white woman in months, let alone one as innocent as those ladies, will pour in here with their bags of gold to bid on the privilege of being first with them. We'll make a small fortune, and by morning the ladies . . . well, they won't be ladies anymore, will they? They'll know by then that they have to go along with what we want."

"So you can kill Salty and Pete and me," Frank said.

"Exactly."

"Would you have done the same thing with Jacob?"

Fiona shrugged. "I might have given Mr. Trench the opportunity to join us in our enterprise once I got to know him, like I did with you, Frank. I might not have. Who knows? And it really doesn't matter now, does it?"

"Nope," Frank said heavily. "It doesn't."

Salty said, "I'm surprised the Mounties are lettin' you varmints get away with this. Last I heard, there was a constable posted here in Whitehorse."

"There was," Hargett admitted. "He's dead now. My men and I run Whitehorse."

Just like Soapy Smith in Skagway, Frank thought, although Hargett had evidently gone further and indulged in outright murder, of a lawman, at that.

He looked back and forth between Hargett and Fiona and said, "You two knew each other before, didn't you?"

"We met in San Francisco years ago," Fiona said. "We've been partners ever since and pulled off some nice jobs. None of them ever had the potential to be as lucrative as this one, though. This is just the start, too. There's a fortune to be made in the Klondike, Frank. More money than you could ever imagine!"

Frank started to laugh. She had no idea she was talking to one of the richest men west of the Mississippi.

Fiona's face flushed with anger. "What are you laughing at?" she demanded. "Shut up!"

"Let's get on with this," Hargett said. "Bring the girls out so they can have a look at these three and see that they're still alive. Then we can lock them up again and let the customers in."

Fiona jerked her head in a nod. "All right." She looked at Frank. "Just so you know, the opening bid for each of them will be a thousand dollars. More than ten thousand dollars in one night, Frank, maybe twice that much . . . and you could have had a share in it."

"I wouldn't touch money like that to save my life."

"Well . . . we're past that point, I'm afraid. Nothing will save your life now." Fiona tossed back the rest of her drink, set the glass on the bar, and took one of the .32 revolvers from a pocket in her dress. She went up the stairs to the balcony and moved along it, knocking on each of the doors as she passed them and calling, "Come on out, ladies. It's almost time for you to meet your . . . suitors."

None of the doors opened. Fiona waited a moment, then said angrily, "Come out here. You won't like it if Jack has to send some of his men in to get you."

Someone jerked a door open. Frank wasn't too surprised when Meg came striding out onto the balcony. She looked furious. She wore a thin, low-cut shift that must have been cold in the chilly saloon. She glared at Fiona and said, "I can't believe we ever trusted you."

Fiona smiled. "People are always eager to believe what they want to hear. I promised you a new life.

Well, that's what you're going to get, honey." She went to the next door and slapped it hard with her free hand. "Get out here, now!"

The other doors opened and the women came out slowly and reluctantly onto the balcony. They were dressed like Meg, and as they lined up along the railing, Frank knew the miners waiting anxiously outside would be happy to bid on them. Some of the miners in the area really would have preferred wives, but men like that probably wouldn't come to a saloon auction of brand-new soiled doves in the first place.

Lining the women up like that and putting them on display had another effect. It drew the eyes of the two men holding shotguns. They stared up at the half-dressed women and forgot for a second about their job. Even Jack Hargett couldn't help but look up at them with an expression of mingled lust and greed on his face.

Frank saw that and knew this would be his only chance to act.

"Ready, ladies?" Fiona asked mockingly.

"Yeah," Meg said, "I'm ready . . . bitch!"

She launched herself at Fiona, knocking the gun aside and tackling the older woman. Both of them crashed against the balcony railing, which broke with a sharp crack under the impact. Suddenly Fiona and Meg were plummeting toward one of the tables below.

Frank couldn't wait to see what happened when they landed. He spun, grabbed the barrels of one of the Greeners, and wrenched them upward. The weapon came out of the hands of the distracted guard. Frank slammed the twin barrels into the middle of the man's face and felt bone crunch under the impact.

"Kill 'em, damn it, kill 'em!" Hargett yelled.

The second shotgunner had his hands full with Pete Conway, though. Conway grabbed the gun with both hands and jerked the man against him, trapping the shotgun between them. The muzzles jabbed up under the man's chin, and he just had time to widen his eyes in shock and terror before Conway shoved the weapon up, tripping both triggers. The double blast blew the man's face off and threw him and Conway apart.

Meanwhile, Frank hit the first guard again, this time driving the shotgun's butt into his already shattered face. The man went down with a bubbling moan. Frank spun when he heard the blast. He saw Conway staggering backward, covered with blood, and yelled, "Pete!"

"I'm all right!" Conway shouted. "Help Salty!"

The old-timer was wrestling with Hargett. Both his hands were locked around the wrist of Hargett's gun hand. Hargett slammed his other fist into Salty's face and knocked him loose, sending the old man stumbling back a couple of steps. Hargett brought the pistol up.

"Hargett!" Frank called.

The man was fast. He whirled and actually got a shot off, sending a bullet whipping past Frank's head. Then Frank touched off one barrel of the shotgun he held and planted a load of buckshot in the middle of Hargett's suddenly bloody chest. The charge blew Hargett back against the bar, where he hung for a second, eyes wide with pain. Then the life went out of those eyes, and he flopped forward on his face to lie there on the plank floor in the middle of a slowly spreading pool of blood.

Finally, Frank had a chance to glance toward the table where Meg and Fiona had landed. It had collapsed under their weight. The other women had rushed down the stairs by now and were helping Meg to her feet. She appeared to be shaken but all right, so Frank turned his attention back to other matters.

He bent over and started checking the pockets of the man he had knocked out. He found a handful of shotgun shells and brought them out. "Pete, reload!" he said to Conway as he tossed a couple of the shells to the young man. He broke open the Greener in his hands and replaced the round he had used to kill Hargett.

The doors of the saloon were locked, but men were slamming against them. Probably Hargett's men, Frank thought as he closed the shotgun, trying to get in here because of the shooting.

With a splintering crash, the doors popped open. Five men spilled into the room, holding revolvers, and Frank recognized them as some of the men who'd been in the saloon when he and the others first arrived.

"Hargett's dead!" he shouted. "Drop your guns!"

The hardcases didn't follow his advice. They jerked their weapons up to fire, but Frank and Conway let loose with the Greeners first. At this range, the spreading charges of buckshot cut the men down like a reaper with a scythe. Their bloody bodies clogged the doorway.

There might be more of Hargett's men, Frank thought, so he threw a couple more shells to Conway and used the last two to reload the shotgun he held. But before they had to use the weapons, a man outside shouted, "Did you hear that? Hargett's dead! Let's get those bastards who work for him!"

Men yelled and cursed and shots rang out in the street. But that racket lasted only a few moments before it was replaced by screams of pain and fear, and then those grim sounds died away as well. Evidently Hargett and his men had been ruling Whitehorse with iron fists, and when that happened, the oppressed always rose up against the oppressors when they finally got the chance.

Meg came over and touched Frank's arm. "Frank," she said. "She wants you."

He didn't understand at first what Meg meant. But then he looked around and saw Fiona still lying on the floor amidst the debris from the wrecked table. Even at first glance he knew something was wrong, and as he came closer, he saw what it was. Her neck was twisted at an unnatural angle. She must have broken it when she landed.

Frank handed the loaded shotgun to Salty and said, "You and Pete keep an eye on the door." Then he went to a knee beside Fiona and looked down into her eyes.

"F-Frank," she said in that hoarse voice that had intrigued him from the time he first met her. "Frank, I . . . I'm sorry . . . it turned out . . . like this . . . You should've . . . taken me up on it . . . such a . . . damned shame . . ."

"Yeah," he said. "In a lot of ways."

But she was beyond hearing him. She had died as those final words came out of her mouth.

From outside the broken doors, somebody called, "Hey, in there! Don't shoot! Is it true that Hargett's dead?"

"Durned tootin' he is!" Salty replied.

"Thank God! Hold your fire!" A man moved into the doorway, his hands raised to show that he meant no harm as he stepped over the crumpled corpses of Hargett's gun-wolves. He was dressed in a thick coat and floppy-brimmed hat and had the look of a prospector about him. "You don't have to worry about the rest of his gang," the man went on. "All the fight's gone out of 'em. The ones who are still alive, that is."

Frank rose from where he knelt by Fiona's body. He said to Meg and the other women, "You ladies get back up there and get dressed." As they hurried upstairs, he stepped over toward the bar to pick up the .38 Hargett had dropped. He asked the man, "Who are you?"

"Name's Keenan. I've got a claim not far from here."

"You came into town for the auction?" Frank asked in a hard voice.

"Hell, no!" Keenan responded. "I was over at the general store with a bunch of fellas who didn't like Hargett and his plans any more than it looks like you did, mister." He glanced at Hargett's body as he spoke. "We're the ones who went after Hargett's men. The bunch who came for the auction scattered when the shooting started. Gold or no gold, most of 'em were no-accounts anyway." Keenan paused. "You're the fella we heard them talking about. The gunfighter. Frank Morgan."

Frank nodded. "That's right."

"All right to put my hands down now, Mr. Morgan?"

Frank gestured with the Smith & Wesson. "I reckon so."

Keenan lowered his hands and went on. "If you'd like a job, Mr. Morgan, we've sure got one for you. Marshal of Whitehorse! We haven't had any law and order here since Hargett back-shot Constable Fleming."

"The Mountie who was posted here?"

"That's right. Hargett's been riding roughshod over the whole town since then, and nobody dared to stand up to him. You changed that in a hurry."

Frank lowered the .38 and said, "I'm not a lawman, Keenan." He pointed at Salty. "There's your man."

"Wait just a gol-durned minute!" Salty protested. "There's still bodies leakin' blood all over the floor, and you got me wearin' a badge already? I done told you, I'm goin' to Mexico!"

"Not for a while yet," Frank said as the women, fully dressed now, began to come back down the stairs from the second floor. He saw how Keenan's eyes followed them with interest, admiration, respect, and a touch of lust. He struck Frank as a decent hombre, but that didn't mean he didn't like to look at a pretty girl. Frank went on. "Remember, we're stuck here in Whitehorse until the spring."

Salty lowered his shotgun and scratched at his beard. "Yeah, there's that to consider, I reckon," he admitted. "Marshal. Don't that beat all."

"At least until the Mounties show up again," Frank added. "I'm sure somebody will come to find out what happened to Constable Fleming."

Salty nodded and said, "All right, Keenan, you got yourself a badge-toter . . . on one condition." He jerked a thumb at Conway. "I want this young feller as a deputy."

"Wait a minute!" Conway exclaimed. "I came to look for gold, not wear a badge!"

"I reckon you'll have plenty o' time for prospectin', too," Salty said. "'Cause as long as I'm marshal, Whitehorse is gonna be a plumb peaceful place!"

Chapter 33

Frank stood at the railing of a ship called the *Jupiter* and watched the wharves at Skagway coming closer. The town had grown in the months since he had been here last, he thought. It had a ways to go yet, but it was actually starting to look respectable.

Salty Stevens flanked him to the left, Meg Goodwin to the right. Meg leaned closer to him and said, "Are you sure you want to do this, Frank?"

"It needs doing," he said.

"And you're too danged stubborn not to do it," Salty said. "Might as well not argue with him, gal. He ain't gonna change his mind."

Meg smiled her crooked little smile. "He wouldn't be the man I think he is if he did."

Salty's stint as marshal of Whitehorse hadn't lasted long, only a few weeks. Then a whole troop of Mounties showed up, rumors having reached Dawson about Constable Fleming's disappearance. They left a couple of men in Whitehorse to keep order, but by that time the settlement had gotten pretty much back to normal anyway.

Over the next several months, most of the respectable miners and businessmen in the area for a hundred miles around paid court to the ladies who had come to Whitehorse for husbands. They might not have been mail-order brides, as they had thought, but by spring they were all brides, Jessica marrying Pete Conway, Lucy marrying Vic Keenan, and the others all finding suitable mates . . . except for Meg. She had steadfastly refused to get involved with anyone, even though Frank had just as steadfastly insisted that a romance between them wasn't in the cards.

But when the time came for Frank and Salty to leave Whitehorse, Meg had gone with them. Nothing would sway her from that decision. Instead of going back over the passes, they had ridden south through British Columbia and eventually back to Washington. It was a long trip through rugged country, and there had been a couple of late spring storms to cope with along the way, which slowed them down even though the storms weren't as bad as the blizzard that had punished them on the way to Whitehorse.

Frank didn't mind the delays. Stormy, Goldy, and Dog were always good company, and Salty and Meg were, too, even though Salty was still a little scandalized by the idea of a young woman traveling with a couple of men, neither of whom was her father, brother, or husband. Meg, as usual, didn't give a damn about that.

When they finally made it back to Seattle, it was

summer, and Salty wanted to keep going south. Frank still had an errand to take care of, though. He told Salty and Meg to head for the border country with a promise to catch up to them later. Meg had said nothing doing to that, of course, as Frank expected, and Salty had stubbornly tagged along, too.

So now it was midsummer and absolutely gorgeous in Alaska as the *Jupiter* docked at Skagway and Frank, Meg, and Salty disembarked. Frank was back in boots, jeans, a faded blue shirt, and his high-crowned Stetson. Salty wore overalls, a red-checked shirt, a cowhide vest, and a battered old hat with the brim turned up in front. Meg was dressed like something out of a Wild West show, in Salty's opinion, in a fringed buckskin shirt, jeans, and a brown, flat-crowned hat. If she was going to be improper and scandalous, she said, she might as well go all the way and wear trousers like a man.

"All right," Salty had agreed reluctantly, "but if you go to chewin' tobaccy and spittin', then I ain't gonna let on I even know you!"

As they walked along the dock, the first thing Frank noticed was that there were a number of soldiers in evidence. The U.S. Army had come to Skagway. He spotted a young officer and said, "Excuse me, Lieutenant, but what's going on here? Why is the army in Skagway?"

"Not that it's any business of yours, mister," the lieutenant replied, "but we were sent in to quell the riots."

"Riots?" Salty repeated. "What riots?"

"The ones that broke out after Soapy Smith was

killed, when his men went to war among themselves trying to seize power."

"Smith's dead?" Frank asked sharply.

"That's right. He shot it out with a member of the vigilantes that were organized against him and his cohorts. Both men were killed, and after a few days the rest of the vigilantes succeeded in driving Smith's cronies out of town." The lieutenant sounded a little disappointed as he added, "We really didn't have that much to do. Most of the trouble was over by the time we got here."

Frank nodded slowly. "Thanks," he said. He turned and started back toward the *Jupiter*.

"Hey!" the officer called after him. "Didn't you just get off that boat?"

Frank looked over his shoulder. "Yeah. But there's no reason for me to be here now."

Salty cackled as the three of them headed for the ship. "You didn't get to shoot him after all. Don't that just beat all?"

Meg linked her arm with Frank's and smiled up at him. "It's not that bad," she said. "Now there's nothing stopping us from going to Mexico, is there?"

Frank grinned back at her. "Not a thing in the world," he said.

THE MOUNTAIN MAN SERIES BY
WILLIAM W. JOHNSTONE

Available Wherever Books Are Sold!

Visit our website at **www.kensingtonbooks.com**